Find Me in Paris

ROSEWOOD PRESS

979-8-9904728-4-6

Find Me in Paris

Copyright © 2025 Megan Leavell

All rights reserved. Except for the use of brief quotations in review of this novel, no part of this book may be reproduced in any form or by any electronic or mechanical means, including information storage and retrieval systems, without written permission from the author.

This is a work of fiction. Names, characters, businesses, places, events and incidents are either the products of the author's imagination or used in a fictitious manner. Any resemblance to actual persons, living or dead, or actual events is purely coincidental.

Also by Olivia Miles

Stand Alone Titles
The Gift of Christmas
The Starlight Sisters
A Wedding in Driftwood Cove
The Heirloom Inn
Christmas in Winter Lake

Sunrise Sisters
A Memory So Sweet
A Promise to Keep
A Wish Come True

Evening Island
Meet Me at Sunset
Summer's End
The Lake House

The Sweeter in the City Series
Sweeter in the Summer
Sweeter Than Sunshine
No Sweeter Love
One Sweet Christmas

The Blue Harbor Series

A Place for Us

Second Chance Summer

Because of You

Small Town Christmas

Return to Me

Then Comes Love

Finding Christmas

A New Beginning

Summer of Us

A Chance on Me

The Oyster Bay Series

Feels Like Home

Along Came You

Maybe This Time

This Thing Called Love

Those Summer Nights

Christmas at the Cottage

Still the One

One Fine Day

Had to Be You

The Misty Point Series

One Week to the Wedding

The Winter Wedding Plan

The Briar Creek Series

Mistletoe on Main Street

A Match Made on Main Street

Hope Springs on Main Street

Love Blooms on Main Street

Christmas Comes to Main Street

Harlequin Special Edition

'Twas the Week Before Christmas

Recipe for Romance

Find Me in Paris

OLIVIA MILES

One

ISABELLE

Isabelle Laurent loved little more in this world than her daily walk to work. It wasn't a short one, but it wasn't too long, either. It was, like so many other things about Paris, perfect.

On rainy days, there were plenty of awnings under which she could duck for cover, and on clear, blue-skied mornings, such as this one, she was free to take her time, watching the vans throw open their back doors to unload flowers of every color to the local florists, and letting her eyes roam the narrow streets filled with cafés, shops, and bistros, until she reached the Quai des Grands Augustins and the entire city opened up, stretching as far as the eye could see. Many days she paused here to take in the limestone buildings with their ornate architecture, the bridges that crossed the sparkling river, and each time she saw something new, something that made her smile, and that she would always notice again, because who could ever forget Paris?

The apartment was another wonderful thing about her life here—a gift, really, left to her from her paternal grandmother last year, because her sister Camille would never have wanted it, and their half sister, Sophie, lived much too far away to ever put it to use. Isabelle had always assumed that the apartment would be passed down from her grandmother to her father, but by the time she died quietly in her sleep at the age of eighty-nine, Grand-mère was well aware of her only son's restless spirit. He wouldn't settle in one city for any longer than he would stay with one woman, something that aggrieved both of Isabelle's sisters greatly.

Isabelle, however, had come to accept her father's wanderlust and had even married a man with a similar urge, a man who, up until last year, she used to travel the world with—him overseeing hotel expansions and her collecting art, discovering new voices, and now, featuring them in her little gallery on Île Saint-Louis, and it went without saying that while small, it was, well, perfect.

Each morning, Isabelle locked the door to her fifth-story apartment on a winding road in Saint-Germain-des-Prés and took the same path to her gallery, so she could first pop into her favorite café for a quick (by French standards) *café au lait* and croissant, where she liked to sit on the *terrasse* and watch passersby start their day. From there, she wandered up to the Seine, where the *bouquinistes* were just opening the stalls to sell books throughout the afternoon. She had been born in Paris and spent the first nine years of her life here, and even though she once again called this city her home, she'd never quite gotten comfortable enough to take it for granted. Maybe it was because its vastness was too overwhelming, its buildings too beautiful, or maybe, to hear her sister Camille tell it, it was because she'd learned at a young age that anything and everything could be snatched out from under you in the blink of an eye.

Especially something you loved. And oh, did Isabelle love Paris.

Sure, London, where she'd moved with her mother and sister when she was nine, was nice, but it didn't inspire her the way her childhood city did. It didn't make her slow down and appreciate the beauty of the buildings, the food, and the art. But it had led her to Hugh, her husband. Her best friend. Her soul mate.

Smiling, she checked her watch as she crossed the Pont de l'Archevêché, then raised her chin to admire the Notre-Dame, before hurrying toward the second bridge on her journey, the one connecting Île de la Cité with the second, smaller island that sat in the middle of the Seine, this one offering a sweeping view of the right bank.

Her gallery was on a long cobblestoned street flanked with small boutiques, ice cream parlors, and the occasional musician who would roll out his upright piano on warm summer days near the sweet old man who would park himself outside of the cafés with his marionette puppets, delighting children while their parents relaxed at nearby tables under the shade of the tree branches.

It was still early. Shops were just opening for the day, and while Isabelle didn't expect many visitors, she did have a show she was most excited about in only a few weeks, one that would require a fair bit of planning, not that she minded. She was her father's daughter in that sense, and she wasn't too proud to admit it. While Paul Laurent may not have been the most present father, and certainly not the most faithful husband, he was a true creative, filling his children's young minds with an appreciation for the creative arts, and that was one gift she was forever grateful for.

Isabelle popped the second key on her chain into the lock of the tall glass door and pushed into the small space, which would be better lit this afternoon, giving new life to the colorful assortment of watercolors that currently graced the narrow walls of the gallery. Soon, they'd be replaced by the moody oils of an up-and-coming artist she was lucky enough to feature for his opening, but she couldn't work on the arrangement of the paintings until she had the last one in her possession, something Gabriel Duvall promised to deliver here yesterday, and the day before that. Isabelle wasn't worried—yet. Growing up with an artist for a parent had exposed her to the temperament that often accompanied a creative mindset, and she knew that the process couldn't be rushed or forced, so she didn't press the artist for his final piece, even though the collection would feel incomplete without it.

Besides, she had bigger, more personal concerns at the moment.

Isabelle walked straight to the back of the room, where an antique desk she'd moved from her grandmother's apartment sat facing the windows, giving her a full view of the activity on the street and a vantage point to greet any guests. There were the occasional tourists, who were usually just browsing, or the locals, who had done their research and knew when she had something new and exciting to see, but most days were quiet, just her in these four walls. And even though she was alone, she never felt lonely. Not with all of Paris right there on the other side of the glass.

Today she certainly couldn't feel alone. Hugh was returning from his latest business trip that had kept him away for the past three weeks. She would take her usual path home—different from her morning routine, so she could stop at her favorite boulangerie along the way to grab a baguette for dinner, unless they decided to go to their favorite bistro for goat cheese salads and roasted chicken. She wasn't drinking wine at the moment —not until she knew for certain what the future held—but a sip wouldn't hurt, and Hugh's return was cause for a celebration.

She set a hand to her stomach and took a steadying breath. She'd gotten ahead of herself yesterday and started thinking of baby names, something that she wouldn't dare share with Hugh because he didn't even know that she might be pregnant. It wasn't like they were trying. She was just...hoping. Longing, really. Whereas Hugh was content with waiting. His business was busier than ever, she knew, with over ten new luxury hotels opening across the globe this year, but she wasn't getting any younger, either. And they were settled, after years of bouncing from city to city and hotel to hotel. The apartment was large with three bedrooms, a spacious living room, and plenty of light thanks to the tall windows. The way she saw it, there was no reason to wait. The way she saw it, she had waited long enough.

Her phone rang before she could settle into her desk, and she smiled when she saw her husband's name appear on the screen.

"Hugh?" She pulled out her chair and powered up her laptop. "Don't tell me you've already landed? I would have taken the day off from work." As it was, she had scheduled two phone meetings with collectors this morning, and she still needed to go over the responses to the invitations for Gabriel's opening.

"So sorry, darling." Hugh's familiar British accent couldn't stop her heart from sinking. "Change of plans."

"Again?" Isabelle sighed. How were they ever going to start a family if Hugh was always away?

But then she glanced at the baby furniture catalog she'd accidentally left on her desk yesterday and remembered that maybe they had already started one, and in due time, her life wouldn't just be perfect, it would finally be complete.

"I need to stay in Tokyo for at least another few weeks," Hugh continued. "I hope you didn't make big plans."

"No, not really," Isabelle said distractedly. She had the Duvall opening to plan, and plenty of work to consume her until his return. "I hope you'll still make it back in time for the show. It's going to be the biggest one of the year." Really, the biggest one of her career.

Several galleries had noticed Gabriel's work thanks to a recent article in *Paris Match*, which featured one of his paintings in the apartment of a well-known fashion designer. After a little investigating, Isabelle had discovered that Gabriel was a professor at an art college, that he'd only painted the landscape as a gift to a friend, and that he was a fan of her father's early work.

It was just the edge she needed, and she took it. Camille would grumble if she ever knew, but Isabelle didn't talk to her sister much, and they talked about their father even less.

The opening was expected to be big. She'd hired a publicist to send out teasers, and she'd put out feelers with all of her collectors who were always on the lookout for a breakout artist.

It was an opportunity that wouldn't present itself again, and one that she knew could help her make her mark among the more established galleries, maybe even land her in a guidebook.

But more than anything, she hoped that its success would finally convince Hugh—and maybe herself—that she'd made the right choice by staying here in Paris instead of continuing to travel.

"I'll do my best," Hugh said, but his tone didn't hold any promises. "You know how these acquisitions can go."

Yes, she did. And she also knew that her husband loved his job and that she wasn't going to be one of those wives who told him to cut back or to stay home more, even though that's exactly what he accused her of doing when she set up home in the Left Bank apartment and rented this gallery space.

He wasn't happy about her decision to stop traveling so much with him, but he understood what made her happy, and so, somehow, they'd made it work. She'd agreed that twice a year she would accompany him somewhere she longed to visit, for vacation or to explore the local art scene, and once a month he would return to Paris, where he'd stay for a few days, sometimes even a week, always insisting he loved this city more than he remembered, before jetting off again.

"Well, don't work too late," Isabelle said, calculating the time difference.

"Just room service and an early night for me," Hugh replied. "And—oh. My dinner is here."

"You go eat and relax," Isabelle told him. "We'll talk tomorrow."

She felt her shoulders sag as she listened to the sound of a food trolley being wheeled into Hugh's room, the clanking of dishes drowning out the polite conversation in the background before suddenly, the phone was turned off.

Isabelle stared at the dark screen of her phone and then lifted her gaze to the window, watching the shop owners and early morning tourists stroll the narrow road, wondering why, if her husband was stuck in Tokyo, she could have sworn that the hotel worker she'd just heard had been speaking in French.

By the time Isabelle had collected her baguette from the boulangerie and rounded the corner to her apartment that evening, she had nearly convinced herself that she had misunderstood what she had heard. It was one of those funny things about being raised bilingual and then picking up bits of other languages from school and travel. Sometimes she dreamed in French when she was still living in England with her mother, and sometimes, especially at museums, she heard someone speak a line or two of a foreign language that she understood, only to later determine that it had been Italian or Spanish.

The hotel worker had probably been speaking English, which would make sense, considering that Hugh didn't speak Japanese, and because Isabelle had lived in France for so long, and because she simply knew that she understood what was being said, her mind played tricks on her.

Yes, surely that was it.

Or maybe... Dare she even hope? Maybe it was baby brain.

A little flutter went up in her stomach as she collected her mail and then let herself into the tiny elevator that carried her up to the second to the top floor of the apartment building, and not because she was anxious that it would stall halfway up, or worse, drop to the bottom. Those were childhood fears, made worse because her father loved to thrill his daughters with wild stories, one of which involved a fictional account of the time that he nearly plunged to his death in this old contraption that could hardly fit more than two people at a time. For years,

Camille would fight back tears at every creak and groan when they visited Grand-mère, and each time Isabelle could have sworn she saw a twinkle in her father's eye.

Thinking of her sister and feeling the need to banish any lingering doubts about that strange conversation with Hugh from her mind, she dialed Camille the moment she slipped off her shoes and deposited the baguette in the small but tastefully decorated kitchen. As it often did, the call went to voicemail, and Isabelle knew that her sister never bothered to check those messages. She'd simply see that Isabelle had called and get back to her when she had a free moment, which was rare, but not rare enough for Isabelle to take it personally. Like herself, Camille had a busy career, but unlike herself, Camille also had a child to raise.

Fighting off a wave of self-pity and then another swell of hope, Isabelle riffled through the mail, smiling at the latest postcard from her father, this one from Portugal.

"Will be in Paris soon. Hope to see you all."

She frowned at this. Her father was coming to Paris? And what exactly did he mean by wanting to see them *all*?

Both implied herself and Camille. But *all*? Did he mean their mother? She nearly laughed out loud at the thought of her stoic, self-possessed mother willingly being in the same room as her ex-husband—she'd only survived Isabelle's wedding with the help of several ice-cold gin and tonics and the self-restraint that came with age and distance.

Unless he meant...Sophie? Isabelle dismissed that idea immediately. Her half sister lived in New York. The last time Isabelle had seen her had been five years ago, at her wedding, and their communication since had been limited to holiday and birthday texts and cards, most of which Isabelle sent from the far reaches of South America, Asia, or other European cities. Surely Papa wouldn't think that Sophie would cross the Atlantic to have a family dinner—the first since he'd left Sophie's mother when she was twelve and Isabelle and Camille had stopped visiting each summer.

There was only one way to find out, and only so much suspense that Isabelle's nerves could handle. Waiting to find out whether or not she was finally going to have a reason to set up a nursery in the small corner bedroom with the lovely view of the neighboring park was one thing, but trying to decipher her father's note was another.

She pulled his name up on her phone and dialed, and, unlike her sister, he answered on the very first ring.

"*Ma belle!*" *My beauty*. His term of endearment always made her feel better, even now, when she was well into her thirties.

"Hello, Papa," she said warmly. "I hope I'm not interrupting your dinner."

"Nonsense! I always have time for you!"

Isabelle narrowed her eyes at that remark, knowing that Camille would have snorted over it. She pressed her lips together, refraining from stating the obvious, which was that Paul Laurent hadn't made a habit of making time for his daughters any more than he had for their mothers.

"I see you'll be in Paris soon," she said, turning the postcard over in her hand to admire the scene of Lisbon at sunset.

"Yes, and I hope to be able to have dinner with all of you too."

There it was again. And so was the skip of her heart.

She sat down on the nearest armchair, the one that lent a view of the buildings across the street, one that she preferred above all the other sitting areas in the apartment. When she was younger, she loved to try to look through the windows, wondering what other people were doing, what kept them busy, what made them laugh. Usually, it brought her comfort to know that in a city as big as Paris, she was never alone. Today, there was a fat chance of that.

"All of us?" she repeated weakly.

"You and your sisters!" He said it as if it should be obvious. Or easy. But that was Paul Laurent for you. He didn't understand practicalities any more than he embraced responsibility.

Expecting to see his youngest daughter in Europe in a matter of weeks was about as far-fetched as spending time with his ex-wives.

And expecting to see Camille... Well!

"Camille is in London and Sophie is in New York," Isabelle reminded him in case he had forgotten—which was entirely possible.

"Surely they'd all welcome a visit to Paris! Who wouldn't?"

Camille, for starters, Isabelle thought wryly. She didn't know what would convince her sister to make the rather short journey other than—

She felt the blood drain from her face.

"Papa," she said nervously. "Is everything...okay?"

"Is it so preposterous for me to want to have dinner with all of my daughters?" he replied, sounding both amused and a little stung.

Oh, her father. That was his way. He didn't understand that his behavior had consequences. That he'd hurt people. That maybe some of them wouldn't want to see him.

Or that a dinner with his three daughters was preposterous.

Not just because they all lived in different countries, but because they'd never once gathered with him as adults.

Or even with each other.

Which again begged the question: Why now?

Dread made her breathing turn heavy, but then Isabelle thought of the baby—or the possible baby—and tried her best to relax.

This was probably one of her father's whims. One of his impulsive ideas, like the time he'd started making wire sculptures out of clothes hangers. Like the time he decided, after ten years of marriage to her mother, whom he claimed was his first true love, to run off and marry an American!

"A dinner all together sounds lovely," Isabelle said honestly. "I'm just not sure how realistic it is."

"*Ma belle*," he said patiently. "Didn't I teach you that in life, anything is possible?"

She smiled now, breathing easier. It was something he'd taught her, long ago, something that mattered much more than the birthday gifts he forgot to send, or the important school events he missed. He'd given her the passion to explore the world, to see beauty in things so many others simply overlooked.

And above all to believe that anything was possible.

She set a hand to her stomach. Anything.

"The thing is, Isabelle," he said, his tone turning more grave, "I don't speak to your sisters as often as I do to you."

This was not new information, though Isabelle was mildly surprised that her father had even taken notice of this lack of contact. Or that he seemed, dare she say, embarrassed by it.

"Would you like me to suggest they visit?" she asked, fighting back a sigh. She was still picking up her father's messes, just like she had when she was eight and he'd stayed out too late at the café around the corner from their apartment in Montmartre, drinking too much and with God only knew who else in retrospect.

"Don't tell your mother," he'd pleaded in a whisper when she'd emerged from her bedroom, her eyes heavy with sleep, confused by the request. "I'll just curl up here for a bit," he'd said as he stretched out on the sofa and plumped the throw pillow under his head. "It's like I fell asleep watching television. She'll never have to know."

By then, Isabelle's mother had taken to going to bed by eight, the same as her daughters, with the help of a sleeping pill, and Papa usually rolled in an hour or so later, having been working all day in various cafés or parks where he was always searching for inspiration.

Isabelle had kept her father's secret that day, thinking that she was helping, just like she helped when he walked out the door for good twelve months later, and she had to bring her mother endless cups of tea and then pack up the beautiful Paris apartment so they could move back to her mother's home country of England.

She was the good daughter. The helper.

And some roles never changed with time.

"Oh, thank you, Isabelle," her father said now with obvious relief. "I knew I could count on you."

"You're sure there's nothing you want to tell me, Papa?" Isabelle asked again. "Something else I could...help you with?"

But instead of confiding a health crisis or some other personal disaster, her father just laughed and said, "Just organizing this *soirée* is all the help I need! Shall we say two weeks from today? All of you?"

Isabelle stared out the window, looking down onto the streets of Paris, the city she'd grown up in, the one she loved. The one that Camille loathed and Sophie had never had a reason to visit before now.

She knew she shouldn't promise anything, but she also knew, like Papa always said, that in life, anything was possible. Even this.

"All of us," she told her father.

Two

CAMILLE

Two missed calls from Isabelle. In one day. Meaning that Camille would have to get back to her, tonight if possible. Only right now it was half an hour past their usual dinnertime, she'd had a morning phone meeting with her editor that ran straight through lunch, and now her stomach was making more noise than the song playing on the radio.

And she still had to cook. And she'd meant to go to the store on the way home but now she was running so late that to make another stop would only make the evening more harried and cause her to become even more hungry.

Camille swore under her breath as she hit the third red light in a row, eliciting a tsk of disapproval from the back seat.

"How come you're allowed to swear but I'm not?" Flora questioned for not the first time.

Camille kept her eyes on the road when it was safe to turn. It had started to rain and her windshield wipers were distracting.

"Because I'm an adult," Camille replied, even though most days she didn't feel like one. Most days, she felt at best like a teenager bumbling through life without much of a plan, dealing with the fallout of the ones she bothered to make. On days like today, when everything seemed to go wrong and she was tired and cranky and oh so hungry, she felt not much older than the daughter who, from one glance in the rearview mirror, made it clear from her expression that she wasn't buying the excuse, either.

"Dad doesn't swear," Flora pointed out.

"That's because your father is perfect," Camille said without the faintest bit of resentment or sarcasm. Rupert was perfect. Tall, handsome, an excellent cook, and an even better father as it turned out. He was kind to animals, kind to all. He was a thoughtful gift-giver and he never forgot an important event or date. He had a killer sense of humor, too. And an even better smile, one that curled at the corners of his lips and formed little lines around the deep-set brown eyes that Flora had inherited.

It was a shame that she'd never married him. Well, not really. But sometimes, usually after a glass or two of wine, friends would point out all of Rupert's qualities and ask her why she was still single when the perfect man was right in front of her.

What they didn't understand was that singlehood suited her just as much as her arrangement with Rupert. She couldn't explain it but it worked quite well. Rupert was her best friend, just as he'd been all through college, save for the night of their graduation, which they'd both agreed had been a mistake, but not a huge one because it had brought them the perfect child. One whom they co-parented with joy and mutual support.

Really, what more could she want?

"Speaking of your dad," Camille went on. "Why don't you

call him and put him on speaker for me? He's meeting us at the house and I want to let him know we're running late."

They tried to eat together as often as possible, if only so that Flora always had a chance to see both of her parents each day. Oh, friends raised their eyebrows at this and told Camille that she'd never, ever meet someone once he caught wind of this arrangement until she pointed out that it didn't stop Rupert from meeting other women, and then their looks turned to ones of pity.

Camille sighed as Flora happily took out the shiny new phone that she'd received for her twelfth birthday—apparently, years after all the other kids at school had access to one. It was one of the many things that Camille and Rupert agreed upon, yet another small relief compared to the endless differences in opinions that her friends complained about having with their spouses. Yet another reminder that her path was the right one, even if others might not see it that way.

"I'm just pulling up." Rupert's voice filled the car after Flora greeted him and transferred him to speaker.

"And I'm afraid we're at least ten minutes out," Camille all but shouted.

"Mu-um." Flora dragged out the word. "I told you, you can speak at a normal volume. He can hear you."

"Oh, right." There she went again. Showing her age. Who knew that thirty-four could feel so old and young at the same time?

"I can hear you," Rupert agreed. "And I can go ahead and get dinner started. I swung by the store on my way over. I saw you were low on staples yesterday."

Camille could have wept with gratitude. Instead, she said,

"Rupert, that would be wonderful. What would I do without you?"

"Luckily, you'll never have to wonder." As usual, Rupert's voice was full of warmth. "So, does a little fettucine sound good to you ladies?"

"It sounds like a taste of heaven," Camille said.

"Mum." Flora groaned. "Must everything be so dramatic?"

Camille pulled to a stop at another red light and turned to raise an ironic eyebrow at her rather dramatic preteen. The little smile Flora gave her in response showed that her point was noted.

"Drive safe. I'll see you soon," Rupert said.

"See you soon," Camille said before Flora disconnected the call.

And suddenly, the entire day felt much better, indeed.

Dinner was, as always when Rupert cooked, delicious. Camille sighed as she sat back in her chair and sipped her wine. Flora had run upstairs to her bedroom to work on her homework, and the kitchen was quiet without her endless chatter about the happenings at school.

Rupert gave her a lazy smile across the farmhouse table that Camille had bought at a rummage sale and carefully restored when she was still in her early twenties and money was tight. Even though her career as a book illustrator had come with more success than she'd ever expected and could easily afford her a new table, she was comfortable with the one she had, scratches and all. It was a reminder of her early days of motherhood, but it was also a reminder that some things were constant.

Some people, too, she thought, warming under Rupert's presence.

"I ate too much," Camille told him. "I'm going to put on weight and it will be all your fault."

"Ah, and then you'll never find a man and that will be my fault, too?" His dark eyes glimmered.

"Of course it will be your fault. Just like it's your fault that I haven't had a date in…" She started to do the math and then stopped when she saw his raised eyebrow.

"About as long as it's been since I've had one?"

Camille did feel bad about what happened with Janine, who did have a problem with Rupert spending so much time here, not that Camille had admitted that to any of her friends, who would be sure to just give knowing nods. But she knew that Rupert didn't blame her for the breakup any more than he would be willing to sacrifice the cozy, albeit unconventional, little family they'd created since Flora had arrived.

"No one understands what we have," Camille concluded.

Rupert drained the rest of his wineglass. "Sometimes I don't even understand it myself."

Camille frowned. "What do you mean by that?"

Rupert hesitated and then shook his head. He pushed his chair back and started collecting the plates. "Nothing. I just mean, well, it's strange, isn't it? We're best friends. We talk all the time. See each other even more than that. And we're raising a child together."

"It's rather perfect, isn't it?" Camille mused, but Rupert stood silently at the sink, his back to her, until she grew worried. It was the first time there had ever been a seed of doubt—well, on his end. She'd had plenty over the years, ones that she kept fiercely to herself until they subsided, and they always did. The Christmas mornings when they were all laughing and opening their gifts. The birthday parties when Rupert carried a big cake into the garden and Flora blew out all her candles and they squeezed together for a family photo wearing lopsided party hats. The vacations they took every summer to Spain because it wasn't like Camille was ever going to step foot in France again.

It was all so wonderful that it was sometimes tempting not to wonder if there could be something more.

But every time these thoughts took hold, Camille reminded herself of what she already had.

And what she stood to lose.

"Rup?" she prompted, swirling the wine in her glass as she eyed him. A knot had formed in her stomach, and she didn't like the way it felt any more than she liked where this conversation was headed. "What we have is special. We both know it. We always say how lucky we are when we see all those other couples bickering while their kids sulk miserably."

He nodded because, like her, he'd been one of those kids, but still he kept his back to her. "What we have is special."

She carried the remaining plates to the counter and stood beside him, stealing a glance at his noble profile as he began to scrub at the saucepot with a little more force than usual.

"Are we having our first argument?" she asked, trying to keep her tone light and playful. Her stomach felt a little funny while she waited for his reply. It was a feeling that she didn't typically associate with Rupert of all people. Usually, when she felt anxious or worried it was Rupert who had a way of making all those uncomfortable sensations go away.

The tension in Rupert's face was replaced by a smile that had the calming effect she had been waiting for.

"Don't be crazy. Us? We don't argue."

"No," she said a little breathlessly. She busied herself by loading the dishwasher. "We don't. And I like it that way. I like everything about this relationship."

"It's just..."

Camille's eyes widened as she slid another plate into the rack. She was grateful she wasn't facing him right now or she might not be able to stop herself from making up an excuse and fleeing the kitchen.

"Yes?" she squeaked.

"Do you ever think we're playing it too...safe?"

Ah. A question she could answer, and with conviction.

She gave him a long, hard stare, but she was smiling, because she knew that this time, like the time that Rupert was miserable in his banking job and needed a little push to start on a more fulfilling career path in personal finance, which he had done quite successfully thanks to his excellent people skills, it was she who needed to reassure him.

"Rupert," she said calmly and surely. "Safe is good. You and I both know that. Look at what we grew up with! Chaos, that's what."

Rupert's father had been an alcoholic, his mother a classic enabler. And her own family. Well! She had been the only girl in her class to have a father disappear overnight to start a new family in the States, and then to have to leave Paris under a shroud of shame and confusion.

"And look at what we're giving our daughter! Two happy, healthy parents who laugh and actually enjoy each other's company and always look forward to seeing one another. Parents who agree on, well, everything."

Everything except, she was beginning to fear by the doubt that persisted in his eyes, the status of their relationship.

"You never wonder what might have been if we'd tried to have a go at a real relationship?" Rupert asked, squinting at her

Of course she had! She questioned it even before they'd conceived Flora, after their daughter was born, and every year that followed. But she'd never actually entertained the idea. To do so would be foolish. Careless, really.

She had Flora to think about. And giving her the stability that she'd never had growing up.

"We do have a real relationship," she told Rupert. The best one she'd ever had. The only one she'd ever had, because he was the only man in her life who she'd kept around—and who'd stayed.

"I meant something more," Rupert said patiently.

"And what if we did?" she asked. It was meant to be a rhetorical question, but Rupert's eyes widened with alarming interest. Quickly, she stood a little straighter. "I'll tell you what would happen. Suddenly, you'd feel trapped, living here, in this little cottage instead of your sleek flat. Cooking dinner for us would no longer feel special, it would become thankless."

"You'd never be thankless," he said softly. Then, his mouth curved into a hint of a smile. "The way I cook? Impossible."

She swatted him with a dish towel.

"Things would change, that's all I'm saying." And she'd had enough change for one lifetime. "You'd grow bored of me. I'd stop making you laugh. We'd have laundry lists of resentments, and we'd start arguing over stupid things like the temperature of the thermostat. And we could never undo it."

Oh, they could, she knew. Legally speaking. But the damage would be far deeper than dividing assets.

"Just so you know," Rupert said softly as he went back to scrubbing the pot. "I would never be able to resent you. You're basically my favorite person in the entire world."

"Besides Flora," Camille pointed out, meeting his eye.

"Well, that goes without saying," Rupert replied.

As so many things between them did. They understood each other. They supported each other. They stood by each other. For better and worse.

Camille let her gaze drift and then cleared her throat. She felt the need to change the subject—and quickly. "My sister called. Twice."

"Twice in one day?" Rupert frowned and handed her the pot to dry. "That's not like her."

"No," Camille agreed. "I hope that nothing is wrong."

"You can go call her if you'd like. I'll finish up here," Rupert said.

Camille hesitated, sensing that there was still something unspoken between them, only this time, something that ran the risk of being misunderstood.

She opened her mouth and then closed it again. "Okay. I think I will."

She took her cell phone from the pocket of her cardigan and went into the living room, where she curled up in the armchair in front of the roaring fire, one that Rupert had started before they'd gotten home. It was nice, she admitted, coming home to find the lights on, the kitchen smelling of roasted tomatoes and garlic, and a warm fire to dry out the rain that had fallen on their shoulders in the dash from the car.

And it was nice to sit here, knowing that her daughter was

upstairs and that Rupert was just one room away in the kitchen, humming one of those tunes from some nineties rock band, because, like her, at least according to Flora, he was rooted in the past.

But Camille was rooted in a different kind of past. The kind of past that she didn't want to repeat.

With a sigh, she called Isabelle, hoping that nothing was wrong. It was usually Camille who was calling her older sister with updates about their mother, who lived in London and rarely went outside the city limits, even to visit her only grandchild.

"Isabelle?" she said when her sister answered. "I saw you called. Is everything okay?"

"Of course!" Isabelle replied, but there was something tense in her voice. "I was just calling to invite you to my gallery opening!"

Camille couldn't have been more shocked than if Isabelle had announced that their parents were getting back together.

Isabelle lived in Paris. And Isabelle knew *exactly* how Camille felt about that place. Did she seriously expect Camille to go there?

"Now before you say no," Isabelle said hurriedly, "I know how you feel about Paris. And I wouldn't ask if it wasn't important to me. This is going to be a very big show and…well, it doesn't look like Hugh is going to make it."

Ah, Hugh. He was always traveling. Camille often wondered how Isabelle felt about that, but she rarely complained.

Until now.

"That's disappointing," Camille hedged.

"It is," Isabelle said matter-of-factly. "He's been out of town more and more. He was supposed to come back from Tokyo today but now...I don't know when he'll be back."

Camille frowned. Was there more that her sister wasn't telling her? They were close, but they'd been closer as children. Distance and phases of life had inevitably led to them growing apart a bit. Isabelle was a jet-setter, and now she was focused on her gallery. She didn't understand what it was like to center one's life around a child any more than Camille could understand how on earth Isabelle could not only live in Paris but love it!

"Is this the artist you told me about last time we talked?" Camille vaguely remembered something about an up-and-coming painter, one that dozens of galleries were wining and dining. It had left her feeling unsettled the next time she sat down at her desk and stared at her own illustrations, daring to imagine for one fleeting moment what it would feel like to not just explore her work but be honored for it, before she reminded herself that she'd purposefully chosen a more stable path. One where her focus could be on her daughter.

"It is!" Isabelle sounded so overjoyed that Camille was momentarily ashamed because she'd only been half listening while baking brownies with Flora for a school event.

"It really means a lot to you," Camille commented, thinking of the countless times that Isabelle had come straight to her side when something important happened in her life. But those were big, life-changing events, like Flora's birth, or later, yes, her birthday parties. But Flora only turned eight or nine once in her life. Whereas the gallery...

It was all Isabelle had, Camille reminded herself, because that's what Rupert always told her when Camille vented to him about her sister. While she couldn't personally understand it, she knew that she should support her sister and the things that were important to her.

"I know how you feel about Paris," Isabelle said gently. "But it's been years, Camille. Decades. It would feel different to you now. We could have some proper sister time, lounge at sidewalk tables, and catch up over wine and cheese and chocolate. Or shop. Of course, I do have a fair bit of work to do. And I know you have Flora."

Flora was now back in the kitchen with Rupert. From the short distance, Camille could hear bits and pieces of their conversation. They were talking about their plans for the weekend, when Flora stayed at his apartment, even though Camille usually ended up staying, too, in the guest room, because, well, like Rupert had said, he was her favorite person in the entire world. Other than Flora.

"When is the opening?" she blurted before she could think of a better plan.

"You mean you'll come?" Isabelle sounded startled.

Camille glanced back into the kitchen while Isabelle gave her the details, smiling when Rupert gave Flora a little twirl on the floor that sent her into a fit of giggles but then feeling her stomach twist when he caught her eye and gave her one of his warm, slow smiles.

She'd go to Paris. Of all places. She would go. It would be good to see Isabelle. Good to support her.

And maybe some distance would be good. For all of them.

Three

SOPHIE

Sophie Laurent eyed the corner of her computer screen, waiting for the moment when it finally struck noon. The last few minutes seemed to drag by slower than usual, and she already had a firm grip on the leather straps of her handbag by the time her lunch hour officially began.

Not wasting a second, she pushed back her chair, speed-walked to the elevators, and pressed the down button. Twice.

She could feel the precious seconds being frittered away while she waited for one of the sets of doors to open, and once she was inside the car, she pressed the lobby button, twice, and then jammed her thumb against the button to close the doors before anyone could delay her further.

Once downstairs in the marble-floored lobby of the Manhattan high-rise where she spent more time than anywhere else, she pushed through the revolving doors and was immediately swept up by the bustle of traffic. She joined the throng of other New Yorkers who had no time to waste, and all but jogged in her kitten heels to the corner, where she turned right.

If she was lucky, she'd have exactly forty-five minutes to sit and relax and enjoy a nice conversation with Jack before he had to get back to his law office and she to her job.

That's all it had ever been to her. A job. Not a career. Certainly not one she wanted. It had been arranged by her mother shortly after her college graduation, who had called upon a favor from one of her sorority sisters to grant Sophie an interview. At first, it had seemed fitting, to work for a publishing company while she was writing her novel. But years had passed, she hadn't moved up the ladder, and she hadn't finished her manuscript yet, either.

The one thing she hadn't considered was that if she spent all her time working on other people's books, she'd have no time left for her own.

Her mother didn't see a problem with that, even though Sophie did. But like many things when it came to her relationship with her mother, Sophie learned that it was better not to bother bringing it up. It was always easier to let her mother have her way.

Jack was already waiting for her at the sandwich shop where they met twice a week. It was a good time for them to properly catch up because they were both putting in so many hours that they were usually too tired to do much more than eat takeout and watch Netflix in the evenings. Weekends were better unless Jack had a big case and was called into the office, which Sophie didn't mind. She liked having her space—if anyone could call the cramped apartment they shared spacious.

From the moment she sat down at the table, though, Sophie detected that something was not quite right. Jack's smile was tight. He didn't quite meet her eyes when she started telling him about her morning, and how she'd found another gem in the slush pile—but she didn't tell him that every time she did, it made her heart sink a little further when she thought of her own unfinished book.

"Jack." Sophie stopped talking and frowned at him. "Is everything okay at work?"

"Everything is fine at work," Jack said. "Couldn't be better, actually. I got put on the Nelson case. I think I might make partner sooner than I expected."

"That's fantastic!" She raised her glass of iced tea to his. "So what's the problem?"

"More hours." He sighed. "Less time for us. I hope you'll understand."

"Oh." Sophie took a long sip of her drink, thinking of the best way to respond. "You know I support your career."

"I know, but we'd talked about taking a vacation soon. I'm not sure I can get away now."

Oh. Well, this *was* disappointing. They'd talked about Bora Bora. Or Italy. The Bahamas. The mere thought of the sun on her face and the sand in between her toes had kept her going most days. But then, as Sophie's mother liked to point out, often with a pinch of her lips, Sophie had always been a dreamer.

Like her father. Even if her mother didn't say it, Sophie knew that she was thinking it.

The vacation had been loosely planned for months. Sophie had spent her free time window shopping for cute swimsuits and sundresses, but in the back of her mind there was a small worry—one she no longer had to bother with, she hoped.

No vacation meant no chance of a romantic seaside proposal. Sophie had been dating Jack for two years now, and while she loved him, she wasn't ready for the next step.

And she feared that he was.

"Well, there's always another time," she said brightly as the waiter appeared with their sandwiches. Jack had taken the liberty of ordering their usuals, and she dug in hungrily, glancing at the time on her phone, knowing she'd have to chew quickly if she didn't want to be late for her one o'clock acquisitions meeting.

"Did I ever tell you that you're the best?" Jack asked with a relieved smile.

"All the time," she said as she pushed back a wash of guilt with another bite of her lunch.

The afternoon dragged on as workdays always did. Jack would be working late, which meant that she would have the apartment to herself for a few hours. Meaning that there was no excuse not to work on her novel, except that she was so tired of staring at the computer screen, reading, and typing, that all she wanted to do was curl up on the sofa with the remote control, a bowl of ramen, and a big glass of wine.

She was just emerging from the subway in Greenwich Village when her phone rang. She couldn't help it. Her entire body tensed and she closed her eyes for a beat, wishing for not the first time that she was not an only child, only to remember that she wasn't technically an only child at all—she was just her mother's only child, and therefore her mother's entire focus in life, even at the age of twenty-eight.

Her mother called her daily, usually when she was just getting home from work, drained, tired, and aching to relax. Talking to her mother was not relaxing, even if she wished it was. And she'd tried. Oh, she'd tried to suggest they have coffee or meet for a glass of wine. Now that she was an adult, she hoped that they might take their relationship into a new phase the way some of her friends did with their parents. But her mother didn't drink coffee. Certainly not wine. And she still saw Sophie as the twelve-year-old girl she needed to hover over and check in on. Daily.

Sophie wouldn't have minded the frequent chats if they didn't all feel like an interrogation and if she didn't feel like every answer she gave was somehow the wrong one. That was the problem between her and her mother. Her mother wanted the best for her, but what she wanted for Sophie and what Sophie wanted for herself had always been two very different things.

Case in point: Her mother wanted her to marry Jack. Jack was, in her mother's mind, the ideal husband. He was nice, that was the word most people associated with him. Relatively handsome. He didn't have the best sense of humor, but Sophie's mother didn't see a problem with that. What she saw a problem with was that Sophie didn't seem to be as in love with him as he was with her.

Sophie's mother would be very upset to hear that their vacation would be canceled. Like Sophie, she fully assumed that a proposal would take place at sunset on a tropical beach.

But as Sophie glanced down at the screen, she saw that it was not her mother calling at all. She stared at the phone, at first not understanding all the numbers until she saw the location listed underneath them: Paris, France.

Her heart began to hammer in her chest as she slowed her pace, forcing another commuter to ram her shoulder as they brushed past her.

Paris. It couldn't be her father. Even though he hadn't sent a postcard in a while, she knew that he hadn't lived in Paris in years. Besides, she had his number stored in her contacts list, not that she ever pulled it up.

That left only one person.

Warily, she put the phone to her ear. "Hello?"

"Sophie?" Isabelle's unmistakable British accent brought a smile to her lips.

"Isabelle?" She couldn't believe that her sister was calling her, when usually at best she mailed a card around the holidays or on her birthday. Isabelle was nine years her senior, a married woman with a busy life. They were more like cousins than sisters, really, but that never stopped Sophie from admiring her ever since she was a little girl and her sisters were still visiting each summer. "Is everything okay?"

Even though she wasn't close to Papa anymore, the thought of something happening to him made her feel suddenly sick with fear.

"Everything is more than okay," Isabelle said with a smile in her voice. "I've called to ask you something."

A favor? Or just a question? Either way, Sophie felt honored to be considered, when of course, Isabelle and Camille had always favored each other, both in looks and in preference. At first, she'd blamed it on the age gap, lagging a solid six years behind Camille, who was anything but pleased by a younger sister's presence. But as they grew older, their bond became more evident, and Sophie began to feel more and more like an outsider on those summer visits when Papa would take them all to the beach on Long Island and Isabelle and Camille would lie side by side on beach towels, whispering and giggling to each other, Camille often switching to French when Sophie tried to join in because she knew that Papa had never taught her his native language. Sophie had longed to be included in their duo, to share their connection, to be able to enjoy their company full-time, which seemed like something that they took for granted when they squabbled and argued over silly things. But now Isabelle was reaching out to her. Acknowledging her as a proper sister. One who was more than eager to fulfill her sisterly responsibilities.

"I've called to invite you to Paris," her sister said simply.

Paris. Sophie was still numb by the time the call ended a few minutes later, after Isabelle had told her all about her upcoming opening, the things they could see and do together, and of course, the apartment, which had three large bedrooms, plenty of room for her to stay.

Sophie plopped down on a bench in Washington Square Park before going home, trying to unpack the conversation, which had ended with Isabelle telling her to think about it, and Sophie, fumbling for an excuse, saying that she wasn't sure she could get the time off from work.

Going to Paris at all—and ever—was not something she had considered. At least not in a long time.

Once, it would have been her dream—back when Paris, France, and everything French felt like part of her identity. When she'd studied the language until she was nearly fluent, or close enough, because even though her father was French, he'd only ever used a few fleeting terms and phrases here and there, and knowing Papa, most were profane. She was his American daughter, he liked to boast, as if that made her special, instead of setting her apart from Isabelle and Camille, when there was already such a line dividing them.

But not every dream was meant to come true. Not every

desire would be fulfilled. And sometimes you had to tuck away a part of yourself until it wasn't buried but forgotten.

Only now, thanks to Isabelle, it was once again a possibility.

Deciding she would think more clearly in the morning, Sophie stood and walked the remaining two blocks to her brownstone, climbing the stairs to her third-floor apartment deliberately, eager to keep her mind from replaying the conversation with her sister, from reading too far into it, but she couldn't quite keep the flutter out of her chest.

An invitation to Paris.

Deciding that she couldn't go home just yet, she stopped on the second-floor landing to knock on the door to the apartment directly below hers, hoping that her friend Erin was already home from her job at the clothing boutique on Broome Street. Sophie sighed with relief when a short moment later, she heard the locks being turned and the door opened to the cramped hallway that was identical to her own, only painted a deep indigo in contrast to Sophie's creamy white walls.

Erin was wearing one of the designs from the shop—leather pants and a shaggy pink sweater. "You're just in time! Let me get out of this uniform and into my sweats!"

Erin wasn't into fashion, but she did want the shop to succeed. A practical woman with an eye for business, she handled all the branding and marketing, and it helped that she looked like she could have modeled in the window.

"Jack working late?" Erin asked from the bedroom just off the front hall where she changed behind a half-closed door.

Sophie let herself into the small living room and plopped down on the velvet sofa Erin had excitedly bought off a neighbor who was moving out last month. She hugged a throw pillow to her chest.

"Yes, but I can't stay too long. I'm feeling tired. I had the strangest phone call from my sister."

"Your sister?" Erin appeared in the hallway again. She'd wasted no time in putting on her college T-shirt and pulling her hair into a messy bun. "Which one?"

Erin was one of the few people who knew all about Sophie's unconventional family. They'd spent hours talking over shared bottles of cheap wine in the six years they'd lived in the building.

"Isabelle, obviously," Sophie replied. Camille had barely tolerated her when they were younger and now, as adults, they were complete strangers, which always made Sophie feel a little sad. But Isabelle had doted on her, which, in hindsight, had probably only added to Camille's resentment.

"And? What was the reason for her call?" Erin pulled a bottle of wine from the small fridge in the kitchen that was barely larger than most people's closets and carried it to the coffee table along with two glasses.

Of course, there would be a reason for Isabelle's call. The sisters didn't speak without reason, which meant that they didn't speak much at all.

"She wanted to invite me to Paris," Sophie said a little breathlessly.

Erin's eyes widened. "Paris!"

"She's having a big event for a new artist," Sophie explained. "I think I told you that she opened an art gallery."

"After she moved into her grandmother's apartment." Erin nodded along as she poured two glasses of white wine. "I mean, *your* grandmother's apartment."

"It's okay." Sophie took a sip of her drink. "I never met her. Papa never took me to Paris. He always said he would but…"

They fell silent, both knowing how that sentence would be finished. But then he met another woman. Moved halfway across the world. Broke Sophie's mother's heart.

And hers, as well.

"You'll go, of course?" Erin said eagerly.

Sophie shifted uncomfortably on the couch. "I don't know if I'll go."

Somehow not going felt easier. Safer. For the first time in as long as she could remember, she understood why her mother lived as she did, going about a simple routine, embracing the boring, not wishing or trying for more.

The thought of putting her heart on the line, of daring to remember the girl she used to be and the hopes that she'd once held, only made her think of all the ways it could end in hurt and disappointment.

"What? But you have to go! You always wanted to! You speak French. You decorated your entire childhood bedroom in posters and photos of the city!"

Until she ripped them all down.

"That was a long time ago," Sophie said. "I gave up on that dream at some point."

"So?" Erin's tone turned gentler. "Who says you can't find it again? It's still in there, Sophie. It was a huge part of you."

"I haven't thought about going to Paris in ten years," she said, feeling an old, familiar hurt creep into her voice.

And eventually, she stopped longing for it. It all became a lost dream, replaced with reality instead of hope.

Her mother was relieved when Sophie stopped talking about Paris, or "the nonsense" as she called it. And Sophie was relieved when the thought of Paris no longer hurt her or made her ache for more.

"I've made a wonderful life for myself here in New York," she said firmly. "I have a great job. A great apartment. A great friend."

"I'll believe the last one," Erin said with a grin.

"A great boyfriend," Sophie went on, taking another sip of wine, hearing the lack of conviction in her tone and feeling terrible about it. Jack was everything that her mother said he was: predictable, dependable, reliable. Nice. So nice. All good adjectives.

But...there was always that missing piece that she just couldn't identify, and maybe she never would. Maybe the hole in her heart would never be filled, and she had to stop thinking it could be.

"I suppose you'd see your father if you went," Erin said delicately.

"Oh, no. My father hasn't lived in France in years," Sophie replied confidently. Where he lived at the moment, she wasn't even sure. He wasn't one to be tied down to one place. Or one person.

"So your mother shouldn't have an issue with you going," Erin said brightly.

Sophie gave her a long look, one that Erin understood without explanation. Sophie's mother could never know about Sophie going to Paris, but she wouldn't have to, because Sophie wasn't going.

"It was just an invitation," Sophie said dismissively, even as her chest began to ache. "A nice thought for a moment or two."

"But it doesn't have to stop there." Erin looked at her thoughtfully. "Can you take the time off from work?"

Sophie thought about the trip with Jack that was no longer taking place. "Yes."

"Then what's stopping you?" Erin asked.

Sophie looked at her friend, trying to think of a way to respond without saying the one thing she didn't want to admit to herself.

Paris was a possibility once again. The dream had been resurfaced, and every part of her ached to hop on that plane and go.

But the thought of opening that part of her heart again, indulging in the life she'd always wanted, scared her.

Because it was one thing to take a vacation. But it was another to face the life you always wanted, and then compare it to the one you'd been living instead.

A glass of wine later, Sophie trudged up the last set of stairs to the top floor, eager for a hot bath, pajamas, and hopefully no more thoughts about Paris. A decision would have to be made—she had told Isabelle she'd get back to her by the end of the week, using work as the excuse. And work could be an easy excuse.

It always was.

She turned the key in the lock, fumbling as she always did because it didn't fit easily, and impatiently pushed the door open, but she stopped cold when she saw the hallway, lit by floor candles, strewn with rose petals.

Her heart began hammering and for a moment she wondered if she'd let herself into the wrong apartment, but no, there was her trench coat, hanging on the hook beside her umbrella.

"Hello?" she called weakly from the doorway, afraid to take another step.

Jack was supposed to be working—he'd made that more than clear. And besides, what reason would Jack have to do this other than—

Oh, no. No. He couldn't.

But as Sophie slowly walked down the hall and almost fearfully glanced into the living room, she knew that he could. And he was.

Jack was down on one knee. Holding a ring box.

"Jack—" She needed to stop him from opening that box. From saying another word.

"Don't say a word," he said instead. "I need—"

"Please get up," she pleaded, feeling on the verge of tears.

Jack looked at her with confusion. "Sophie." His voice was barely a whisper.

"Please, Jack. Don't do this."

He stared at her for a moment and then, to her relief, stood and jammed the ring box into his pants pocket.

"So?" he finally said. "What do you have to say?"

She took a breath, steadying herself, feeling more miserable than she thought possible. She'd hurt him, made a big mess of things, and that was the last thing she wanted.

Well, other than a big romantic proposal.

"You don't want to marry me?" His tone was so incredulous that she wondered if he even knew her at all.

Sophie pulled in a breath, hating what she was about to say but knowing that she had to be honest because the alternative was to accept the ring, plan a wedding, and commit to a future that she couldn't envision.

"I don't know if I ever want to get married to anyone," she

said sadly. Seeing the hurt in his eyes, she added, "You know I don't have a great track record with marriage."

"Your *parents* don't have a great track record," he replied. "Or your father, I should say. My parents are divorced, too, I'll remind you."

Maybe, but his father didn't walk out the door when he was twelve and move overseas, rarely to be heard from again, and certainly never seen, at least not on this continent.

"I'm just saying, I think we should take things slow," she said calmly.

"Slow? We've been dating for over two years! We live together!" Jack closed his eyes and shook his head. He began pacing the small living room, making it feel even more cramped than it already was, thanks to Sophie's mounting collection of books that took up every free surface.

He stopped a few feet from where she stood and said, "I thought we were happy."

"We *are* happy," Sophie said, but the words didn't sound any more convincing than they felt. Right now, she felt anything but happy.

Jack blinked at her, as if not understanding, and she fought for words to salvage this night—the relationship. She might not want to marry him, but she didn't want to lose him. She'd lost enough people, including, she was beginning to feel as she stood in the cramped space, in the middle of the city that she'd lived all her life and never really left, herself.

"Look, this came as a bit of a shock," she started to say.

She saw his shoulders come down a bit. They were getting somewhere.

"You caught me off guard," she told him.

"I was trying to surprise you." Jack's eyes pleaded with her. "I was trying to be romantic."

"And I appreciate that, but..."

His face hardened again.

At that moment, her phone rang. She didn't need to look at the screen to know that this time, it was her mother.

"Please don't answer that," Jack said wearily.

"If I don't, she'll just keep calling until I do," Sophie pointed out, and they both knew from experience that this was true.

With a sigh, Jack nodded, and Sophie picked up the phone, trying to keep her growing emotions from showing in her tone.

"Hey, Mom, can I call you back in a little bit?"

Immediately, her mother grew suspicious. "Is something the matter?"

"Nothing is the matter, I'm just in the middle of something is all," Sophie replied, praying her voice remained light, but her heart was pounding when she glanced at Jack.

"Too busy to talk to your mother?" Her mother's voice pitched with the accusation.

Sophie felt the tears spring to her eyes. The weight of the day was coming down on her. Jack was staring at her intensely, waiting for an answer. Her mother was on the other end of the line, demanding more than one child could ever be expected to give. And tomorrow would be more of the same.

"I'll call you back in a bit, Mom," she said, and, knowing she couldn't hold it together much longer, she disconnected the phone.

Her mother would not be happy. Jack was not happy.

But Sophie was not happy, either. And she hadn't been in a long time.

She set the phone down and took a step back, away from the device. Away from Jack. She needed to create some distance between them and this entire night, even though she knew that she couldn't without hurting him more. She licked her lower lip, knowing at once that her decision was made.

"I was on the phone with Isabelle earlier," she said, her heart beating so hard she felt like it could push right out of her chest. "I'm going to Paris. This weekend."

Her mind was spinning, and it didn't feel real, but it was. It could be. Technically, Isabelle had mentioned next weekend, but if she was too early, she could find a cheap hotel. She'd use her time off. Stay a full two weeks until the gallery opening. What she'd say to her mother she didn't know or even care right now. She'd find an excuse.

"So you see, now isn't the best time to be thinking of the future," she said gently.

Jack's eyebrows shot up. "Oh, I think this is the perfect time to be thinking of the future."

"What's that supposed to mean?" she asked as he brushed past her toward the door.

"I mean, I think that you should go to Paris. I think the timing couldn't be better. We need some time apart, Sophie."

"Where are you going?" she asked when he set a hand on the front doorknob.

"To my brother's." He opened the door and stepped one foot into the hallway. "I started this night hoping to spend the rest of my life with you. To wake up every morning next to you. But right now, I think space would be good."

"Are you breaking up with me?" Sophie's voice rose in alarm. That wasn't what she wanted; she just didn't want...this. This argument.

Or maybe that ring.

"Shouldn't I be asking you that?" Jack replied. He shook his head and then said, "Don't answer that. Not now. We'll talk when you're back from Paris."

"The phone works over there," she said gently, maybe even hopefully, but maybe, from the look on his face, not hopefully enough.

"We need this time apart," Jack replied, and even though Sophie knew that it was true, that it was the reason she'd blurted out her plans in the first place, hearing it come from him only made this entire situation feel all too real.

About as real as the possibility of going to Paris. Could she really do it, now, after all this time?

She thought back on her call with Isabelle, and her talk with Erin. And then on the awful conversation with Jack.

He was right. A little time apart would be good for them if only to lessen the hurt from this evening.

And Erin was right, too. Paris wasn't just a dream, it was a part of her, and not just because her father was French.

This time it was about her. About finally getting to the root of her deepest self.

Or at least finding her truest self again.

Four

ISABELLE

It wasn't until a few days later, when Isabelle was sitting with her usual breakfast of a croissant and *café au lait* at her favorite café near the gallery, that she realized it was her five-year wedding anniversary.

Five years. It seemed impossible for Isabelle to believe that she'd been married to Hugh for so long; almost more impossible to believe that somewhere in all those years they hadn't found the time to start a family. They'd been too busy traveling, enjoying their freedom and their youth, until suddenly she realized that she wasn't so young anymore. She'd been thirty-six when she inherited the apartment, and that had seemed like a good age to settle down.

Hugh was still in Tokyo, of course. They'd talked last night, briefly, but long enough for Isabelle to rule out all her suspicions as a trick of the mind. There were no familiar sounds in the background, no sounds at all, actually. Hugh had been tucked into his hotel room, and she had absolutely nothing to worry about.

The thing was, that up until that strange call the other day, she hadn't ever worried about Hugh. Sure, he traveled a lot, but that didn't mean he had a wandering eye. She knew that her sister thought otherwise, even if she was too polite to say anything. But Camille didn't trust any men, well, other than Rupert, but not enough to marry him.

Hugh had always been attentive and loyal, and as much as he didn't like being tied to one place, he'd never insinuated that he didn't want to be tied to one woman. He'd proposed, after all, after just a year of dating. They'd had a big wedding near London, with all their friends at the time, friends who had by now gone off on the domestic path, something that she and Hugh used to shudder over while they fastened their seat belts for landing in yet another new destination.

Until Isabelle started craving that life, too.

She felt her stomach flutter as she stood and finished her walk to the gallery. Today was her wedding anniversary. It seemed like a sign.

Today was the day she would take a pregnancy test. She just had to get through the workday first.

Two dozen pink peonies were waiting for her outside her apartment door when she arrived home an hour earlier than usual, hurrying in the early spring drizzle that had started midafternoon. She would have jogged home if she wasn't worried about slipping or catching one of her heels in the cobblestoned roads or, worse, looking like a tourist.

She picked up the enormous bouquet wrapped in brown paper and tied with twine and inhaled the sweet aroma. Her favorite. Hugh had remembered, not just that it was their anniversary but that these were the very flowers she'd had in her bouquet all those years ago.

A door across the hall opened and her neighbor's friendly face appeared.

"I signed for you," the man, Antoine, said. At least she thought that was his name. They'd only briefly exchanged pleasantries and that had been when she first moved in and then a few times afterward when they both happened to be collecting mail in the small vestibule near the front door. "They just arrived about twenty minutes ago, so they are still fresh."

His English was excellent, accented heavily by French.

She smiled. "*Merci beaucoup*."

"*Très jolie*," Antoine said, giving her a slow smile. *Very pretty*.

She frowned a little, wondering if he even knew she was married, but then realized that of course he was talking about the flowers. "*Oui*. They are." And they were also her favorite.

She thanked him again and slipped inside, eager to get the bouquet into water. She found a vase on a high shelf in the kitchen and soon had the arrangement centered on the coffee table in the living room where she could admire them all weekend, mentally scratching one item off her endless to-do list before her sisters arrived. Preparing the apartment for their earlier-than-expected arrival had kept her nearly as busy as her gallery all week—and now she wouldn't have to worry about buying fresh flowers, not that she ever minded that task, or any that kept her mind off the possible life growing inside her. The sun was still shining bright in the sky, but she knew that it would be several hours ahead in Tokyo. Hugh had a dinner meeting tonight, meaning that she might still have a chance to order a surprise for him before he returned.

But first…

Isabelle inhaled sharply and then, feeling as nervous as she had as a schoolgirl about to deliver a valentine to her childhood crush, she forced herself down the hallway to the bathroom. She rummaged under the sink for the test she'd bought weeks back, hidden in its plain white paper pharmacy bag, even though she was the only one here these days.

She took it out and read the instructions carefully, and then read them again, to make sure she wasn't going to do anything to interfere with the accuracy of the results. With shaking hands, she opened the box, said a silent prayer, and took the test.

She decided to fill the wait time by preparing for her sisters' visit. Sophie would be arriving tomorrow morning, and Camille the day after. With her mind still spinning with the realization that her entire life might be about to change in a matter of minutes, she forced herself to make sure that both guest rooms were ready for her sisters, pulling stacks of towels from the linen closet and setting them on the antique chests of drawers, still half in disbelief that not just one but both of them had actually agreed to visit.

She glanced at the bathroom, then checked her watch, deciding that she would give it an extra minute, just to be sure.

Her stomach swooped as she walked into the living room, dropped into her favorite chair, and called Hugh's office here in Paris before they closed for the day.

His assistant answered in a professional tone; it wasn't often that Isabelle called his direct line when she could try his cell instead.

"Hello, Celine. I'm trying to reach Hugh."

"You weren't able to reach him on his cell?" Celine replied, naturally.

"I was hoping to surprise him," Isabelle confided. "I just realized that I don't have the name of the hotel he's staying at in Tokyo." The hotel chain owned many properties in each city, and in one as big as Tokyo, it could have taken her twenty minutes to find the correct one.

And she couldn't wait that long to find out the results of her test.

"Tokyo?" Celine sounded dumbfounded. "There must be some confusion. Hugh isn't in Tokyo."

"He's not?" Isabelle wondered if Hugh had a last-minute request to fly into another city. It wouldn't be the first time he'd been asked to put out a fire. Unless... Had he left today? As a surprise? For their anniversary? Was he about to walk through the door at any moment, in time to read the test together, in time to celebrate?

"Hugh hasn't been to Tokyo since last summer," Celine replied in a tone that said Isabelle should know this.

And she should. She should absolutely know where her husband was—if he was in Tokyo or if he was not.

Just like she should know when he was lying to her.

A dozen questions ran through her mind, but she settled on the one that would bring her the most pertinent information. Isabelle stood, clutching the phone close to her ear.

"I'm sorry, I must have gotten the cities mixed up," Isabelle managed to say in an eerily calm voice. She started to pace. "Then...where is he?"

"*Paris, madame.*" The woman sounded sincerely confused.

Isabelle stopped walking and stared out the tall windows of her living room, onto the rooftops of the very city where her husband currently was. Where he might have been all this time, while she was unaware.

While others, like Celine, knew.

"Paris?" Isabelle managed to whisper.

"*Oui, madame.* He's been staying at our premier property while overseeing the new acquisition. Would you like me to connect you to his room?"

Isabelle opened her mouth to speak but no sound came out. Hugh had been in Paris all this time? All those calls, all those conversations, and he'd never been in Tokyo at all! There was no extended business keeping him somewhere he'd never been in the first place. No excuse to skip their anniversary. No reason to miss her upcoming opening that he knew would be the biggest of her career.

All this time, he's been right across the Seine. Lying to her.

"*Madame?*" the woman asked again.

"*Non,*" Isabelle said quickly. "*Non, merci.*"

She hung up without another word. Maybe the woman would say something to Hugh in passing, or maybe she'd forget all about this conversation, and not say a word.

Maybe Hugh would never know that she knew. And what would he do then? Keep up this ruse? Eventually stop by the apartment for a few nights, feigning jet lag, talking about his next trip—a trip that might not even exist?

A trip that was just a walk across the Seine?

Isabelle stood up, grabbed the vase with the two dozen pink peonies, marched into the kitchen, and slammed the flowers into the trash. Then she walked into her bedroom and opened the closet. She didn't know what she was looking for, exactly. A trace of lipstick on one of Hugh's collars? A receipt for a lingerie store or a restaurant that she'd never dined in before?

She didn't need more evidence, not when she already had it. Hugh had been lying to her. And there could be only one reason. He'd met someone. Maybe he intended to keep it on the side, or maybe he planned to leave her. In time, she'd know how this all ended, because that's the only outcome there could be. It would end. Her marriage. The life she was living.

She brushed away a hot tear before it slipped, wishing that there was someone she could talk to, but Hugh was the one she preferred to talk to, and that was no longer an option. And that, perhaps more than his lies, hurt the most. There would be no more long conversations over lazy dinners at the bistro on the corner. From now on it would just be her.

Alone.

She blinked, suddenly remembering the pregnancy test waiting for her in the bathroom, and hope felt all at once restored. There was still that wonderful possibility, still the chance to have a child, even if it wasn't under ideal circumstances, maybe somehow something good still came from all of this.

Maybe all was not lost.

Barely able to breathe, she moved slowly to the bathroom. She'd left the door open and the light on, but she couldn't make out the indicator strip from a distance. She closed her eyes just as she approached the room, pausing to inhale deeply, and then looked.

She registered the results before her eyes even seemed to understand what they were seeing. Her emotions swirled from hope to shock to complete disbelief.

Denial.

And then, despair.

It was negative. As clear and sure as the woman on the other end of the phone had just been.

There was no baby. There was no marriage.

There was nothing but this apartment in Paris. A little gallery on Île Saint-Louis.

And two sisters who were soon going to descend on her. And who could never find out about any of this.

Five

SOPHIE

The plane touched down with a bump early Saturday morning, Paris time, rousing most passengers from their sleep, but Sophie had been up for the past hour, and not only because it hadn't been easy to get comfortable at the back of the crowded plane. She had booked a window seat, and she craned her neck for the first sight of land. Of France! It seemed ordinary at first, countryside, really, but how could it be ordinary when she had traveled across the globe, overnight, and was now looking down on a completely different continent?

Only mildly disappointed that she had not been able to spot the Eiffel Tower or any of Paris from her view, Sophie wasted no time in hurrying through customs to get her baggage from the carousel.

With Jack staying at his brother's apartment in Brooklyn, she'd been using her evenings to brush up on her French, and she felt almost confident as she approached the taxi stand, hoping that her accent was acceptable and that her understanding of the spoken language was better than it had been while binge-watching French-dubbed Netflix shows for the past week, all the while wondering why she hadn't thought to do this sooner until she'd remembered that she'd let that part of her die off—or so she'd thought. But all it took was a few minutes of watching some online language tutorials, and half an hour in front of the television to revive that part of her that she'd thought was gone forever. Her heart beat a little faster all week. She smiled a little more. She didn't even mind listening to her mother remind her to schedule her biannual dentist appointment or question her about her upcoming performance review because all she could think about was…France!

"*Bonjour*!" Sophie greeted the driver when she reached the front of the taxi line. He wasted no time in grabbing her two suitcases and tossing them in the trunk. She handed him the address she'd written down as she settled into the back seat. "*Saint-Germain-des-Prés, s'il vous plaît.*"

The 6th arrondissement! The Left Bank! She couldn't believe it! She was on her way, nearly there! There had been a time when that neighborhood was all she could think of, somewhere she hoped to live, to study. She imagined long afternoons in cafés, sipping coffee or cocktails and scribbling in a notebook. She had thought the words would just flow from her fingers, and they once had. But not in a very long time.

As the driver pulled away from the airport, she fired off a text, replying to one of the many her mother had sent since she'd departed New York. She'd told her mother she was in London, at a publishing conference. It was the first lie she'd ever told her mother, but she'd done it to spare them both.

The taxi pushed forward on the highway, and the traffic was surprisingly light. Sophie knew from her research that it wouldn't take much more than thirty minutes to get into Paris, maybe less, and she stared out the window, looking for a glimpse of the world she'd only dared to dream about. The highway seemed to drag on, soon replaced by industrial-looking buildings, until the car suddenly exited, took a turn, and there, right in front of her was—

"The Arc de Triomphe!" Oops. She'd squealed that. She caught the driver's gaze in the rearview mirror, too excited to be embarrassed, and shamelessly rolled down her window, hanging her arms out so she could get a good picture.

But before she could soak in the magic of the moment, the car continued down a wide road flanked by trees and large storefronts.

Blinking quickly to gather herself, Sophie realized that this wasn't just any street. This was the Champs-Élysées! The very street she'd imagined strolling as a teenager. And now it was right in front of her, not just a picture she could stare at in a guidebook but a real place that she was seeing with her own eyes. It was just a quick plane ride away all this time, all these years. She'd woken up and here she was, not just on a different continent but in Paris. And she wasn't still dreaming.

"*Regardez*," the driver said, pointing to the right. "*La tour Eiffel.*"

And there it was, standing even taller than she imagined it would. The Eiffel Tower! She gazed in the distance as the car drew closer to the river, the firm reminder that she was here. That she'd made it. Or more like she'd done it. Past disappointments couldn't hold her back anymore.

Maybe nothing could.

She sat back against the seat, staring out the window, taking it all in, the architecture, the buildings that were even bigger and more beautiful than she'd imagined, the people bustling on the sidewalks and walking across the bridge as the taxi crossed the Seine, where boats passed lazily underneath and locals picnicked on the riverbank. Here, on the other side of the city, the streets were tighter, the shops charming and inviting, and the driver wound through a maze of buildings, past cafés and delicious-looking pastry shops and art galleries, until he finally came to a stop.

"*Voilà*," he said and promptly exited the car.

Sophie had been in such a trance watching the city pass her by that she felt startled and had to rouse herself. She'd been so excited about finally being in Paris that she'd nearly forgotten the other part of this trip. Seeing her sister, her favorite sister, after so many years.

A flutter of nerves swept through her stomach as she pushed out into the warm spring morning and looked up at the building where Isabelle lived.

It was classic Parisian, Sophie noted with satisfaction. The building was a light gray stone, six stories tall like its neighboring ones, with a wrought-iron balcony running across the third and fifth floors. Tall windows cased in ornate frames lined the entire facade, with dormer windows at the very top, tucked into the roof. She stared up at the building, wondering which set belonged to Isabelle, when the front door opened and a woman with dark shoulder-length hair, wearing a navy linen shirtdress, walked onto the sidewalk.

Sophie watched as the woman's pretty face broke into a huge smile. "Isabelle? Isabelle!" she exclaimed, forgetting her bags as she rushed to hug her oldest sister.

Isabelle laughed as they embraced and then finally pulled back. "Let me get a good look at you!"

But it was Sophie who was staring at her sister, who seemed to have only grown more elegant with time. There were fine lines around her bright blue eyes, the only thing that gave away her age. Her makeup was minimal, and her face was nearly as familiar as it was foreign.

"It's been so long," Sophie breathed, daring to think back on the last time they'd all been together. It had been five years, and before that was the summer before Papa left Sophie's mother—and her—when she was twelve and Isabelle was a grown-up already at twenty-one. A college girl studying at Oxford, so worldly and sophisticated, embodying everything that Sophie ever hoped to be.

"*Too* long. The last time you saw me I was in a wedding dress," Isabelle said with a smile that didn't quite meet her eyes. "And it certainly wasn't here in Paris."

She didn't seem to want to dwell on the memory as she quickly paid the driver before Sophie could protest, and promptly whisked one of the bags through the doorway into a tasteful vestibule containing brass mailboxes. There was a small marble table with a bouquet of flowers and a stand for umbrellas, and, farther into the lobby area, an elegant—yet positively ancient-looking—elevator with a retractable iron door.

"Are we going to take that?" Sophie asked a little nervously, calculating if they could even both fit along with her two large luggage pieces.

"It's this or the stairs!" Isabelle motioned to the winding staircase that seemed to climb all the way to the roof. "I'm on the fourth floor. That's the fifth for you Americans since we call this level *le rez de chaussé.*"

You Americans. Sophie knew that Isabelle meant no harm, but the point was clear. Isabelle was European, and Sophie was not. And though they were sisters, their differences were clear.

"The elevator it is, then," Sophie said, all too happy for the full Parisian experience. Once they were crammed inside and the car started to screech as it carried them slowly up, she tried to hide her doubts.

"Camille is scared to death of this thing," Isabelle said with a laugh. "Just you watch. She'll be carrying her luggage up the stairs on her own when she arrives."

For a moment, Sophie forgot all about the rickety elevator. She even momentarily forgot that she was in Paris.

She stared at her sister, replaying the last words, trying to make sense of what she'd just heard and hoping that she was mistaken.

"Camille is coming?" she asked breathlessly.

Isabelle raised an eyebrow. "I'm as surprised as you are, given how much she despises Paris. But yes, she's arriving tomorrow afternoon. Like you, she seemed willing to spend a little extra time here before the opening, not that I'm complaining about an extra week with my sisters. It will be a long overdue reunion. Just us girls."

Just us girls.

Once, this would have thrilled Sophie, and a part of it still did, if only because she never stopped longing for a relationship with these women. Only Sophie couldn't shake the discomfort she felt at how Camille would feel about this.

Or if she even knew that Sophie was here at all.

The apartment was exactly as Sophie imagined it would be— only better. She resisted the urge to take out her phone and start snapping photos to send back to Erin, knowing that there would be plenty of time for that later. The living room was spacious, with faded rugs covering the herringbone wooden floors and a marble fireplace anchoring one of the walls. Sun filled the space from the tall windows that looked out onto the street below. The furniture was a mix of old and new, leading Sophie to believe that her sister had kept much of it the same from when their grandmother lived here.

Sophie took in the polished and long dining room table at the far end of the room, the cluster of chairs that were grouped near the hearth, and imagined what it might have been like to spend time here as a child the way her sisters had done. She tried to imagine her father's mother opening the door and welcoming her inside, into a world that she had never been a part of—until now.

Isabelle walked over and opened one set of windows, and the noise from the street filled the silence.

"This is beautiful," Sophie said, meaning it sincerely.

"I can't take any credit for it," Isabelle said. "It is beautiful, and I'm grateful for it every day. I used to love visiting Grand-mère here when I was a little girl."

Sophie could only nod. She'd never met her father's mother and had certainly never visited this apartment. It was an experience that Isabelle shared with Camille alone, another link in their chain, bonding them together, reminding her that she was still an outsider, and not just because of her American accent.

"Is this her picture?" she asked, crossing the room to the fireplace where several gilded frames were artfully arranged on the mantel.

Isabelle came to stand beside her, smiling sadly at the photo. "She was a beauty, wasn't she?"

Sophie picked up the black-and-white photo of her grandmother in her younger days, wearing a chic, formfitting satin dress and holding a glass of champagne. She was laughing in the photo, a candid, Sophie's favorite kind because they captured who the person really was, instead of making her guess what lingered behind the smile.

"She enjoyed life," Sophie remarked, smiling back at the still image of the woman she'd never known.

Isabelle gave a nod and then her smile turned rueful. "Papa learned it somewhere."

There was a brief silence while Sophie returned the frame to its original setting. She didn't want to talk about Papa right now any more than she wanted to think about her mother and all the texts she'd sent since Sophie had let her know she'd landed safe and sound, not when it could spoil this moment. She already had Camille to worry about without inquiring if Isabelle had any updates on their father.

Instead, she picked up the wedding photo of Isabelle and Hugh. The couple were hand in hand, running down the aisle through the garden where they'd been married, laughing as the guests showered them with rose petals.

"What a happy moment," Sophie said fondly, searching for herself in the crowd.

"Mm," Isabelle said noncommittally.

Sophie frowned a little, giving her sister a longer look, but Isabelle had moved on to the luggage now, her smile reappearing when she pointed down a long hallway.

"There are three bedrooms here. Mine is at the end. I thought I'd put you right next to me."

Sophie couldn't help but feel special at the gesture. Maybe Isabelle really did want her here, maybe she did view her just as much a sister as Camille. Maybe this time, now that they were all adults, it would be different than when they were kids and their age gap made them sisters only, not friends.

Sophie took one last look at the wedding photo. She'd been a bridesmaid, along with Camille, only Camille had stood beside Isabelle on that day, just like Camille had been the one to fluff her dress and help pin her veil, while Sophie stood awkwardly to the side. At the reception, Camille barely spoke more than two words to Sophie, focusing on her daughter and her daughter's father, her date even though she'd made it clear that they were not romantically involved, giving the briefest of introductions, referring to Sophie by name only, not by any sort of relation.

Papa had been there. It was the last time that Sophie had seen him, and the first time since he'd moved out and, more upsetting, moved on.

And when he'd crossed the tent and held out a hand, flashed that devilish smile of his that made his blue eyes twinkle, and gallantly asked her to dance, she wanted to say no. But she couldn't.

She could never resist her father. Few women could. She just never thought she'd be one of the many he left with a broken heart.

"Let's get you settled in your room," Isabelle said, rousing Sophie from her memory. "And then we'll go for lunch at this great little café around the corner."

Lunch at a Paris café? Sophie almost pinched herself, not wanting to wake up from this dream.

Until she remembered that it might all come to a premature end tomorrow when Camille arrived.

Six

CAMILLE

Camille didn't need to look up the address of Isabelle's apartment. She rattled off the cross streets to the taxi driver and sank back against the leather seat, closing her eyes to the view of Paris, focusing instead on her breathing, like she'd done on the Eurostar, only then it was because she was trying to take her mind off the thought that she was not only on a train going to her childhood city but, worse, in the Chunnel.

 For an agonizing thirty-five straight minutes, she focused on not hyperventilating while the train moved under the body of water separating England from Europe, because there wasn't exactly any hope of dealing with a medical emergency from the depths of the English Channel. Isabelle used to tell her that she worried too much; later, that she was a pessimist. Camille knew it was more than that. Her mind was on overdrive, capable of going to all sorts of dark places about what could go wrong. She had her dear Papa to thank for that—for the creative spirit that his daughters had inherited in their own, unique ways, and for proving that her suspicions were right. You couldn't trust anything or anyone. And so, the moment the train began its descent into the tunnel, she'd closed her eyes, gripped her seat handles, and focused on her breathing. She didn't relax again until light filled the cabin and the tension finally left her body. Even if, by then, she was in France.

But now the tension was back with each turn they took, bumbling down cobblestoned roads, turning right and then left, screeching to a halt for people on bicycles, no doubt. She didn't know. Her eyes were closed. She simply imagined.

Sometimes her imagination was her worst enemy. But sometimes, when she wanted to escape reality, it was her best friend.

Right now, as the taxi carried her toward Grand-mère's apartment, Camille thought of what Flora and Rupert were doing.

It had been a cheerful, typical late Sunday morning when she'd zipped her luggage closed, meaning that Rupert was making breakfast, like he always did, the only surprise being what was served. Today, he'd put together a special menu filled with all of her favorites, and she knew without him saying it that he'd done it because he knew how difficult it was for her to make this trip.

He just didn't know the real reason why she'd decided to go.

Sitting at the table, eating blueberry pancakes and drinking milky coffee, she'd had to all but force herself to finally walk to the door, and even then, she'd hesitated. It would have been so nice to stay in that world—just like it would be so easy to make that sort of morning a permanent thing.

But it was permanent. A constant. And committing to it, making it official, would only change things, and not for the better.

So now Rupert and Flora were probably taking a walk, or a bike ride, or maybe dusting off their tennis racquets for the season. And as much as she longed to be right there with them, to join in the laughter and the closeness and the fun, she knew that it was best that she wasn't.

She was here to clear her head. To remind herself of just how wrong love could turn out. And where better to do that than Paris?

She didn't even realize she was smiling until the car came to a firm stop, the driver's-side door opened, and Camille felt her spirits droop. She climbed out of the car and collected her bags, then paid the driver and slogged over to the door just as a handsome man was leaving the building.

He gave her a flash of a smile, one that reached his dark eyes, and Camille couldn't help but feel a little perked up. There were other men in this world, men other than Rupert, that is. She knew. She'd dated here and there over the years, but nothing ever serious. Maybe she'd even start up again. Have a French fling.

The thought made her almost laugh, but the man's smile broadened when he caught her grin.

"*Avez-vous besoin d'aide?*" the man asked. *Do you need any help?*

Camille had forgotten to prepare for this, the language barrier, and she was almost dismayed to realize that after all these years away, she was still fluent.

Or at least semi-fluent, she thought, stumbling over how to respond. The truth was that she wouldn't mind having some assistance with her heavy luggage, but she also didn't want to invite any further complications into her life.

This was supposed to be a girls' trip. Isabelle had said so herself. And that's what it would be. Two sisters, catching up and laughing over wine—and cheese. At least she was promised that much. So they'd be in Paris. At least she could indulge in some good bread.

"*Non, merci*," she told the man and rolled her luggage across the marble lobby. She eyed the elevator sternly, remembering how terrified she'd been every time that gate closed and the creaking sounds began, how a five-story climb felt like an eternity, how she nearly wept with relief every time it finally stopped, and she'd fling open the gate and jolt out onto the landing on shaky knees.

The six-year-old version of herself couldn't trust that elevator.

The thirty-four-year-old version of herself couldn't, either.

With a very deep sigh and yet another moment spent questioning her decision to come back to the scene of her best and worst memories, she hoisted her tote bag deeper onto her shoulder, grabbed each piece of luggage by the top handle, and began dragging herself up the winding stairs, her bags bumping along awkwardly behind her.

Each landing had a window, some to the street, some to the courtyard, but she didn't look out and admire the view. She knew the view. She'd climbed these stairs plenty of times, and nothing had changed in all these years. That was the thing about this city, and maybe life in general. Years could pass but the things that mattered stayed the same.

She was out of breath and hot and, admittedly, badly tempered by the time she finally reached the second to the top floor. Grand-mère's door was the second on the left, across from that deathtrap her sister called an elevator. She raised her hand to knock, remembering the last time they'd been here, when Camille was still wearing her blond hair in braids, when her family still felt complete.

That was back when things like the elevator just felt scary because of her imagination. That was before she knew that the things that you came to count on the most could be snatched away without any warning.

Grand-mère had been hosting Christmas Eve, as she loved to do. She'd opened the door and they'd stepped inside to see a tree fully decorated, sparkling in front of the large windows, with all of Paris illuminated in the darkness behind it. A fire crackled in the marble fireplace, and an antique record player filled the living room with Christmas songs. There was champagne flowing, trays of fruit and cheese, and pastries from the little shop around the corner that Grand-mère knew the girls enjoyed. She'd given them each a gift that night, wrapped in gold paper and tied with a bow. Two matching porcelain dolls in lavish dresses with hair colors that matched theirs, blonde for Camille, and brown for Isabelle, both with bright blue eyes and a sweet painted smile.

"Two sisters," she'd said. "A pair." And that's what they'd been.

And if Camille had any say in it, that's how it would have stayed. Two sisters. Their mother, their father, their grandmother, all tucked into this apartment, toasting to the season, to the new year, to each other.

Camille shook away the cobwebs and knocked on the door. Isabelle was expecting her; she'd be home. Sure enough, the locks turned and the door opened, only it wasn't Isabelle who greeted her.

It was someone she hadn't expected to see. Someone she didn't want to see, if she was being honest.

Someone who wasn't supposed to be here. Not in Grand-mère's apartment. Not in Paris. Their Paris. The city that housed their memories alone.

It was her other sister. The sister she'd gained by the loss of everything else. The one who didn't know what it felt like to have her father disappear at such a young age or to leave the only country you'd ever lived in, to worry what tomorrow would bring and what would come crashing down next. The one who had laughed all those years that Camille had cried.

The one Isabelle never mentioned would be here. And once again, Camille cursed to herself for coming here. She should have known better, expected the worst, or at least imagined it.

Because nothing good ever happened in Paris. And like so many other things, time hadn't changed that, either.

Isabelle could tell that Camille wasn't happy with her if her tense smile and wide eyes said anything. That was fine, Camille thought. Served Isabelle right, really.

After an awkward greeting, the eldest Laurent sister suggested they all get out and enjoy some fresh air, and Camille and Sophie eagerly agreed, because even Camille would rather take in the sights of this awful city than be trapped within four walls with two sisters she wasn't exactly pleased with at the moment. Soon, they were sitting at a café terrace a few blocks from the apartment, one of many that lined the streets in this neighborhood. At least here there was the distraction of the scenery, other people, and the very (very) occasional interruption from the waiter.

Camille had forgotten how in Paris you could linger for hours at a table with just a beverage. There was no one to rush you along or push you out. The sisters could spend the rest of the day here if they wished, and maybe they would.

Or maybe Camille would go back to the train station and put her return ticket to use.

If she could stomach the thought of that Chunnel again.

When they'd left France the first time, they'd taken the ferry, something she hadn't been able to face again even if it probably was a safer bet.

Instead, she gave Isabelle another long, silent look over the small table that was filled with three kir royales, a small bowl of nuts, and an untouched cheese plate.

It was coming on the time of day known to the French as the *apéro*, when drinks and snacks were consumed before dinner. As a child, it had been Camille's favorite time. It was when life slowed down, work and school were over, and evening hadn't yet set in, but somehow all the tough parts of the day were behind everyone.

If only that were the case now.

"So Sophie," Isabelle began, refusing to react to Camille's glare. "Are you dating anyone?"

Camille turned to Sophie with only mild interest. She had to admit that Sophie was a pretty girl. She had their father's dark hair, like Isabelle, but otherwise, she mostly resembled her mother, a woman whom Camille had made a point of never getting close to, and who had left most of Camille and Isabelle's care to Papa, anyway. Looking back on that time, which Camille tried not to do, she saw Sophie's mother in the shadows during those short summer visits. At the time, she'd assumed that her stepmother wasn't interested in forging a relationship, but now she saw it differently. Sophie's mother was focused on her own daughter, who was six years younger than Camille, and just a newborn when the girls started visiting.

Even then, Camille always resented having to share their father with Sophie during those precious fourteen days. And she resented even more having to board the flight back to England, while Papa returned to his new home with her new sister. Her replacement.

"Oh." Sophie's cheeks colored as she glanced at the table. "Yes. No. Sort of."

Isabelle smiled. "You sound like Camille."

"She sounds nothing like me!" Camille bristled. Then, a little softer, "You know I don't have a boyfriend, of any sort."

Isabelle merely raised an eyebrow at that.

Camille heaved a sigh. "Go on. Out with it."

"Out with what?" Isabelle said primly. Sophie darted her head from one sister to the other.

Camille leaned back in her rattan chair. "Isn't this the part where you tell me that I have issues? That I have a great man right in front of me that I don't even notice?"

"You know that I refrain from commenting on your love life," Isabelle replied.

"As I do yours," Camille said.

Color bloomed in Isabelle's cheeks and she reached for her glass. Camille decided to drop it. While she'd kept her mouth shut, and not without some effort, when Isabelle first introduced her to Hugh on a rainy summer night some six years ago, her eyes shining with joy, alarm bells went off in Camille's head. She braced for it—the inevitable tear-filled call, Isabelle working her way through a carton of ice cream to nurse her broken heart.

Only it was Camille who ate the ice cream while she sat

alone on the sofa most nights after Flora had gone to bed, listening to Isabelle on the phone, talking about her travels and her happiness. And it was Camille who'd eaten the cake at Isabelle's wedding, where she glowed from within, nearly casting aside all of Camille's doubts. But not all of them.

There was this whole business of Paris, the apartment, and then the gallery. Camille couldn't quite understand how her sister could be content to spend so much time in this city, especially when her husband continued traveling the globe—without her.

But then, who was she to talk? She liked her space, too. She was taking it right now from the man she loved most, only in her case, she rather hoped it would change the way she felt about him, whereas it was clear from the mere blush when Hugh was mentioned that Isabelle was still mad for her husband.

"Back to you then, Sophie," Camille said, and she realized that it was the first time she'd spoken directly to her younger sister since she'd arrived in town, and before that, all the way back to Isabelle's wedding. She'd done her best to avoid her then, too, but it was Papa's presence that had really unsettled her, stirring up emotions that she tried to keep from bothering her, reminding her of the little girl with braids she'd once been, even when she'd had her own little girl with braids sitting right beside her.

"Oh." Sophie's cheeks also turned pink. Camille refused to go so far as to think it was a family trait. One that she hadn't inherited.

"Who is this man? Is he cute?" Camille wasn't really interested, but she would rather talk about Sophie's love life than think about her own. Or her lack of one.

Isabelle laughed. "I'm sure he's handsome! Look at how beautiful Sophie has turned out!" She shook her head. "I still remember when you were a pudgy little baby. I used to love pushing your stroller around. Papa always let me."

Camille pursed her lips. Who could forget the early years of their visits when Isabelle played house with baby Sophie? She was like a little doll to Isabelle. Camille always preferred stuffed animals, especially after that last Christmas here in Paris. The sister dolls served as a constant reminder of the magical holidays that they'd never again celebrate in the beautiful apartment. She'd been happy when they'd been packed away for the move and then never removed from the trunk.

"Anyway, it's not what he looks like that matters," Isabelle went on. "It's how he treats you."

"Oh, come on," Camille chided. "It's not like you didn't marry a handsome fellow."

"And it's not like Rupert doesn't treat you like a queen," Isabelle shot back, smiling.

"Jack is very handsome," Sophie said a little reluctantly.

"Jack!" Isabelle nodded with approval. "I like that name. And where'd you meet him?"

"At lunch," Sophie said. "We always went to the same place, halfway in between our offices. I noticed him, and I guess he noticed me. And then one day he happened to be standing next to me in line. We got to chatting, and... Well, that was two years ago."

"Two years!" Isabelle looked surprised. "That sounds rather serious."

"Well, we live together. Unofficially. He still has his old apartment he shared with his brother." Sophie opened her mouth and then stopped. "We're taking some space."

Camille felt an unfamiliar sense of kinship for Sophie, but she quickly shrugged that off.

"Well, there's certainly no better place for a little time to yourself than Paris!" Isabelle grinned as Camille scowled.

Sophie, however, beamed. She swiveled her neck, looking up and down the street. They were seated at a popular café, right on the corner of a bustling area of Saint-Germain-des-Prés. There were three other cafés at this intersection, and others in between, along with a bookstore, a clothing boutique, and a chocolate shop that Camille had to admit smelled heavenly.

"I still have to pinch myself to believe I'm really here."

Camille fluttered her eyelids. Of course Sophie would think Paris was the best place ever—if only because Camille found it to be the worst. It was just further confirmation that they had nothing in common then or now.

"But you live in New York," she insisted. "Surely, you can't be that impressed by Paris."

"How can I not be impressed?" Sophie's eyes were wide. "The architecture. The cafés. The people walking by with fresh baguettes! And the language! Oh, I can't believe that I went so many years without speaking or hearing any French."

"It's amazing how quickly it comes back to you," Isabelle said, looking pleased.

Camille could only grunt, even though she secretly agreed. At least it would help her get by. Make her stay a little easier.

"Papa never taught me the language," Sophie said, a disappointed edge creeping into her tone, one of the first hints that she wasn't anything but completely enamored by their father. She'd practically swayed to every dance with him at Isabelle's wedding, after all.

"Well, we lived here for a big part of our childhoods,"

Isabelle reminded her. "We had no choice but to know the language."

The table fell silent. Their life here was rarely ever spoken about—regardless of Sophie's presence.

"How's Flora?" Sophie finally asked. It was the first direct question she'd posed since Camille had arrived. Was it possible she disliked Camille or resented her? But that was impossible. Camille had done nothing to this girl other than fail to embrace her with the same open arms as Isabelle.

Camille relaxed a little bit at the thought of her daughter. "She's getting tall. A little sassy, too."

Isabelle again raised a single eyebrow. *Like mother like daughter*, she was no doubt thinking.

"And where is she staying while you're away?" Isabelle asked.

Camille knew that Isabelle knew better than to assume Flora was with their mother. Despite living only an hour from Camille's little house, she wasn't the kind of grandmother who stopped by with a warm dinner when Camille came down with the flu or offered to bake cookies with Flora after school. She'd struggled enough with raising her own two girls once her marriage broke down, choosing to throw herself into an interior design career the moment she was back on British soil, a business that she still ran to this day.

"She's with her father, of course." Camille felt Isabelle's eyes on her as she rearranged herself in the chair to reach for her phone. Could the tables be any tighter? Desperate to avoid talking about the man who was perfect on paper and in real life, she scrolled through some photos and leaned into Sophie, only then realizing just how desperate she was.

"Oh, she's a beauty!" Sophie said, and her tone sounded truly sincere. "She looks just like you did at that age!"

Camille blinked at her, startled by this confession. "I didn't realize that you remembered me at that age."

"I remember everything about both of you," Sophie said, grinning widely. "What you would wear. How you would style your hair. The boys you liked that year. What you ate. What you talked about—or what I could try to overhear, at least. I looked forward to those summer visits all school year."

Whereas Camille had dreaded them.

Momentarily at a loss for words, Camille glanced at the phone again. "Speaking of Flora, I should call her. A mother never gets a break," she joked.

Isabelle's lips pinched before she took another sip of her cocktail, reminding Camille of the underlying tension that had been there ever since Flora was born. She knew that Isabelle felt pushed aside, and maybe she had been, but not by choice. By circumstance. And reality.

But Flora wasn't a baby anymore. And a call could wait a little bit.

Especially because a call to Flora would only make Camille think of Rupert, and right now she wanted to do anything but that.

She signaled to the waiter for another round of drinks, prolonging their return to the apartment, hoping that by the time they did, she could drop into bed and fall blissfully to sleep.

"Maybe a small break is okay once in a while," she said to Isabelle with a conspiratorial grin.

Maybe, this time, it was necessary.

Seven

ISABELLE

Isabelle knew that she should have told her sisters about their father's request, just like she should have probably warned each of them that the other was coming to Paris. She had made the conscious choice to leave that part out, and not because she was naive enough to think that now that they were all adults they might all be able to get along. Their time at the café had snuffed out that remaining hope.

She wasn't surprised that Camille wasn't happy to see Sophie any more than she wasn't surprised that Sophie was visibly tense around Camille. And it was for that reason that she had purposefully kept their invitations to herself. If she hadn't, then she stood a chance of neither of them agreeing to come and stay, and where would that leave Papa?

But now she felt guilty for bringing them here under somewhat false pretenses, sensing that both of her sisters continued to hold a less than favorable opinion of Paul Laurent, even though she hadn't been sure where Sophie stood until now.

It was clear that neither of them had spoken to their father since her wedding, something that Papa had alluded to and something that made her sad, especially now in light of his surprising request.

She considered blurting it out the next morning over croissants and coffee, but Camille was still asleep by the time she and Sophie finished eating and she hoped to spend a few hours at the gallery today.

"You can join me if you'd like," Isabelle told Sophie as they cleared the dishes, leaving two croissants in the bakery bag for Camille. "Unless you wanted to see the sights first?"

"I'd love to see your gallery!" Sophie said with sparkling eyes, and Isabelle couldn't help from reaching out and hugging her, holding her tight, this young woman who was still just a little girl in her mind and maybe always would be.

No, now was not that time to blurt out that Paul Laurent was requesting their presence. Now was the time to be grateful that both of her sisters were here, and that one had such an appreciation for it that it was almost contagious. Who couldn't see the bright side of the day with Sophie's overwhelming excitement?

They took Isabelle's usual path to work, stopping every so often so Sophie could take photos of cafés and storefronts that Isabelle passed every day but never thought of as particularly special until she saw the way her sister lit up with excitement. When the winding street eventually opened up onto the Quai des Grands Augustins, she heard Sophie gasp, and even she stopped to appreciate the view. There, just across the river divided only by its ornate and impressive bridges, was all of Paris, the Louvre spanning a sizeable part of the Right Bank in the distance, and the Notre-Dame in plain sight on the nearby

Île de la Cité. Isabelle played the tour guide, pointing out the highlights, even as she felt like she was seeing the city for the first time. Through Sophie's eyes.

"I'm sorry," she felt the need to say when they reached a quiet spot.

"Sorry?" Sophie stopped walking and stared at her in confusion.

"For not telling you that Camille was coming," Isabelle explained. *Or for why I invited you here in the first place.* "The truth is that I was afraid you wouldn't come if you knew she'd be here."

Or the whole truth.

"More like she wouldn't have come," Sophie said, showing a frown for the first time that morning.

Sophie was correct, not that Isabelle would admit it. Isabelle had hoped Sophie was oblivious to Camille's coldness to her when she was younger, but she was old enough to see it now and mature enough to understand it.

If only Camille were mature enough to see the situation for what it was, too.

"She's a great person once you get to know her," Isabelle said, hoping to bridge the gap between her two sisters.

"She doesn't let me get to know her," Sophie replied. "How can I ever connect with her if she's so determined to shut me out and treat me like a distant cousin?"

Isabelle had no excuse for her sister's treatment of Sophie other than the obvious. "I'm afraid that Camille never really recovered from Papa leaving."

"Another thing we have in common," Sophie said with a wry smile. "It's amazing how all these years later, one person can still have that much influence. He doesn't deserve it, really."

No, Isabelle supposed in some ways he didn't, but she also knew that it wasn't that simple.

"I don't think Papa set out to hurt anyone," she tried to explain, as she'd managed to convince herself over the years.

"But he did," Sophie said simply. "Relationships end, I get it. But the way Papa ended things is what makes it all so wrong. If you love someone, you don't just...disappear."

Isabelle could barely swallow as they continued the walk. No, you didn't just disappear if you loved someone, and that's exactly what Hugh had gone and done, wasn't it?

She glanced across the river, to the Right Bank, where most of the big hotel chains were located in the 1st or 8th arrondissements, closer to the tourist spots like the Champs-Élysées and the Louvre, many with views of the Eiffel Tower for lucky, or affluent, guests.

Was Hugh up there now, looking out the window onto the Left Bank? Was he thinking of her at all?

But he couldn't be. If he was thinking of her, he would have called. He wouldn't be living in a hotel, in the same city, pretending that he wasn't. If he loved her, he'd come home.

Camille had said those words to her years back, when she was only six, and Isabelle was nine. Papa had been gone for days, and this time, it seemed that he wasn't coming home. Still, Isabelle insisted he would. Maybe it was denial, or maybe it was hope, or maybe it was faith. She saw the hurt in her little sister's eyes, the tears that flowed each night when darkness came and another day ended, and as they lay in their twin beds, side by side, divided by only an antique nightstand filled with books and toys and treasures that they'd collected from the streets of Paris, she promised Camille that tomorrow Papa would come home. That he loved them. She said it every night, if only to convince herself, until one night, Camille stopped crying, gave her a stony look, and said firmly that if Papa loved them, he'd come home.

And he never did.

Deciding that was enough talk about Papa for now, and more convinced than she'd been earlier that she was right in not saying anything about his invitation yet, Isabelle linked Sophie's arm, the one good thing to have come from that painful part of her past, eager to catch some of Sophie's excited energy. She didn't want to think about Hugh or Papa. And she wasn't about to put a damper on Sophie's fun or cloud this beautiful spring day.

She had enough to worry about without upsetting Sophie, too.

With every step she took, her eyes darted, looking for a glimpse of Hugh. She knew that it was ridiculous. Not only was the city huge, and packed with tourists who flocked here every spring to see the cherry trees in bloom, but it was the start of the workweek, and Hugh's office (like his hotel and current place of residence) was across the river. He had no reason to be on the Left Bank, and he certainly wouldn't risk crossing one of the *ponts* knowing that he might get caught.

She didn't even realize she was scowling until Sophie nudged her carefully. "Is everything okay?"

"What?" Isabelle shook her head and forced a smile. "Oh, just thinking about the big opening. All the work I have to do."

And it was true, as a fresh surge of anxiety made her heart begin to race. She still had to finalize the guest list, confirm the menu with the caterer, and decide on the arrangement for the exhibit, which was her favorite part of her job and also the most important. Art wasn't always about something of beauty. Each piece was meant to evoke emotion, good or bad, or trigger a memory, hope, or loss. When people came in for the Gabriel Duvall exhibit, she wanted to give them an experience, not hit them square in the face with the biggest and brightest piece.

But she couldn't do that until Gabriel delivered the final painting.

"I'm happy to help," Sophie suggested almost hopefully.

"I can't put you to work!" Isabelle quickly dismissed the idea even though it was appealing.

"Are you kidding me? Spending time in an art gallery, on an island in the middle of the Seine, in Paris? That's hardly what I classify as work." Sophie's eyes went wide as if she'd realized her faux pas. "Sorry. I didn't mean—"

Had Camille said this, Isabelle would have taken offense, because Camille had a way of insinuating that her life was far busier and more important than Isabelle could ever understand, but coming from Sophie, Isabelle laughed, feeling better than she had just a moment ago. "I know what you meant and you're right. Even I can't call it work most days. I'm lucky to do what I love. In the city I love."

Even if she wasn't lucky in love.

"You are lucky," Sophie said softly as they walked.

Isabelle glanced at her. Now she was the one who felt concerned.

"How do you like your job? It must be exciting working at a major publishing house in New York City."

"At first, but then, it just became a job." Sophie hesitated. "I guess I always hoped that someday an editor would be reading my book. Instead, I'm the one editing everyone else's work."

Isabelle remembered clearly the little girl who used to scribble in her notebook on their holidays together. She'd always ask to read one of the stories but even then, Sophie had been fiercely private about her creations.

It had reminded Isabelle of Papa, when he was in the beginning stages of a new idea, and it was too precious to share.

"You're young," she told Sophie. More than nine years younger than herself. She realized that somehow that age difference felt huge, that she hadn't even been dating Hugh when she'd been Sophie's age. She hadn't traveled to dozens of countries yet. She hadn't moved into Grand-mère's apartment. She hadn't decided to open a gallery or dare to go through with it.

Everything had still been possible at that age. Unknown, but possible.

And now, everything felt cemented in stone. As firm as the bridge they now crossed. She'd made choices. She was settled.

And she was alone. And childless.

"Working at the publishing house must help your writing," she said, forcing her attention away from her own problems and onto Sophie's dilemma.

"If I could find any time to write," Sophie said a little wistfully.

"Maybe you'll find the time while you're here." Isabelle opened her free arm wide, sweeping the panoramic view. "Or the inspiration."

"Maybe," Sophie said, brightening. She sighed as she stopped halfway across the bridge to take in the view from all sides. "Do you ever feel like you're living a dream?"

Isabelle wanted to say that right now she felt like she was living a nightmare, but then she followed her sister's gaze, seeing

Paris as if for the first time, the landmark sites so close that it almost did feel surreal.

"Why haven't you visited until now?" she asked her sister suddenly. For a woman who was this enamored by Paris, it seemed strange that she hadn't come sooner.

"Oh." Sophie started walking again, looking distracted as she stared at the island they were quickly approaching, greeted at the base of the bridge by a cluster of charming cafés with tables set up under the fanning branches of tall trees. "After college, I went straight to work for the publishing company. I guess it just...never occurred to me that I could come, you know?"

There was something in the way she said it that gave Isabelle pause, but by then they were already approaching the gallery, and she had to fish for the key in her bag. She had only just turned the key and flicked on the lights when her phone started ringing.

She stared at the screen, her heart thumping so hard that she was sure that Sophie could hear it as she crossed the room to admire some of Isabelle's favorite acquisitions.

Isabelle knew that she had to make a decision quickly. She and Hugh hadn't spoken since the day after their anniversary, and then it was only long enough for her to choke out a comment about the beautiful flowers that she'd tossed in the bin. Since then, they'd texted briefly; knowing that she had her sisters in town ensured that he gave her space.

But now he was calling. And if she didn't answer, she would only delay the inevitable.

"I need to take this," she said to her sister before slipping out the door onto the narrow cobblestoned street. Then, upon connecting the call, she managed, "Hello?"

"Well, hello to you," came Hugh's rather chipper voice. "I hope I'm not interrupting sister time."

Her eyes narrowed. Since when did he care about her welfare? Not in a while, clearly. But for how long she wasn't certain. Months? Years? The entire time she'd been settled in Paris? Was that when it started? Had her moving into the apartment and him joining the Paris headquarters cemented their fate?

She could picture some young French woman working in the office, now lying in his bed.

She had to steel herself from not lashing out right here and now. But she wouldn't, and not just because it was a Monday morning and she was standing on a public street and Sophie could easily see her through the window.

She wouldn't because that would be rash, and right now, she needed to think clearly. Gather the facts, try to make sense of this. Prepare for the next steps, whatever they were.

Divorce. Just the thought of a life without Hugh felt impossible, but it was the bigger vision that made her heart ache in a way that it hadn't since she was nine years old, crossing the English Channel on that ferry.

It was one thing to lose a husband. But another to lose all hope of a child. And that was something she wasn't ready to let go of just yet.

She walked down the street until she reached the small parkway near the bridge that led into the Marais, all the while listening to Hugh talk about his make-believe business meetings in Tokyo. She finally found a bench in the shade, where she sat, not even trusting herself to speak, because she had only two choices: to feed into his lie or to call him out on it. Neither felt like an option at the moment. Not when she was tired. Confused. Hurt.

"How are your sisters?" Hugh luckily asked, changing the topic rather quickly, she noted.

"Sophie's thrilled to be in Paris," Isabelle said. "Camille... I'm not even sure why Camille came."

"Because you asked her to," Hugh replied.

No, thought Isabelle, there must be more to it, and it was only now, talking to her lying spouse, that her general suspicions began to grow. She'd invited Camille and Flora to Paris countless times, wanting them to stay at Grand-mère's apartment, wanting to show Flora all of the city's charms. Each time Camille made it clear where she stood; she didn't even bother with a polite excuse. But now, of all times, she'd come, and not for a short stay, either.

The question was: Why? And why now?

But that was a question for another day because there was a bigger one looming. Why was Hugh lying? And why was he bothering to call?

"Sophie's helping in the gallery today," she said quickly, before she asked a question she wasn't ready to hear the answer to just yet. "The show's coming up soon. Do you think—do you think you'll be back in Paris by then?"

"Oh, I don't know, babe. But I'll try," Hugh said without the slightest hint of dishonesty.

And it was that part that made Isabelle's breath lock in her chest and stay there, tightening it so hard that she wasn't sure she'd be able to breathe again.

He was lying to her, and she'd never have been able to tell.

Because maybe, just maybe, she didn't know him as well as she thought she did. Maybe she'd never really known him at all.

Maybe, just like with Papa all those years ago, she'd seen what she'd wanted to see. Believed what she needed to believe. Her father had taught her that anything was possible, but maybe some things simply weren't, no matter how much you wished they could be.

Eight

SOPHIE

Sophie walked the perimeter of the small gallery space, stopping before each piece to admire it, the way she'd been trained to do as a little girl when her father used to take her to the museums on Saturdays. But today, she wasn't as interested in the art as she was in what led her sister to acquire each piece. She wanted to see what Isabelle saw. To understand her sister better. To connect on a level that they hadn't before but maybe finally could.

She turned at the sound of the gallery door opening, expecting to see Isabelle but instead coming face-to-face with a man, and a good-looking one at that. He was tall, broad-shouldered, with dark brown hair that cut across his forehead, and Sophie found it a little hard not to stare. But it was his eyes that held her attention, unwavering in their deep-set intensity, as if he was expecting something from her.

Maybe wanting something.

Unsure as to what to say to greet this potential customer, she gave him a nervous smile while her mind went blank, losing all the French she'd managed to remember in the past week.

Finally, she gave up and said, "I don't work here."

"I know," the man replied in a heavy French accent.

"And how is that?" Sophie was curious, wondering if this man had frequented the gallery before.

His dark eyes raked over her. "Because you look and sound like an American."

Even though Sophie was, in fact, an American, and therefore should look and sound like one, she knew an insult when she heard one. "Very astute. Today is my third day in Paris."

The man gave a little smirk. "I see. So you thought you'd visit a small gallery, and snap a few photos for your social media, after eating the required croissant for breakfast, of course. Tell me, do you plan to take a river tour after this?"

Sophie's face flushed with heat. She *had* hoped to take a boat cruise today. A ride down the Seine checked off one of many lifelong dreams, and it would be a great way to see the buildings and soak in the reality that she was here, and that against all odds, she'd made it happen.

The man jutted a finger at Sophie's large tote bag, which still hung from her shoulder since she hadn't known where to set it and didn't want to take liberties by resting it on Isabelle's small polished desk, which appeared to be an antique.

"You might want to get a bag with a zipper," the man advised. "You don't want to lose your wallet."

Oh. Well, that was almost nice. "Thank you," she said pertly.

"People like you are prime targets for pickpockets," the man said.

"People like me?" she asked, barely suppressing her anger. She clutched the straps of her bag a little tighter.

"Young. First time in Paris. Maybe a little…we have a word in French… *naïve*?"

Sophie felt her nostrils flare. "It's the same word in English."

This earned her a little smile. "Ah. Well, isn't that nice?"

Nice? There was nothing nice about this conversation. And she intended to end it, immediately.

She opened her mouth to tell this man to come back another time, preferably when she was back in New York, but just then the door opened and Isabelle breezed in, looking more than a little rattled, with a pinch between her brow and a faraway look in her eyes.

"Ah, Gabriel!" Isabelle quickly composed herself and greeted the man with a broad smile. "I hope you haven't been waiting long."

"I just walked in," he replied, kissing her on each cheek.

Sophie's own cheeks warmed, and she wondered if she was expected to do the same or if the moment had passed. She hoped that it had and that she wouldn't have to get within an inch of this rude man.

"I see you met my sister," Isabelle said proudly. "She probably knows even more about art than I do, and she's certainly far more creative. It seems that the artistic gene missed me." She gave a little smile, not at all bothered by this. "But then, it just makes me appreciate what others can do all the more."

Sophie stood a little taller in Isabelle's presence. It was impossible not to bask in the light that her older sister always shone on her. Now it was her turn to give Gabriel a smug look.

"We didn't have the pleasure of being introduced. Gabriel Duvall." Gabriel crossed the room, and Sophie felt her shoulders stiffen as he set a hand on one and kissed each of her cheeks, finally giving her a proper greeting. He smelled like fresh soap, and even though the gesture was customary, she knew, nothing more to it than that, somehow, it felt...affectionate. If she didn't know better she'd say that he'd lingered a little longer with her than he had with Isabelle.

But then, Isabelle was a married woman. And probably five years his senior.

"Sophie Laurent," Sophie said, feeling a blush warm her face.

"An American sister?" Gabriel asked, glancing at Isabelle in confusion.

"Yes," Isabelle said with a smile in Sophie's direction. "We share a father."

"Ah," Gabriel said with a simple nod, as if that was that.

And any of the awkwardness that might have been there disappeared. There was no need for an explanation or expectation of a juicy story to tell. Isabelle was French and British. And Sophie was...

Staring. She didn't realize it until she felt Isabelle's gaze pull her away from this infuriating man, and one look at Isabelle's knowing expression brought a full blush to Sophie's cheeks.

So the man was attractive in a classic, if not slightly unkempt way. Jeans and a leather jacket, even on a warm day. His curly dark hair was tousled and his thick eyebrows framed his intense hold on her, which she had no doubt held oodles of judgment.

Self-consciously, she smoothed her hair with her palm.

"Gabriel is an artist," Isabelle explained to Sophie. "And not just any artist. My star artist. It's Gabriel's opening that we're prepping for today."

Sophie tried not to show her surprise. This was the guy that her sister couldn't stop talking about? The new talent that every gallery had hoped to feature for his debut? The one who all the press would be featuring?

Isabelle had portrayed him to be a quiet creative, someone who kept to himself. But all Sophie saw was an arrogant cad.

And a handsome one, which probably only added to his ego.

Sophie refused to feed into it by fawning over him, instead opting for a tight smile of recognition.

"So, Gabriel," Isabelle said as she moved to the back of her desk. She seemed a little harried, Sophie thought, and it wasn't like Isabelle to be anything other than composed.

Or so that was what Sophie always thought. But what did she really know of her sister in fairness? She hadn't seen her in five years, and before that, nearly eleven years had lapsed, painful teenage years when Sophie longed to reconnect with her older, sophisticated sister. To know that even though Papa was barely in her life anymore, her sisters still could be.

Now, though, seeing Isabelle check and then recheck her cell phone and then finally shove it into her handbag, she saw a more human side to Isabelle. Something more relatable. Something that almost made her feel like she was on equal footing.

Isabelle took her seat at the small desk and folded her hands in front of her, giving Gabriel a huge smile. "I'm dying to see your final painting. Now I can strategize the order of the pieces."

Gabriel shoved his hands into the pockets of his faded jeans. "That's why I'm here. I'm afraid I need a few more days to get it just right. I hope that's not going to be a problem."

"Not at all!" Isabelle said, but Sophie could tell by the high pitch of her voice that it was going to be a problem, at least a small one.

Maybe this explained the way Isabelle was behaving. This gallery show meant a great deal to her if she invited both Camille and Sophie to attend. In the excitement of coming to Paris, Sophie had managed to almost overlook the true purpose of her visit.

All the more reason to help her sister, she decided. Sure, she longed to see the sights, and positively ached to get outside and wander the streets, but there would be time for that.

Right now, her sister needed her. And it had taken twenty-eight years for her to be able to say that.

"I hear your show is going to be a big success," Sophie said to Gabriel, trying to control her stomach from fluttering when he stared at her from the hood of those thick eyebrows. "I'm actually in town to see it."

He looked surprised, or maybe flattered. It was impossible to know and Sophie wasn't sure she wanted to find out. Right now, all she wanted to do was make her sister's day a little easier, and ensure that this show was the success she deserved it to be.

"You came all the way to Paris for my opening?" He frowned at her, his eyes narrowing in suspicion.

Sophie's cheeks didn't feel like they could burn any hotter and she wished she hadn't said anything. Of course she hadn't flown halfway across the world just to see a random artist's opening, even if her sister did own the gallery.

She'd come because she finally had an excuse. After ten long years.

"Well, I came to visit my sister. Sisters," she corrected her, feeling the heat in her face rise by a few degrees.

She glanced at Isabelle, hoping to be saved, but Isabelle was frowning over some paperwork now, so Sophie was on her own.

With this man. Who would not stop staring at her, his mouth twitching, no doubt wishing he could insult her again, had Isabelle not been present.

"Sisters?" Finally, Gabriel turned his attention to Isabelle, forcing her to look up at him again. "How many Laurent women are there?"

Isabelle laughed. It was a lovely sound that made Sophie relax. "Three of us. My middle sister, Camille, just came over from London yesterday. I'm afraid she's still jet-lagged."

Gabriel frowned. "From a short train ride?"

Now Sophie had to bite back her smile. Maybe Gabriel wasn't so bad after all.

"And how long are you here for?" Gabriel asked her.

"I leave a week from Sunday," she replied, already sad that two nights had ticked by so quickly.

"You're in town for a while then," he remarked. Then, with a little smirk, he said, "I hope that there are enough tourist traps to keep you busy."

Sophie glowered at him, but Isabelle seemed to have missed the slight. Instead, she brightened and said, "Oh, Sophie can't wait to take in all the sights of Paris!"

She grinned at Sophie, who felt her own smile wither.

"To really appreciate Paris, you have to see it like a local," Gabriel said, his gaze locked on her in a way that made Sophie shift on her feet, feeling unsettled.

"Of course!" Isabelle said, nodding enthusiastically. "I hope to give Sophie more of my time, but I'm so caught up in preparing for your show."

Gabriel's dark eyes didn't waver. "I can show you around the city. If you'd like."

"Oh, no—"

"Of course she'd like that!" Isabelle said at the same time.

"Don't you need to finish that last painting?" Sophie stammered. Her cheeks felt like they were positively on fire now.

But Gabriel just shrugged and said, "I can't work all the time. I'm French!"

At that, he and Isabelle shared a laugh, one that Sophie couldn't quite match, and she gave her sister a nervous smile and a less-than-subtle look that Isabelle either didn't catch or chose to ignore.

"Well, speaking of work, I should be going," Gabriel said. "It was a pleasure." He gave Isabelle another kiss on each cheek with the promise to call and then pushed through the door, giving Sophie a little wave before disappearing down the street.

"Isabelle!" Sophie couldn't help it. She felt anxious. Nervous. Even distressed. But not in the way she did when she was around Camille. Now, this was more of a tightness in her stomach feeling. Apprehension, she realized.

Or maybe…more like…anticipation.

Nonsense! The man was a jerk, completely infuriating.

Handsome, but truly…loathsome.

"What?" Isabelle blinked at her innocently as she stood to fetch a glass of water from the small bar cart in the corner.

"You know that I have a boyfriend," Sophie said as she followed her.

Isabelle looked up at Sophie with a little smile. "I know you've been dating a man named Jack for two years. And that you're taking some space. Is that how they classify a boyfriend in America?"

Sophie swallowed back her answer, knowing that she wouldn't be able to explain any of this to Isabelle, at least not easily, or quickly. And Isabelle was stressed out about all the work she had to do. The last thing Sophie should be doing was adding to it right now.

"But I'm supposed to be helping you in the gallery," she said as Isabelle started riffling through a box next to her desk.

"You are helping me," Isabelle said, stopping to look at her squarely. She huffed out a breath before speaking. "Gabriel needs some watching over, especially if he's ever going to finish that last painting. This is his first opening, and he's never created an entire collection before. I'm afraid that without a bit of pressure, this last piece will never be finished. He may have downplayed the event just now, but trust me, he knows just how big it's going to be."

"I don't doubt it," Sophie said.

"What do you mean by that?" Isabelle asked, amused.

"Just that he doesn't seem to be lacking in the confidence department," Sophie said knowingly.

"Oh." Isabelle waved a hand through the air. "He's French!"

Yes. And so was Papa. And Sophie had had her share of French artists for one lifetime. It would seem, however, that Isabelle had not.

"You love this gallery," Sophie commented, looking around once more, thinking of the work that must have gone into making the space as it now was. Even though it was full of other artists' work, and an eclectic mix at that, Isabelle's stamp was all over it. There was warmth, beauty, and accessibility to everything about the space.

Seeing the distress in her sister's face, Sophie suddenly felt bad for resisting Gabriel's offer. "Do you really need that last painting to complete the collection?"

Isabelle didn't need to think about it. "Yes. He's been dropping hints about this particular painting all over town. The anticipation has been great for business, but people will be coming to the opening expecting to see it. If he doesn't deliver…"

"He will," Sophie assured her, even though she wasn't so sure. She didn't know this man, and Isabelle wasn't the type to worry without good reason. And right now, she was clearly, visibly concerned. "Unless…I can't speak to his character."

Other than to say that he was smug, rude, full of himself, and extremely outspoken. Throw overconfident in there and it was a truly unappealing mix.

"Oh, he's a great guy," Isabelle assured her. "And a brilliant artist. Just…temperamental, you know?"

Sophie raised an eyebrow, and they shared a small smile. They'd both grown up with the same father, if not under the same roof or at the same time.

"If you spend a little time with Gabriel, you can help me by putting the pressure on him, and asking about the painting a bit, subtly, just to encourage him." Isabelle tipped her head. "Plus, you'll get to see all the best parts of the city, I'm sure of that."

"I suppose that it *would* be nice to have a tour guide," Sophie admitted, especially since it was clear that Isabelle would be otherwise unavailable for several hours each day. And it would be an excuse to get out of the apartment and away from Camille for a bit, too.

"Absolutely!" Isabelle agreed with a firm nod. "Trust me,

Gabriel knows all the best spots in Paris. You want to see the real Paris, not just what the guidebooks tell you to see."

"I just don't want him to think of this as a date," Sophie said.

"So what if he does?" Isabelle shrugged. "He's single. You're...taking space. And you're in Paris!"

Sophie looked out the window onto the narrow cobblestoned street, at the antiques shop across the road, and the iron balcony with cascading flowers overhead. In the distance, she could hear the sounds of music from a street artist, like something out of a story. A movie. Or a dream.

Yes. She was in Paris, at long last.

"Make the most of it!" Isabelle went on. "Have the whole Parisian experience. The food. The sights. Maybe even the romance." Isabelle waggled her eyebrows and Sophie felt her stomach go all funny again.

"Maybe there's a better way to encourage Gabriel to finish the painting," she said, feeling desperate. "I don't see how I could have any influence over him. Besides, won't spending time with me take him away from his work?"

"Even an artist needs to replenish his creative well. And if you are worried about how it will look, think of it as research then!"

"Research?" Sophie asked weakly.

"For your novel." Isabelle seemed surprised to have to clarify, and it dawned on Sophie that Isabelle didn't have any reason to question Sophie's ability to finish a book, and finish it successfully.

She had faith in her.

If only Sophie could find it in herself.

Nine

CAMILLE

When Isabelle suggested lunch on Wednesday, Camille waited until her sister said, "Just the two of us," before accepting.

It had been a strained few days, and Camille had spent most of her time alone, walking the streets of Paris, strolling the long halls of museums, zigzagging through the Marais, and crossing back over the Seine late in the evenings, hoping to avoid too much "sister time" even though that's exactly what Isabelle had promised with this trip.

Camille told herself that the trip wasn't completely in vain. She was successful in avoiding Rupert for a bit, even if she did still think of him, especially when he sent her texts, updating her on the day with photos of Flora, and even more so when Flora herself texted from her shiny new phone, this time with photos of Rupert. Camille always felt a lift when her phone pinged, reminding her of the people back home, and the wonderful life she had waiting for her.

That was until she looked around, felt the pull of the city drawing her in, bringing her back to those happy childhood days spent walking these very streets, stopping in patisseries for her favorite treats on Sunday mornings, sitting at cafés sipping *chocolat chaud* on crisp autumn afternoons, or relaxing in one of the parks, her favorite being the Luxembourg Gardens with the large fountain and view of the Eiffel Tower on a clear day. And then she'd stop and remember how it felt to lose something you loved.

Because she had loved Paris once.

With that in mind, she kept her replies to Rupert brief and centered around their shared responsibility of caring for their daughter. That was what bound them, after all. That's what she would focus on.

"Sophie's going sightseeing with one of my artists," Isabelle added.

Camille couldn't help but bristle. In Paris for less than a week and Sophie had already found a new friend? It seemed that she was the only one immune to her sister's charms, and she didn't like referring to her as her sister. Or even by name. She preferred not to think of her at all.

That's what she'd done as a child. Out of sight, out of mind. If Sophie didn't exist, then maybe their father had a chance of coming back. They could go back to their old life, and all would be right again.

They could come back to Paris.

But they never had, and neither had she. Until now.

She swallowed back that hurt and grabbed her handbag from the small desk in her bedroom where she'd camped out while she wasn't roaming through Paris until late in the evening, avoiding dinners even though she longed to spend some quality time with Isabelle. Finally, that time had come, and Camille was determined not to mess it up by talking about Sophie or thinking about Papa.

"Where to?" Camille asked. They stepped out into the hallway, and Isabelle for once didn't chide her about the elevator when they left the apartment, instead, moving toward the sweeping stairs, which were admittedly easier to walk down than up.

"There's a little spot closer to the Seine that has delicious *crêpes*," Isabelle suggested, pronouncing the last word with a flawless French accent.

"You know me," Camille said. "If it's food, I'll eat it."

Isabelle laughed. "And as you know, in Paris, it's all good food."

That was true, and it made Camille think of their lazy weekend afternoons with Papa, when they'd walk for hours, stopping here and there for a snack or a small bite, eventually establishing their favorite places, and later, in Grand-mère's small kitchen, where she'd whisk up an omelet for dinner with fresh herbs from the terracotta pots she kept on her balcony. Those days felt so long ago now that they almost didn't feel real, but more like a story she'd heard about another little girl, one whose entire way of life didn't suddenly change and alter course.

"I took Sophie there for dinner on Monday night and she loved it," Isabelle said, and Camille glared at her when they reached the small apartment lobby.

The insinuation, of course, was that Camille had missed dinner, just like she'd missed last night's meal, too. She couldn't feign jet lag, so instead she'd used Flora as her excuse, hiding away in her bedroom with the phone, catching up on her daughter's day, whilst eating the baguette and brie she'd bought for herself on her way home both days.

"Is that how we're going to spend our time together?" Camille asked. "Talking about Sophie?"

Isabelle looked tired as she sighed. "Would you rather talk about Rupert?"

Point taken. Pinching her lips, Camille pushed outside into the warm sunshine, grateful for another beautiful day, even if it was in Paris.

The walk was short, and Isabelle filled it with details about her gallery, but by the time they'd reached the café, they'd covered that topic, and that just left a few things to discuss. And there was no way that Camille was going to talk about Rupert.

"So, Sophie is out on…a date?" Camille asked once they were settled at a sidewalk table. It was the lunch hour and the restaurant was crowded, but Camille knew that they wouldn't be rushed along, and she appreciated it. She wouldn't mind a long, lazy afternoon with Isabelle. It had been too long since they'd had time like this, and she felt like that was mostly her doing.

Besides her reluctance to come to Paris, she knew that her priorities had changed once Flora came along, and how could they not? She had gone from having to think about only herself to having to worry about a small human twenty-four hours a day, every day. Even now, when she was enjoying some "sister time" with Isabelle, a part of her mind was back in England.

She knew that Isabelle hadn't understood her sudden lack of availability once Flora was born any more than Isabelle could understand just how tired or busy Camille was all the time. Camille recalled being relieved when Isabelle met Hugh so that she wouldn't have to feel guilty about never being available unless it was on Flora's schedule. Then, Isabelle and Hugh started traveling, and as Flora grew older and more independent, Camille had more freedom and suddenly it was her sister who was no longer available to her.

Maybe that's why Isabelle had wanted her to come to Paris. Maybe she felt bad about that. Maybe they were both here right now to ease their quiet guilt.

Sure, there was the gallery's show. But it was one of many. And Isabelle wasn't the artist—not that Camille would be pointing that out. It would only lead to Isabelle pressing Camille to do more with her talent, when Camille was quite content illustrating children's books.

"I don't know if it's a date per se," Isabelle said, then paused to place her order in perfect French.

Camille soldiered on, knowing that her verb tenses were not quite perfect, and that her British accent shone through more than her sister's. Still, it was there, that French side of her that she couldn't deny, even if she tried to do just that.

"I get the impression that things aren't completely over with this guy she's dating in New York," Isabelle said.

Camille shrugged, already losing interest. "I wouldn't know. The first I heard of him was this week."

"It wouldn't kill you to be a little nicer to her," Isabelle said quietly but firmly.

"I've been nice!" Camille's voice rose with indignation. "When have I been not nice?"

"You certainly haven't been interested," Isabelle said. "And at best you're cordial, treating her like a distant relative."

"Well…" Camille raised an eyebrow.

Isabelle's lips pinched. "She's our sister."

"*Half* sister," Camille corrected her. "And we didn't grow up together. We saw her once a year until Papa bailed once again, and then we didn't see her again until your wedding. If that's not a distant relative, I don't know what is."

Isabelle seemed to struggle not to sigh while the waiter appeared with a bottle of Sancerre and poured them each a glass before setting the bottle in a bucket of ice and moving on to the next table—a couple in their twenties, clearly in love by the way they insisted on sitting so close they were nearly rubbing noses as they talked.

Camille managed not to roll her eyes. It was all exciting and new now, but she'd give them eight months. Maybe six.

Across the table, Isabelle was still looking at her with obvious disapproval. "She knows you don't like her."

Now it was Camille's turn to sigh. "It's not that I don't like her. I don't even know her."

"You don't *want* to know her," Isabelle said sharply.

Camille sipped her wine. She didn't want to argue with her sister and certainly not about Sophie. Besides, she couldn't exactly argue when Isabelle's point was correct. She didn't want to get to know Sophie—she never had. Sophie just stirred up all the hurt she'd tried to bury.

"It's not like she fared any better than we did when it comes to Papa," Isabelle pointed out.

Camille nodded at that. Again, she couldn't argue. And didn't want to.

"And I get the sense that she's uncomfortable around you," Isabelle went on.

"Around me? But I'm like…the friendliest person in the world!" Camille caught Isabelle's expression and laughed. "Okay, I can be a bit of a grump."

"A bit?" Isabelle raised an eyebrow. "You're a lot older than her—"

"Gee, thanks for the reminder," Camille said wryly, taking a longer sip of her wine.

"She knows you never warmed up to her. And she's old enough now to know why." Isabelle took a sip of her wine, too, and then set the glass back on the table. "She's so excited to be in Paris. Please, just…don't ruin it for her."

Camille opened her mouth to defend herself but then shut it promptly. Sophie was young, and her enthusiasm for this city was obvious.

And Papa *had* left Sophie, too. None of them had been spared. And maybe there was nothing to be jealous of anymore. Maybe there never had been.

"Okay," Camille said, eliciting a little smile from her sister. "I'll do it for you."

Isabelle frowned again. "Don't just do it for me. Do it for Sophie. And…for yourself. Sophie's a breath of fresh air. I think if you got to know her, you'd enjoy her company."

Camille wasn't so sure about that, but she also didn't want to continue this conversation. "I told you I'll make an effort."

Isabelle nodded, seeming to accept her words.

"So," she said, mercifully changing topics. "How's the job? What are you working on now?"

Ah, but not to a safe topic, per se.

Camille told Isabelle about her latest project, illustrating a children's book about two bears who built a tree house in the woods. It wasn't much different from the one she'd recently completed about a family of ducks who built a raft, and while Isabelle nodded along politely, Camille could sense that she was refraining from saying what she really wanted.

"You know that if you ever decided to expand your work, I'd love to showcase it in the gallery," Isabelle offered.

Camille gritted her teeth. It was a kind gesture, but it had a deeper meaning.

"I know you think I should be doing more," she remarked, relieved when the waiter appeared with their lunch.

"I think you should be doing what you love," Isabelle said.

"Who says I'm not?" Camille shot back.

Isabelle hesitated. "I'm just saying that you have a gift that not everyone has. Me, for example."

It was true that poor Isabelle couldn't even play a decent game of Pictionary. No one ever wanted her on their team.

"Just because I'm able to do something doesn't mean I should," Camille said. That applied to many things, she thought. Marriage being high on that list.

She looked down at her crepe, folded into a perfect square, dusted with powdered sugar, and drizzled with caramel that made her stomach rumble from the buttery smell.

She resisted the urge to take a picture of it for fear of looking like an eager tourist, but more so because the only reason she wanted to take the photo was so that she could send it to Rupert, who would appreciate it, comment on it, and inevitably make her laugh.

There would be no texting Rupert pictures of food. No texting Rupert about anything other than Flora's welfare.

She raised her eyes to her sister, waiting for what she knew was going to be said.

"I just worry that you're playing it a little safe," Isabelle said gently. "You're such a talented artist. Your watercolors! The one you gave Mum for her birthday last year was better than most things I see in galleries, and you know I've seen them all on my travels. There's a special quality to your work, Camille. Something that sets it apart."

Camille didn't take too much of what her sister said to heart. Were her watercolors good? Probably. Could she be doing more with her art? Yes.

And was she playing it safe?

Maybe, but so was Isabelle.

Isabelle had decided to open a gallery to showcase other artists, after insisting all her life that she had no talent of her own, even though Camille just believed it was untapped. When Camille had pointed that out one time, Isabelle had grown very defensive, insisting that she loved the gallery and that it was all she had ever wanted.

Funny, Camille had thought at the time. Up until then, Camille thought Isabelle loved traveling with Hugh.

But Camille didn't say that. She knew when not to push.

She lifted her fork and took a bite of her crepe, resisting a groan because then she really would be labeled as a first-timer in France, when in fact, she was one of them. Or she had been once.

"My watercolors are not that special," she told Isabelle after she'd swallowed. Her sister started to argue, but Camille continued, "And my schedule with the publisher is security, not safety. I have a child to provide and care for, and I don't think that sticking with a job that offers good pay and a flexible schedule is playing it safe. I'm being responsible. I don't have the luxury of taking risks."

Or, she didn't mention, the desire.

Isabelle went quiet, and Camille couldn't help but feel surprised. When it came to the topic of art, Isabelle was always eager to talk at length, but it seemed that her sister had decided not to push things, either. Camille studied her sister as she ate, watching as a little frown appeared on her forehead.

"So," Camille said, changing topics. "How's Hugh? You said he was in Japan?"

Isabelle took a bite of her food and nodded. "You know Hugh. Always on the road."

Yes, Camille did know.

"How's Mum?" Isabelle asked.

"Mum is Mum," Camille said, her heart softening when she and Isabelle shared a knowing smile. "She doesn't know I'm here."

"Would she care if you were?"

Camille considered this. Her mother was busy with her own life, the new one that she made for herself immediately upon their return to England. With each passing year, she seemed to throw herself deeper into her business, and with quite a bit of success.

She stopped by for holidays, birthdays, and the occasional school event. They even had the rare mother-daughter phone chat or lunch a few times a year. Their relationship was pleasant, better than some of Camille's friends had with their mothers, but it wasn't what anyone would define as close.

"I don't usually share details of my life with her," Camille replied with a shrug.

But then, she didn't usually share details of her life with anyone. Not even, she realized with a twinge of guilt, with Isabelle.

"You got that from her," Isabelle replied with another conspiratorial smile. "We both did."

"Is there something you're not telling me?" Camille asked, intrigued.

"Oh, nothing like that." Isabelle shook her head quickly. "I just mean that Mum isn't exactly demonstrative. Even when she was married to Papa, he was the one who cuddled us and held our hands."

It was true, not that Camille liked to reflect on that time in their lives or think of Papa as anything other than what he had turned out to be.

"Well, I'm not like Mum when it comes to Flora. She gets all the hugs she wants, whenever she wants, and sometimes even when she doesn't. I tell her I love her all the time. Probably more than she wants to hear. Like, I shout it out the window at school drop-off."

Isabelle laughed. "You don't."

Camille grinned. "I do."

Isabelle shook her head but she was still smiling. "That's the kind of mother I want to be."

Camille's hand froze mid-reach for her wineglass. This was the first time Isabelle had ever mentioned any interest in having a child. Up until now, she'd only ever seemed to find them inconvenient, which of course they would be if you were jet-setting all over the planet.

But now Isabelle was in Paris full-time.

Hugh, however, was not.

Camille opened her mouth to press her sister on this but then decided against it. Isabelle was probably just making conversation, keeping things light and relatable. They didn't have much in common anymore, after all.

"You're a good mother," Isabelle said, and the look in her eyes told Camille that she meant it.

Coming from her sister, who had been there for her on those dark days and months when Camille needed someone, this was high praise. Of all the people in her life, she valued Isabelle's opinion the most.

Other than Rupert's.

Camille pinched her lips. There she went again.

"Flora's growing up so fast," she said wistfully. "Some days, I miss the little girl who used to hold my hand and skip beside me."

Some days? More like most days.

Isabelle nodded along silently, no doubt growing bored by Camille's tales of motherhood. Camille knew how it was. She would have probably been the same way, had she not had Flora.

But she knew just how lucky she was that she did have a child—and how frightfully close she could have come to never knowing her or loving her. Had she and Rupert not crossed the line that fateful night but remained friends, then she wouldn't have her beautiful daughter and all the little irreplaceable moments that had transpired since then.

It didn't seem possible, how close she had come to missing out on the best thing that had ever happened to her.

If she hadn't taken a risk.

If she hadn't opened her heart.

Camille sat a little straighter in her chair. Well, she'd tempted fate once and it had been on her side.

But she wouldn't tempt it twice. She couldn't.

Ten

SOPHIE

Sophie couldn't believe that she had agreed to this, but agreed to it she had. And now here she was, at a café not far from the gallery, tapping her foot and watching passersby stroll past, hoping that her tour guide for the day was a no-show.

She had just finished the last sip of her *café crème* when she spotted him crossing at the corner, wearing the same faded jeans and leather jacket as earlier in the week, but looking even more handsome than she'd remembered—and she didn't seem to be the only one who noticed if the appreciative glances other women gave him meant anything.

Her heart sped up as he approached the café.

Dread, she told herself. And nerves. Spending an entire day with a stranger in a foreign country would unsettle anyone.

She averted her eyes and went back to the notebook she'd bought yesterday, the first she'd purchased in...years. Right now it was still nothing more than a book of blank pages, but maybe...maybe...

She felt the table shake as Gabriel dropped into the chair opposite her, forcing her to look up at him.

No kiss on the cheek today, she noted. Not that she was disappointed. Certainly not!

"*Bonjour*," she said pertly, hoping that her accent wasn't going to spark another round of commentary.

"It is a good day, isn't it?" Gabriel switched to perfect English, and Sophie considered asking him where he'd learned it but decided that she didn't really care to know, or sit through the answer. No doubt it would turn into a comment about how rusty her French was, and she certainly didn't want to have to explain why that was the case.

She firmed her mouth, defiantly looking out onto the street, a little thrill bubbling up inside her again when she remembered that she was here in Paris, yes, with an annoying French guy, but still, she'd done it.

At long last.

"How was your breakfast?" Gabriel asked.

Sophie looked down at the half-eaten croissant, which she intended to finish, whatever opinions he might have about that.

"Delicious," she said honestly.

He gave what appeared to be a sincere smile, one that crinkled the corners of his eyes and made him almost seem…approachable.

"Paris has the best food. I'll show you."

Sophie broke off another piece of her croissant and popped it into her mouth, savoring the buttery taste.

"What do you have planned?" she asked.

Ah. Once again, the smirk surfaced. "No plan. We just…live. We go where the day takes us."

Spoken like a true artist, and she should know, having been raised by one. Papa would sometimes retreat to his studio for days without emerging when he had a new idea, or lapsing into silence at random, unable to think of anything but his newest creation at inconvenient times, like say, in the middle of her tenth birthday dinner. When he was in the zone, he was transported, as if he were in another world completely, and he lost all track of time, not resurfacing until he was satisfied with his current masterpiece.

No wonder her sister was worried about Gabriel coming through for her in time for the opening. She'd grown up with Papa, too.

And as Sophie had come to learn with time, he hadn't changed much over the years.

"Unless…" Gabriel tipped his head and made a show of glancing into her tote bag that sat at her feet. Her open tote bag. "Perhaps you prefer to follow your guidebook?"

The question was posed with a mischievous smile and a devilish arch of his brow.

Sophie felt her eyes narrow on instinct. She'd seen this type of confidence before, the kind that sometimes accompanied handsome men who were used to charming and wooing women.

Men, she couldn't help but think, like her father.

She'd seen this exact kind of smile long before she knew what it meant, when Papa would take her to the grocery store for items for dinner, and women would pause near their cart to comment on how cute she was, only to then let their eyes drift to Paul, commenting on his French accent and wondering aloud where his wife was, wondering if there was any wife at all. She'd seen it at school functions, when he attended, or the trips to the beach when her sisters visited. She'd hear women laugh, and she'd feel special that her father could have that effect on people.

She just didn't realize until she was older what kind of effect it was.

But now she knew. It was charm. Appeal. Physical attraction.

And she felt all three at once from the man sharing her table, not saying anything, and not having to, either.

Sophie took a steadying breath and brought up Jack's familiar face in her mind, suddenly longing for the security and safety he brought to her life. For the ordinary.

But before she could dwell on that feeling for too long, Gabriel said, "*D'accord*. You want a plan? The first thing we're doing is buying you a new bag."

Sophie bit back a sigh of frustration. "You really think I'm going to get pickpocketed?"

Gabriel gave her a sly smile as he lifted his hand from under the table and triumphantly revealed her wallet.

She felt her mouth drop as she stumbled for something to say, but he just let out a laugh, long and rich, and not exactly grating, but oh so certainly boasting.

She snatched the wallet from him and shoved it back into her bag, which she picked up and held against her chest.

The first stop *would* be to buy a new bag. After that, she didn't know.

All she knew was that today was going to be a very long day, indeed.

By the time Sophie checked her watch and realized that it was nearly one o'clock, they'd already visited the Eiffel Tower (because even Gabriel couldn't deny her that experience) and taken a long walk along the Seine, eventually ending up in the Marais.

"Hungry?" Gabriel asked.

"Famished," Sophie admitted.

"There's a place on the corner that makes great sandwiches," Gabriel said, gesturing with his hand to an awning that ruffled with the light breeze. "We can eat in the Place de Vosges."

Sophie didn't dare admit that the Place de Vosges was on her bucket list out of fear that Gabriel would alter their plans, but she secretly smiled and admitted to herself that so far the morning had been almost pleasant. Gabriel had only scowled when she'd asked him to take her photo in front of the Eiffel Tower, but he'd obliged, anyway, and if she didn't know better, she thought she detected a hint of a smile when he rolled his eyes.

Once they had ordered their sandwiches and settled near one of the four identical fountains in the small enclosed park that Sophie knew from all her reading on the plane was surrounded by seventeenth-century redbrick townhouses, she pulled out her phone to scroll through the photos from the morning.

"You're a good photographer," she commented.

And he was. He had artfully captured each image, paying attention to lighting and making sure that there were as few people as possible in the backgrounds.

"It was my first love," he said as he unwrapped his sandwich. He smiled as he chewed. "Actually, my first love was Claire. She lived next door and she broke my heart. I was five," he added, pulling a smile from her.

Sophie supposed that this was the moment when she could

easily ask if he was in love now, but that would just lead to him asking the same in return, and she didn't want to talk about Jack right now.

Jack hadn't texted or called since the proposal that never happened last week.

Last week. It was hard to believe so much could change in just a few days. That one day she could be sitting in an office in New York, and the next day she could be sitting on the grass in Paris, surrounded by beautiful buildings rich with history.

It felt so easy that she wondered why she hadn't come here sooner.

Why she'd let a part of herself slip away. Why she'd stopped fighting for what she wanted most in life.

But then, she knew why. Just like she knew why she hadn't written her book. Why she edited other people's books instead.

Because it was safe.

"And what about you?" Gabriel asked.

"My passions? Or my first love?" Sophie took a bite of her sandwich, savoring the taste of the brie and perfectly baked bread.

"Your passion, I suppose," Gabriel said. "I don't even know what you do."

"I work for a publishing company," Sophie told him. She hesitated, but the intensity of his gaze told her that he would patiently wait for her to answer his first question. "I always loved to write. I guess I always thought I'd be a writer. Instead, I'm an editor."

"And I am a painter." Gabriel nodded. "Sometimes we find new loves when we find ourselves."

And sometimes you lose yourself in the mess of everyday life and all its setbacks and disappointments and responsibilities, Sophie thought.

"So, being an editor is your passion?" Gabriel asked, shifting his position so he faced her better.

"Not really," she told him. "But it pays the bills."

"So why not write on the side?" Gabriel posed the question as if the observation were simple, and maybe it was.

"I work long hours," she started to explain, seeing the lack of conviction in his face. "And I know firsthand just how difficult it is to get published."

"Those are just excuses," Gabriel said, leaning back to take in the view. "If you love something enough, you'll find a way to make it happen. It's no different than being in love with a person. You'd move heaven and earth to be with them, long for them when they aren't there, dream of them once they leave, and only feel whole once you're with them again."

Sophie stopped eating to stare at him, wondering if she had ever felt that way about Jack.

About anyone.

And without having to soul search, she knew that the answer was that she hadn't. She cared about Jack, and even believed that she did love him, but not in the way that Gabriel described.

"It's the same way with painting," Gabriel said. "I dream of painting, you know. I can't stop thinking about it, even when I'm not working. And it's never work, not really. It's...a calling. It's what I have to do. Whether I want to or not, it's not what I do but who I am. I wouldn't be happy without it. I wouldn't be complete."

Sophie nodded, even though she hadn't dabbled in her

writing in years. She'd neglected it, just like she'd neglected her dream of coming to Paris.

Now, though, she wondered if it was more than that.

If somewhere along the way, she'd neglected herself. If the part of her that was missing had been right there all along.

"Speaking of your painting," Sophie said as she folded up her sandwich wrapper. "I should probably let you get back to your studio. My sister will be pretty mad at me if I keep you from finishing in time."

"I will finish in time," Gabriel said with a small smile, and for some reason, Sophie believed him.

He cared far too much about his art to not make it a success.

"Besides," he said with a little quirk of his lips. "Maybe you are my muse."

Sophie's stomach swooped and tightened as she narrowed her gaze on him, determined not to fall for his practiced charms.

"And maybe you're a flirt," she replied lightly.

He shrugged, seeming undeterred. "Is that such a bad thing?"

Yes, it was, and she should have said that, but her cheeks flushed and she hid her face by turning to her left, taking in the cafés that lined the street level of the buildings, imagining what it might have been to live here when it was first built.

A phone rang then, interrupting this perfect Parisian moment. Sophie glanced down at her phone—seeing her mother's name on the screen pulled her directly out of the present and brought her straight back to her life at home.

"I'll call back," Sophie said, quickly dropping the phone into her new bag and zipping it closed. She'd dropped her old tote off at the apartment on the way to their first destination—happy to see that Camille was nowhere around.

But she couldn't avoid her sister forever—or her mother. She just didn't want either of them to spoil this trip for her.

"Well," Gabriel said as they stood and brushed the crumbs from their hands. "I suppose I should get back to my studio—only because I wouldn't want to get you in trouble."

There was a glimmer in his dark eyes that pulled another smile from her, and she sensed that this time he wasn't having fun at her expense, but maybe with her.

And despite her better judgment and all her expectations for the day, she had to admit that she was having fun, too.

At least...a little.

Eleven

ISABELLE

Isabelle sat in her gallery the next day, enjoying the quiet now that her apartment was anything but. It was strange, having her sisters there, even though neither talked very much when the other was around. Still, there was the familiar buzz of life: footsteps down the hallway, the running of the shower, the opening of the fridge.

She hadn't realized how used to living alone she'd become until these sounds became so obvious, and she now pulled up her calendar on her laptop to see just how long it had been since Hugh had last been in Paris—or rather, home.

She frowned as she looked at the screen, telling herself that this couldn't be correct. Last month, between his so-called trips to Brazil and Japan, he'd been here for four days. She remembered now because they'd had a picnic in the Parc du Champ de Mars near the Eiffel Tower, and then strolled home that evening, taking their time meandering through the streets of the 7th arrondissement as it turned into the 6th. For as long as she'd lived in this city, Isabelle always felt like there was something new to discover, and she enjoyed doing it most with Hugh, hoping that with appreciation for the city, he'd eventually fall in love with it, too.

Only it would seem that Hugh might have fallen in love with someone else. Right here in this city where he was spending more and more time—without her.

She scrolled back another month, her hand freezing over the keyboard. That couldn't be right. Had he not been home at all in February? Surely she must have just forgotten to add the dates. He'd been in Paris for Christmas and New Year's, and then he'd stopped by for a weekend at the end of January before flying to Chile. There had been talk of a romantic dinner on Valentine's Day, but now Isabelle remembered that she spent the evening with a girlfriend who worked at the Louvre, talking about art, and Paris, and indulging in good red wine and chocolate *soufflés* at a little bistro in the Marais.

She looked up to see a young mother pushing a baby stroller down the street, and Isabelle knew that she couldn't sit there for one more minute. At least back at the apartment she would have Camille or maybe Sophie to distract her unless she was out sightseeing again—but here, she had only her thoughts, memories, and longings.

Deciding she'd done enough work for the day, especially because she still couldn't begin to plan the installation until she'd seen Gabriel's final painting, Isabelle gathered up her tote. She took her usual route back to Saint-Germain-des-Prés, only it didn't hold the same magic it usually did, and she found herself wishing that Sophie were with her, not just because Sophie's endless commentary was a welcome distraction but because Sophie made her remember why she loved Paris so much. And that maybe Paris would be enough.

It would have to be.

Without Hugh, there would be no baby, and time wasn't on her side when it came to meeting anyone new. And besides, she didn't even *want* anyone new.

But did she still want Hugh?

Her head felt cloudy and her chest ached and she knew that the answer to that should be simple, clean-cut, straightforward—that's how Camille would see it. But Isabelle wasn't Camille and never would be. And this was about more than Hugh. This was about the life they'd shared, and the future she'd hoped they'd have.

And the part of it that depended on him.

Another woman with a stroller passed by her, and something deep in Isabelle physically ached. It wasn't just longing now, but loss, for what she'd wanted so badly and now most likely would never have.

Would the only baby she'd ever push in a stroller be Sophie, who was now a grown adult, not a pudgy little toddler with silky curls and a big smile?

With Sophie in mind, she decided to stop by a patisserie for a special treat. Her sisters hadn't all gathered for a meal since Camille's first day in Paris. They'd have omelets tonight, a good bottle of cold white wine, and something decadent for dessert.

Something that might be good enough to help her forget her troubles for a while.

But even as she admired the offerings in the shop window, she knew that this was wishful thinking. Even Paris, with all its beauty and delicious food, couldn't help her now. And if not Paris, then what?

Isabelle awkwardly carried the grocery bag, her usual leather tote, and a bouquet of flowers, all while trying not to crush the dessert. She managed to do this quite well, even as the sky turned overcast and raindrops started to fall until she reached the apartment.

She stared at the wet cobblestone, and then at her overfilled hands, weighing her options, wondering which object to sacrifice to the wetness so she could fish out her key, when the front door swung open.

Isabelle sighed in relief. "*Merci!*"

She started to move into the small vestibule, grateful to be inside and dry, giving a flash of a smile to Antoine as she went on her way.

He gave her a frown of disapproval. "Let me help."

"Oh…" Isabelle was used to doing things on her own. Her mother had raised both of her daughters to handle their own affairs and especially to never rely on men.

And yet that's what Isabelle had gone and done, anyway, wasn't it? Maybe not financially, but in every other way. She'd assumed that Hugh would take care of her emotionally. That he'd fill her needs by giving her what she wanted most in this world. A life in Paris. A family of her own. A baby.

"It's no problem," she replied with a tight smile. "I can manage."

She'd been managing on her own just fine since she'd moved into the apartment, and she'd have to get used to it full-time if she and Hugh… Her eyes filled with hot tears and she blinked them back quickly, looking away so her neighbor didn't see.

But of course, at that moment, the flowers that she'd rested rather precariously on top of the grocery bag started to topple, and, seeing as Isabelle didn't have a free hand, it was Antoine who stopped them from falling.

"Please. We're going the same way," he told her. "Just let me get my mail."

Isabelle was too tired to argue, and a moment later, she was relieved to be handing off the heaviest of the bags to her neighbor.

They stepped into the elevator, and Antoine closed the gate, locking it.

"This thing always scares me a little," he admitted, giving her an amused look.

Feeling more comfortable, she said, "You're not the only one. My father grew up in this building and he liked to tell scary stories about all the people who would get trapped in here."

"Did people really get stuck?" Antoine looked suspicious.

Isabelle bit back a smile, recalling Papa's fantastical stories.

"Only the ones who didn't fall to their deaths," she deadpanned.

Antoine seemed to pale before they both started laughing, and when they reached the top floor, both of them seemed to move a little quicker than usual to exit.

Isabelle expected Antoine to set the grocery bag outside of her door as she fished for her key. "*Merci beaucoup*," she said again.

"I'm happy to help," Antoine said, showing no signs of handing over the bag.

Isabelle opened her mouth to protest but then decided that she was too exhausted to argue. Besides, a little help *was* nice, and she was far too used to not having any.

She unlocked the door and set the key down on the small entry table, freeing up both of her hands. There was no noise from down the hall, no pages of a book turning or shuffling of feet. She was alone, and she had come here precisely so that she wouldn't have to be.

She reached out for the bag to liberate her neighbor, but something in his dark eyes warmed her, made her feel a little less lonely, for a second at least, and without giving it much thought, she said, "Would you like to come in? For a glass of wine?"

"That would be nice," he said without hesitation, and then proceeded to carry the bags into the kitchen, where he deposited them on the marble counter.

Isabelle narrowed her eyes suspiciously. "You seem to know your way around."

"It's not my first time in this apartment," he said with an easy smile.

Meaning he had probably helped her grandmother a time or two. Still, it was a foreign feeling to have a stranger in her personal space, and Isabelle suddenly felt nervous as she plucked a bottle of Sancerre from the refrigerator. The cabinet fronts were glass paned, and after a nod of approval, Antoine took down two glasses.

"We can move into the living room," she told him, already heading in that direction, eager to get out of the cramped kitchen before she started to regret this decision more than she already did. Really, what kind of message was she sending this man?

But then, they were neighbors. He'd helped her out more than once. There was nothing wrong with being friendly.

She realized as they took the two armchairs closest to the windows that she didn't know the slightest thing about him other than his first name. She knew that he lived alone, but then, she supposed that some people might think that she did, too, given how rarely Hugh was ever here. Like her, he left for work each morning, but she didn't know what that work was.

"How long have you lived in the building?" she asked.

Antoine did a quick calculation as he uncorked the bottle of wine. "Ten years?"

"And you're still scared of that elevator?" Isabelle couldn't help but laugh.

"I'm a rational man," he replied, giving her a small smile. "Anyone who isn't at least a little afraid of that thing is reckless."

Isabelle felt her smile fade then. Maybe that's what she was, reckless. Or maybe she just put too much trust in things, and in people.

Maybe Camille had it right all along. About the elevator. About a lot of things.

She accepted a glass of wine from him and took a sip, hoping to push away her darkening mood for at least a little bit. She had a friendly neighbor to keep her company, the rain was pelting against the long windows that lined the wall of the living room, and it was springtime in Paris. Surely, there was something to enjoy right now.

"It feels good to relax," she said with a sigh. Or try to, at least.

"What is it that you do for work?" Antoine asked.

"I run a gallery," Isabelle explained. "And you?"

"I'm a translator," Antoine said. "I work for the government."

"No wonder your English is so good," Isabelle said. Then, curious, she asked, "If you've been in my apartment before, how well did you know my grandmother?"

A smile lifted his face. "Very well. And I feel as if I know you too. She spoke of you girls all the time."

Isabelle was surprised by this, if only because in the year since she'd moved into the apartment, she'd exchanged only polite and brief words with all of the neighbors.

"I looked out for her," Antoine clarified. "She was an older woman, living alone. I know she was independent and proud. She didn't like to ask for help, but I was happy to offer it. In exchange, she always made me something to eat, and since I'm a bad cook, I was happy to have whatever she was offering."

They shared a smile and Isabelle felt her heart lift for the first time all day.

"She was a very good cook," Isabelle agreed. "I'm afraid I didn't inherit that talent so it will have to be wine from me."

"I like wine," Antoine said good-naturedly. "And good company."

"*Santé*," Isabelle said, giving the traditional French cheer as she raised her glass. "To Marie Laurent. Wonderful grandmother and neighbor."

"The best neighbor and, I imagine, the best grandmother," Antoine said, drinking to it. "She showed me an album once, of when you and your sister were little."

Isabelle knew the one. She found it when she moved in and now kept it on a shelf in her closet.

"My sister Camille and I lived in Paris until I was nine years old. When my parents divorced, our mother took us back to London."

"And how do you like being back in Paris?" Antoine asked.

"I love it," Isabelle said sincerely. "Although I don't think my sister Camille would agree. She's visiting for a bit."

"Ah, the woman with the blond hair?" Antoine nodded.

"She looks like Marie. I noticed her the other day when she arrived. I was going to offer to help with her bags, but I could sense that like your grandmother she would have scoffed at me."

Isabelle laughed. "You're right, she would have!" She shook her head, imagining her sister schlepping all that luggage up five flights of stairs. "Camille is very much like the French side of our family, even if she would never admit it."

"Ah, another Marie trait." Antoine smiled. "You must miss her very much."

"I do," Isabelle said. "After we left Paris, I didn't see her very often. But being back here in this apartment makes me feel close to her. It's almost as if she's right here sometimes."

"I can see you kept a lot of her things," Antoine said, looking around the living room that was a mix of new and old.

Most of the furniture was the same as it had always been, down to the threadbare and fading rugs that Isabelle never planned to replace. But the artwork was mostly new, from Isabelle's personal collection, lovingly acquired on her many trips. With Hugh.

Now she wondered if she'd take them down. Replace it with new work. From a new chapter.

"I needed to make it my own," Isabelle said emphatically, almost to herself. But her own was what it was, wasn't it? She didn't consider until now that Hugh had never put his mark on it. Aside from a few toiletries and drawers of belongings, she'd never have known that Hugh even lived here.

And maybe he never had. Maybe she was more of a stopover than she'd thought. Nothing more than another hotel room.

"And...you're married, right?" Antoine asked, looking only slightly unsure of himself.

Legally speaking, she thought. But she still wore her rings, and she twisted them now, not ready to take them off, not ready to admit that her marriage was over.

"Hugh." Just saying his name made Isabelle's heart start to pound. She swallowed back another sip of wine, barely tasting it, thinking that Hugh could be standing outside the building at this very moment, that he could turn the key, walk in, and find her sharing a bottle of Sancerre with a handsome man.

Even if it was just a neighbor.

"He isn't here often," Isabelle managed to say, hoping that was enough of an explanation. She couldn't exactly say that he traveled a lot, could she? It would be a lie because it was a lie. Hugh wasn't in Tokyo. Who knew if he'd ever gone to Chile or Brazil or any of those other destinations he'd talked about with her so casually.

"Well, if you ever need anything," Antoine said, "I'm just next door."

Isabelle smiled. It was a reassuring thought, even if she'd never act on it. This man knew her grandmother, and in a way, that made him feel like family.

She went to refill their glasses, but she was interrupted by the sound of the locks turning and a moment later, Camille stood in the entranceway to the living room, wearing a look that was a cross between curious and surprised.

"Camille," Isabelle said, rising. "This is my neighbor, Antoine."

Camille crossed the room and glanced at Isabelle before shaking his hand.

"We meet at last," Antoine said gallantly. "Officially, of course."

"Officially," Camille said, giving a guarded smile.

"I must say that you're very strong," Antoine remarked,

fighting off a grin. "It's no small feat to haul all that luggage up all those stairs."

Camille pursed her lips, but it was clear she was trying not to laugh. "Better safe than sorry, as the saying goes. When it comes to protecting myself, I do what needs to be done."

Yes, Isabelle thought, she certainly did. But at what cost?

She thought of Rupert, otherwise known as the nicest guy in the world, and how Camille was committed to keeping their relationship platonic.

But then she considered her own disaster of a marriage, and she supposed that maybe Camille wasn't wrong. Because she had someone to go home to when she left Paris. Whereas Isabelle was going to be all on her own in the city of love...

"Your grandmother always had nice things to say about you," Antoine went on, but Isabelle could have told him that there was no use in trying to charm Camille, who would close up the moment someone tried to flatter or compliment her.

Sure enough, Camille narrowed her eyes at him and then at the side table between the two armchairs, where the half-empty bottle of wine stood between the two glasses.

"This looks cozy," she remarked, meeting Isabelle's gaze with a challenge. "I didn't mean to interrupt."

"You're not interrupting at all," Isabelle said lightly, refusing to feed into her sister's judgment, even if it did trigger something in her. Guilt, she supposed, even though she'd done nothing more than reminisce about her grandmother with a neighbor. Even though her husband didn't feel guilty about his behavior at all. "Is Sophie with you?"

It was a stupid question to ask, but Isabelle felt out of sorts, and desperate for some normalcy.

Camille gave her a funny look. "Sophie's been out since

before I got up this morning. I had some sketches to do, so I sat by the river for a while. I forgot how warm it can get here in the afternoons."

"Then come sit down and join us." Isabelle motioned to the empty chair near the fireplace. "I can get another glass."

"I should call Flora, but..." She looked like she was making a quick calculation and finally said, "I'll get my own glass."

When she disappeared into the kitchen, Isabelle and Antoine shared a small smile. He was right; Camille was just like Grand-mère, in all the best possible ways, infuriating as they sometimes were.

"Flora is Marie's great-granddaughter!" Antoine said when Camille returned, helping herself to a heavy pour before sitting down on the nearest chair.

"She's my daughter, yes," Camille said. "Although she takes after her father much more than me these days."

It was the first time that Camille had mentioned Rupert outright since she'd arrived, and Isabelle leaned forward, happy to talk about him. She'd always liked Rupert, and she'd always secretly hoped that maybe Rupert would develop feelings for her sister because it was clear as day that Camille had always been in love with him, even if she'd never admit it.

She smiled to herself, thinking again of Marie Laurent. She'd been a widow for decades, and never talked about romance, but now Isabelle found herself wondering if her grandmother had ever found it again.

If Isabelle would, too.

If she'd dare to believe. Again.

"And she's the only grandchild?" Antoine looked uncertain, given the possibility, Isabelle supposed, that another might have come along since Marie's passing.

A lump formed in her throat and she forced it back with a sip of wine.

"So far!" she managed. "Our other sister isn't married yet."

"She's our *half* sister," Camille stressed before meeting Isabelle's disapproving glare.

"The American." Antoine nodded, polite enough not to feed into the family drama that threatened to unfold. "I didn't hear as much about her, I'm afraid."

"That's because Sophie never came to Paris until now," Isabelle explained. "Papa never took her. She never even met Grand-mère."

Antoine frowned. "That's a shame."

"Yes," Isabelle said softly, only just now realizing what a loss it was. For both of them. Grand-mère was the ultimate French lady, from her silk scarves to her signature red lipstick. Sophie would have adored her and Grand-mère would have been completely charmed by Sophie's passion for French culture.

She knew what Camille thought, that they'd missed out on so much because of Papa's second marriage. But more and more, Isabelle couldn't help but think of what Sophie had missed out on, too.

Christmases in this apartment, with the tree lit up and all of Paris glistening behind it. Walks through the different arrondissements, always with stops for her favorite apple-filled pastry, *chaussons aux pommes*, and chocolate croissants, or steaming cups of hot chocolate at little cafés. Picnics in the Jardin du Luxembourg. Rides on the carousel at the base of the hill in Montmartre.

There were happy times. If only Camille could remember them.

"Well," Antoine said, glancing a little nervously at Camille, who returned his gaze flatly. Challengingly, even. "I should leave you to your evening."

Isabelle had a strange urge to invite him to stay if only because he had managed to take her thoughts away from the present for a while and put them firmly back on the past, a time she didn't reflect on very often, but when she did, she did with fondness.

Instead, she stood and walked him to the door. Antoine's smile was warm when he stepped out into the hallway, where his apartment was just a few feet away.

"Thank you again," Isabelle said, leaning against the doorjamb. She was feeling relaxed from the wine, and all her earlier stress seemed to have melted away thanks to good conversation.

"Anything for one of Marie's granddaughters," Antoine said with a smile. "Hopefully, I'll meet Sophie before she leaves."

"I'll make sure of it," Isabelle said, giving one last smile before closing the door.

In the living room, Camille was waiting for her with a second bottle of wine and a pert expression.

"What?" Isabelle groaned as she moved back toward her chair.

"I didn't realize you were so friendly with the neighbors," Camille replied. "I seem to recall you telling me you had most of your packages delivered to the gallery since there would be no one to sign for them here at the building and you worried that they might get stolen if they were left in the lobby."

She had said that once, hadn't she? And it turned out it wasn't true. Someone had been looking out for her, all this time, even if she hadn't known it.

"He helped me with some groceries today," Isabelle replied

with a shrug, even as she struggled to meet her sister's eye. "It would have been rude not to invite him inside."

Then, because she could sense that this wasn't enough of an excuse for Camille, she added, "Not everyone cheats on their spouses, Camille."

But her eyes prickled with tears, damn it, and she blinked quickly before they could fall. A part of her longed to tell her sister what was happening in her life, but doing so would just confirm Camille's cynical belief that marriages didn't last, and neither did love.

Maybe she was right. Maybe Isabelle had been foolish and naive. Maybe all this hope for a baby was nothing more than a fantasy, much like her entire life.

"I'm not implying that you were cheating," Camille said tersely. "I mean, you? You'd be the last person to stray."

Isabelle sat a little straighter. "Are you saying that Hugh would stray?"

Camille looked down into her wineglass. "Of course not. I've had a long day, too much sun, and now too much wine. What groceries did you buy? Tell me we still have some of that brie I bought the other day."

Isabelle couldn't help but laugh because it was easier than pushing a topic that she'd rather forget.

"Of course. And something for dessert, too."

"What's the occasion?" Camille asked, perking up.

Isabelle shrugged. "I just thought we could all use a treat, that's all."

"We? Or you?" Camille asked.

"Honestly, Camille, I was just trying to do something nice!" Isabelle was exasperated as she stood but Camille set a hand on her arm, stopping her.

"I'm joking," she said, looking deep into her eyes. There was a softness there, an understanding, a connection that only a shared history could create.

Isabelle once again felt the urge to sit back down, to let the tears fall, and to share everything.

But talking to a stranger was a lot different than confiding in her sister. Isabelle didn't need to hear Camille say that she'd told her so or fight back a satisfied look that would only confirm her cynical view on life and love.

Because just like she saw Paris as beautiful, she wanted to see her marriage as something wonderful, too.

There were good times. She was sure of it.

Even if, like all those other perfect moments here in this city when she was a child, it came to a crashing, crushing end.

Twelve

CAMILLE

Camille woke up with a pounding headache from too much wine that she knew only coffee could cure. She opened her bedroom door, relieved to smell the fresh brew from the kitchen. She walked down the long corridor, expecting to see Isabelle, but instead, Sophie turned to give her a big, toothy smile.

"Good morning!" Sophie said brightly as she filled her mug.

Camille wanted nothing more than to turn on her heel and march back to her bedroom, crawl into bed, and toss the blankets over her head. But that would be rude. And no matter how much Camille might be tempted to scowl right now, she found she couldn't.

Just like she'd struggled to ignore Sophie during dinner last night, which had been, against all of Camille's expectations, relaxing. Even...pleasant. They'd kept the conversation light, mostly talking about movies, books, recipes, and anything else that they might have in common other than a childhood she'd rather forget.

By the time Flora had called and Camille decided to turn in, she found herself almost wishing that she could decline the call for more sister time—until she realized that must be the wine talking.

Still, there was something to be said about Sophie. She made it very difficult to dislike her and Camille wanted to—she really, really did.

Except that she wasn't a child or even a teenager anymore. She was a grown adult with a child of her own. She was old enough to understand the situation. To know better. To do better.

With shame, she gave Sophie a small smile in return.

"You're up early," she commented.

"Oh, not really," Sophie said pleasantly, cradling her coffee mug in both hands. "In New York, I'm up before six every day."

Camille glanced at the clock on the wall, seeing that it was half past seven, and then pulled a mug from the cabinet for herself. "Do you need to be at work that early?"

"Oh, no," Sophie replied. "But I usually hit the gym and then I have to shower, and the commute isn't exactly easy."

Camille nodded, remembering what her life was like in London during her college years, before she traded the city for the quiet life of the suburbs. She'd moved to her country town because it was more affordable with a baby, and practical in every other way, too. She couldn't imagine lugging a stroller up and down apartment stairs, much less groceries. And she used to love taking long walks with Flora, first when she was confined to a stroller, and later, when they'd walk slower, always stopping to admire the flowers, Flora's little hand gripping hers.

"I'm not much of a city person," she confided, surprised that she was only just now putting things together.

All this time, she had thought she had moved out of

London because she had to—now, she knew that she wouldn't have wanted her life to be anything other than how it had turned out.

And that was exactly why she would stop thinking about Rupert and what he'd said and how she sometimes felt. Her life was everything she could have hoped it would be. More, really, considering that she'd never planned to have a child.

Now, she couldn't even think of a world without Flora in it.

"So it's not just Paris then?" Sophie gave a little smile as she lifted the mug to her lips.

Sophie had her there, and Camille didn't see the reason to argue. "I like where I live. Flora has her friends, I have a sunny studio to work in, the neighbors are nice, and there's enough to do that we don't get bored. London is a short train ride away if we want to see a play or do some shopping."

"And Rupert lives close?" Sophie asked.

Camille felt her hand shake as she filled her mug from the French press. "Yes. Rupert lives in town, which is great—for Flora, I mean."

"And your mother?" It was the first time that Sophie had mentioned Camille and Isabelle's mother on this trip, and Camille knew that it was a deliberate olive branch, maybe even a sign of maturity. At Isabelle's wedding, she'd stayed away from the first Mrs. Laurent, aside from a brief introduction at the rehearsal dinner.

Looking into her sister's eyes, Camille saw the compassion that rested in them, and Camille understood what Isabelle had been trying to tell her the other day at lunch. She saw it for herself. Sophie knew that her sisters shared a bond. She felt singled out. Left out.

And Camille had been a large part of that, hadn't she?

"My mother's fine," Camille replied airily. "She spends a lot of her time working. She's a pretty well-known interior designer. I'm...proud of her."

She held Sophie's gaze for a moment, knowing that they both knew the obstacles Camille's mother had overcome.

But she wasn't alone in that, was she?

"How about your mother?" The other woman. It was the first time in Camille's life she'd ever asked about Patricia. When she was younger, the mere mention of Sophie's mother would make her entire body go rigid with anger. She thinly tolerated her presence on those annual visits, and certainly never warmed up to her.

But Sophie's mother wasn't just the woman Papa left Camille's mother for; she was Camille's sister's mother. A woman who had been let down and heartbroken just like the rest of them.

A woman who had been left to raise Sophie all on her own. She was all Sophie had, whereas Camille at least had Isabelle.

As a single mother to Flora, an only child, Camille understood that this bond must be deep.

Sophie looked surprised by the question and took a moment to consider her answer, glancing down at the mug in her hands and swallowing a few times.

"She's...fine. Busy. Well, maybe not busy enough." Sophie gave a little laugh, though she didn't sound very amused. "I always wished she would start dating again, but I don't think she ever will."

Camille said nothing. For the first time, she sympathized with Sophie's mother.

"Does she still work in the theater?" she asked instead.

"Oh, gosh, no!" Sophie looked shocked by the question.

"No, she gave all that up when Papa left. She has an office job now. A sensible job, as she calls it."

Camille was both surprised and not by this news. She understood more than anyone how playing it safe was sometimes easier than putting your heart on the line.

"*Bon matin!*" Isabelle appeared in the kitchen doorway, an uncertain smile on her face when she glanced from Sophie to Camille. "Everything okay in here?"

"Just pouring coffee," Camille assured her.

Isabelle looked from Camille to Sophie and back again, and, seeming to decide that it was safe to enter, pulled a mug from the cabinet and poured herself a cup of coffee.

"I usually stop at a café on my way to the gallery but today I have a lot to do," she said. "No pressure, but if either of you would like to join me, I have some catering details to finalize before the opening and I'd love your opinion."

Camille had planned to visit the Jardin du Luxembourg today and sketch near the fountain, but she could always put that off for a day or two.

"I wish I could," Sophie began. "But Gabriel offered to show me around the city a little more today."

"Then you should go!" Isabelle stirred cream into her coffee. "Has he said anything about the last painting?"

Sophie sighed. "Only that it's not quite finished."

"And how will he ever finish it if he's gallivanting around the city all day?" Camille didn't like the sounds of this Gabriel fellow. This opening meant a great deal to Isabelle if it warranted inviting both her and Sophie to France for it, and the artist was busy playing tour guide.

Or Don Juan, she thought, sliding her gaze to Sophie.

"Artists need inspiration," Isabelle told her. "Besides, he promised me he'd deliver on time."

"And you believed him?" Camille was aghast. Finally, she shook her head. "You're too trusting, Isabelle."

Isabelle opened her mouth to protest but then stopped. "Maybe I am."

Well, that silenced her. Camille stared at her sister, surprised by this admission, and more than a little curious as to where it stemmed from.

"Well, I think he'll come through," Sophie said emphatically. "He's excited about it, and the show. He won't do anything to screw it up."

Isabelle gave Sophie a relieved smile, but Camille just pinched her lips, trying to stop herself from saying what she was thinking.

"Out with it, Camille," Isabelle ordered, looking more than a little annoyed. "You don't think he'll deliver the painting?"

"I have no idea if he'll come through or not," Camille said honestly. "For your sake, I hope he does, but he's not scoring any points with me for delaying things and causing you stress."

"A creative process can't be rushed," Isabelle stressed as she added cream to her coffee.

Camille bit back a sigh. She rushed her creative process all the time when she was on a deadline for her publisher, especially a tight one. A promise was a promise in her book.

But not in everyone's, and Isabelle seemed yet to learn this lesson. Somehow.

"Look, you see the good in people. And you know this guy better than I do," Camille said, trying to be fair and stick to the facts. "I just know what I'm told, which is that he's late delivering the painting, he's spending his afternoons wooing a tourist—"

"He isn't wooing me!" Sophie exclaimed, but her cheeks flushed.

Camille gave Isabelle a pointed look. "And let's just say that I'm not impressed by him being an artist."

"Have you forgotten that you're also an artist?" Isabelle said with a raise of her eyebrows.

"Yes, but I'm not..." Camille shook her head.

"Go on," Isabelle said. "You were going to say that you're not like Papa, am I right?"

Camille said nothing but instead took a sip of her coffee, which was growing cold during this argument.

She was nothing like Papa. She'd made damn sure of that.

"Well, neither is Gabriel. Not every man will let you down, Camille," Isabelle said, but instead of looking satisfied as she normally would in pointing this out, a little pinch of uncertainty formed between her eyebrows, and her hand shook as she brought her mug to her lips.

Camille felt bad. She'd upset her sister, which was the last thing she wanted to do.

"Maybe I jumped to conclusions," Camille said. Then, with a little smile that she hoped would smooth things over, she said, "You know me."

Isabelle eventually smiled back. "I do."

There was a silence in the kitchen, one that seemed to stem from Sophie, who they all knew didn't know Camille, not in the way that Isabelle did, and maybe not at all.

And Camille had the sinking feeling that this was all her doing.

She swallowed hard, pushing back the discomfort that made

her stomach feel funny—telling herself it was just the effects of the wine from last night.

"So. Tell me more about Gabriel, then. How has he managed to get by all this time, if he is only just now being discovered?"

"He teaches art," Isabelle said. "He wasn't chasing fame and glory. He was simply doing it because he loved it."

Hm. Still, Camille was suspicious of this sudden interest in Sophie. She was openly excited about being in Paris. He was familiar with the city. It was...opportunistic. And given that Sophie would be returning to New York before long, it could only end, and only end badly.

"He's a very nice man," Isabelle said, giving Camille a reassuring smile.

Camille would be the judge of that. "Just how old is he?"

"He's only in his early thirties!" Isabelle laughed. "What's with the inquisition? Would you like me to pull his bio up on the gallery website?"

Actually, Camille would like that. What she didn't like was the idea of this man seducing her naive sister and tainting her experience of Paris.

"I'm just saying that you can never be too careful," she warned Sophie. "Men, especially French men, can be very charming."

Now Sophie and Isabelle exchanged a glance of amusement.

"Again, we're talking about Gabriel," Isabelle said, all humor in her voice now gone. "Not Papa."

"I'm not talking about Papa!" Camille shuddered to even think of the man. "I'm talking about this man. A French man. An artist. One who has taken an interest in Sophie under the guise of playing tour guide. Handy excuse, isn't it?"

"I thought it was a nice gesture," Isabelle said.

"He hasn't been inappropriate," Sophie told Camille gently. "And today we're just going to have breakfast and visit some of the smaller neighborhoods that tourists don't always know about."

"And it's probably safer than her wandering the streets by herself," Isabelle said, giving Camille a pointed glance. One that homed in on the fact that Camille hadn't spent any time with Sophie at all this week other than last night's dinner, which hadn't exactly been her idea.

"Fine," Camille said, even though she didn't feel anything of the sort. "Just...be careful. And don't stay out too late. And make sure you have some cash on you in case you need to get your own transportation home. Do you even have any euros?"

Sophie grinned. "I'll be okay. If I can handle New York, I can manage in Paris."

Camille pursed her lips, letting her gaze drift over Sophie's attire. It was a denim skirt and T-shirt, which would have been perfectly fine if the skirt wasn't so short and the top wasn't so tight. "Is that what you're planning to wear?"

"Camille!" Isabelle scolded. To Sophie, who was now looking down, studying her outfit with a frown, she said, "You look beautiful. Perfect. Very French." She gave her a wink. "You go and enjoy your day. I'll clean up here."

Sophie gave her a smile of appreciation. "Thanks, Isabelle. I mean, *Merci*." She grinned, proud of herself, or maybe just excited, and darted out of the room, her ponytail swinging. A moment later, they heard the front door open and then close again.

"What?" Camille asked, noting Isabelle's disapproving

stare. "I assumed you would have been happy that Sophie and I were talking."

"More like you were questioning her," Isabelle said.

"I was looking out for her," Camille argued. She dumped the remains of her coffee in the sink, deciding that she'd get a fresh cup at a café. Preferably, one that was still hot.

"She's twenty-eight years old. She lives in New York City. And she's not your daughter, she's your sister. Not that you've ever acknowledged that relationship before."

"Well, I am now," Camille said with a huff, turning from the sink. "And she may live in New York but she's never been to Paris before and she's looking at it all through rose-colored glasses."

Isabelle gave her a look of warning. "And it should stay that way."

"I just don't want her getting swept up in the romance of this city, thinking it's like something she read in a book or watched in a movie."

"And why can't it be?" Isabelle replied. "Just because you don't like this city doesn't mean plenty of others don't love it. It's her first time here. It may be her only time here. Let it be magical, Camille."

Magical. Camille paused, remembering a time when this entire city seemed to sparkle just for her. When she loved nothing more than staying up late just to watch the Eiffel Tower glitter for five full minutes at dusk.

And as much as she'd blamed Sophie for stealing that joy from her, she knew as a thirty-four-year-old woman that it wasn't Sophie's fault at all. It never had been. And that Isabelle was right. Sophie deserved to enjoy her time in Paris. At least one of them did.

Still, Camille wasn't convinced.

"And does that require this...this...*Frenchman* to be a part of her daily experience?" Camille replied.

Isabelle shook her head with a soft smile. "This is only the second time he's taking her out."

"This week!" Camille huffed. "I'm just being protective."

"You're her sister, not her mother. She has a mother."

"Yes, but I am a mother, and that's just something that you can't understand, Isabelle."

Isabelle's eyes went wide and she opened her mouth and then closed it again, officially silenced.

Camille knew that Isabelle couldn't argue with that statement. Her older sister status ended the day Flora was born, in Camille's opinion. Sure, Isabelle might have more years on her, but Camille had twelve years of experience that she couldn't describe or explain, but which had to be experienced firsthand.

"A mother is who I am at this point in my life and it's who I've been for a while," Camille explained. "Sophie is young and excited, and if she were my daughter in a foreign city, I'd want someone to be looking out for her."

"And you're saying I'm not?" Isabelle looked affronted.

"I'm just saying that I'm the one of us who has experience. I'm a mother," she repeated.

Isabelle blinked several times as she seemed to consider her response.

"Just because I don't have a child doesn't mean I'm not nurturing," Isabelle said, color rising in her cheeks. "I was the one who was there for you all those nights after Papa left."

Now it was Camille's turn to go silent. Isabelle never brought up that time in their lives; she knew how painful it was.

"And I was the one who used to push Sophie's stroller when

we visited Papa every summer. I was the one who used to help wiggle her into a swimsuit when Papa took us to the shore for the day. I used to braid her hair and play tea party with her. You were the one who wanted nothing to do with her!"

Camille stepped back, surprised by her sister's rare burst of emotion. "It's true, I didn't. And you know why, so I'm not going to explain myself. But I'm also not going to sit back while our younger sister goes galivanting around Paris with a strange man wearing a short skirt."

Isabelle rolled her eyes. "You really are cynical."

"Protective," Camille corrected her. "And I could say that you're too comfortable."

"Excuse me?"

"You're too comfortable, Isabelle. You have this cozy apartment that was just handed to you—"

"Hey, we could have shared it," Isabelle said. "Grand-mère left it to both of us, and I was the only one who wanted it."

Camille just stared flatly at her. "You have your gallery. Your marriage. Your world is perfectly laid out for you."

"That would be the way you'd see it," Isabelle said, spilling her coffee into the sink.

"Are you telling me I'm wrong? That your life isn't so perfect? That you've never once stopped to think that maybe it could all be snatched away or suddenly disappear?"

"I didn't ever think that," Isabelle said quietly, and then, with a flash of anger in her eyes, she stopped at the door to the hallway. "Some people just accept happiness, Camille. They let love into their lives. They trust people."

"Well," Camille said with a sniff. "They stand to lose a lot."

Isabelle stared at her sister for a moment, until Camille began to doubt her own words. But just as quickly, she reminded herself that all was not as it ever seemed. Not with her parents, and her so-called happy early childhood. Not even with Sophie, and her mother's marriage to Papa. Not with her and Rupert, who told everyone they were content with their situation even as he questioned it when they were alone together.

And maybe not even with Isabelle. And her perfect Parisian life.

Thirteen

SOPHIE

Sophie's legs were tired from hours of strolling the streets, not that she wanted to stop. Today, Gabriel had taken her to Montmartre, the charming little village perched on a hill where Sophie imagined she might live if she had been lucky enough to have come to Paris when she'd planned. They'd taken the metro together early in the morning to beat the tourists and ascended what felt like dozens of flights of stairs, rounding their way up to the street above as they took in colorful murals painted on the metro walls. Sophie couldn't get enough of every corner of this neighborhood, from the small gardens that were lush with greenery and flowers, to the charming variety of houses in different colors and styles that looked out onto the shops and restaurants lining the winding and narrow cobblestoned streets. She especially enjoyed the Place du Tertre featuring artists who worked on landscapes or painted portraits on-site.

"You know," she said as they leisurely strolled. It was nice to slow down, something that she didn't do often enough in New York. "You still haven't told me what you paint or what your collection is about."

"If I told you then it wouldn't be a surprise," Gabriel said, seemingly amused by her comment.

She gave him a funny look, wondering if he was serious, but then realized that he didn't want to talk to her about his work and that this was his way of telling her so. It reminded her of when she was little and her father was working on something new, something that he didn't want to put into words, but wanted to simply show everyone once it was complete.

"I get it," she said with a nod, because she did. They paused to admire a few more artists, neither of them commenting on the work, but each quietly assessing. She was sure that Gabriel had his own view, as an artist and as a teacher, but she was also sure that as a creative, he was not prone to judge, but rather to study, observe, and reflect.

Perhaps it was why she was so comfortable in his company. In many ways, he reminded her of her father. The good parts of him, at least.

"This is somewhere Papa would have liked," Sophie said, feeling nostalgic. Though she didn't know much of his life in Paris, she was sure that these streets were familiar to him.

"I'm sure," Gabriel said. "Your father is a very gifted artist."

"A tormented one," Sophie said ruefully. "He was always searching for his muse. I'm not sure that he ever found it."

"Isn't that what keeps life interesting?" Gabriel said as they rounded another corner, this one leading them farther up a hill toward the Basilica Sacre-Coeur. They stopped when they reached the top of the steps to look out over the Paris skyline.

Sophie took it all in, imagining her sisters somewhere down there, going about their business, Isabelle in her gallery, Camille probably on the phone with her daughter. And for the first time, even though she was technically removed from it all, she felt like a part of it.

Even, perhaps, a part of the family.

"I suppose that it is," she finally said when they'd seen enough. "But that's not what my mother would say."

"I take it that your mother is different than your father?" Gabriel asked.

Sophie laughed, even though it was far from funny. Once, there had been a time when her mother and father had a lot in common, back when her mother was involved in the local theater, making costumes and working on set designs. It was there that she'd met Papa, when he'd been in New York for a gallery opening and stopped by the playhouse to take in a show.

Her mother hadn't stepped foot in a theater in fifteen years. She hadn't picked up a paintbrush, either.

"My mother believes that life is better spent boring than interesting. That it's better to stay in one place, doing the same thing every day, even if it's something you don't enjoy, than to wish for something more. She's all about…embracing reality."

Gabriel's brow furrowed. "And she was married to your father? The great artist, Paul Laurent?"

Sophie wasn't so sure that her father was a great artist, but one part of Gabriel's question was true. "*Was* married. They divorced when I was twelve. My father loves adventure. And my mother…she loves security."

"She sounds like a woman who has been disappointed by life," Gabriel said sadly.

Sophie glanced at him, surprised by how quickly he picked up on this. "Unfortunately, she wants to keep me locked up beside her. If she had it her way, I'd live a small life, within a ten-mile radius of my childhood home."

"Maybe she's protecting you?" Gabriel said.

Sophie thought of Camille, and how she'd treated her this morning. It had been amusing, even flattering, to feel like her sister cared enough to be worried about her welfare, but now she saw it as something else, too. A symptom of Camille's own fears and worries, an outcome of her disappointments.

Life had let Camille down. And now she was trying to control it.

Maybe the same could be said for her mother. She knew that her mother worried about her, that deep down she only wanted the best for her. But the best for Sophie wasn't to be sitting in a gray cubicle doing a job she didn't enjoy day after day, simply because it paid the bills and came with a health plan. And it wasn't to marry a man she didn't love, either.

She glanced at Gabriel, who was giving her a funny smile, and for the first time in a long time, she felt a connection. Without having to say much of anything, or explain herself, someone simply understood.

Maybe even better than she did.

"Coffee?" Gabriel asked, sensing that she was getting fatigued. "Or...wine?"

"Coffee," Sophie said firmly, and not just because she needed the caffeine. She needed to keep a clear head around this man who wasn't just turning out to be an excellent tour guide, but also, rather worthwhile company.

She'd almost forgotten that she wasn't just spending time with him as a favor to Isabelle, but now she checked herself as he led her to the café across the street.

"You know every inch of this city," she remarked once they'd settled at a wrought-iron table on a narrow stretch of sidewalk, each with a *café au lait* in front of them.

"You'd think I lived here all my life," Gabriel said.

Sophie looked at him in surprise. "You didn't?"

He shook his head. "I only moved here a few years ago. Oh, I visited all the time, of course. But I was born and raised in a village about two hours from here, and that's where I lived until recently."

Sophie stared at him, trying to make sense of this information and how it changed the image she had of him. All this time, she'd assumed that his confidence with this city came from having grown up here. "What made you decide to move?"

"I needed a change," he said simply. "Besides...does anyone ever need a reason to move to Paris?"

She grinned. "So this city is new to you, too."

"Not new," he corrected her, "but, I'm still discovering it. There's always something to uncover."

"I feel like there's more to take in than I could ever possibly see!" Sophie agreed, widening her arms, as if embracing the busy streets around her, wishing that she could take them all with her back to New York.

"So, is Paris everything you hoped it would be?" he asked.

She smiled broadly, feeling her heart swell in a way that she couldn't ever remember it doing. It felt full, when for so long, a part of it was missing, and she hadn't even realized it. Or perhaps hadn't dared to admit it.

"More," she said.

A little wrinkle appeared between his eyebrows. "Why is it that you haven't visited before? You have a sister here."

"Isabelle has only been living in Paris since her—I mean, our—grandmother passed away and gave her the apartment," Sophie said. Even though she knew that technically the apartment had been left to the three of them, Sophie had never even considered asking for it. It wouldn't have felt right.

And Paris...Paris had still felt off the table. A forgotten dream. A forbidden place.

Not wanting to talk about her reasons for never visiting France, she quickly changed the topic.

Thinking of Isabelle's request that morning, she asked, "So...have you gotten much painting done since I last saw you?"

"Are you asking for yourself or your sister?" His mouth twitched when he asked the question, and Sophie felt comfortable enough to answer with full honesty.

"Both, I suppose." She gave a little smile. "I'm curious to know how you work. In fits and bursts? Or...methodically?"

"If I waited for inspiration to strike, I'd be a very poor man," Gabriel said with a laugh. "As it is, I pay my bills by teaching."

"Do you plan to continue doing that if the show is a big success?" Sophie asked. "To hear my sister tell it, this opening could be the start of a big career for you."

"My day job isn't just for the security," Gabriel went on. "I enjoy sharing my expertise."

Ah, the ego had returned. Only this time, for some reason Sophie found it more charming than irritating. Maybe because she'd come to see the person behind it.

"Can I ask you something?" Sophie asked. "If you don't paint exclusively when inspiration strikes, then why has it taken you so long to finish this painting?"

Gabriel raised an eyebrow, drawing a flush from Sophie's cheeks.

"Either you've done your homework or Isabelle's been complaining about me."

Sophie laughed. "I'm not stalking you, just so you know. I have better things to do. Like explore Paris." They exchanged a smile. "And Isabelle isn't complaining. She just wants the show to be a success."

"That makes two of us." Gabriel seemed pensive. "I don't always need inspiration, but with this painting, I do. Objectively, it's finished. But in my gut..." He squinted as he shook his head. "When it's finished, I'll know."

Sophie understood. "When you know, you just know."

"Exactly. It's not an assessment. It's a feeling. Like love."

Sophie knew she was blushing again, and she picked up her coffee to take a sip, nearly burning her mouth because she'd forgotten how hot it was.

Did you just know when you were in love? Did you get a feeling, something to confirm that yes, this was the one, the person who was meant to find you, to complete you, to share your life?

If so, it hadn't happened for Sophie yet. Either that or it had, and she just hadn't known what to look for.

"Even love is never certain," Sophie replied.

"Very true," Gabriel said with a firm nod.

"People marry and divorce all the time. My parents did."

"Are you saying that what they had wasn't love?" Gabriel countered, again with the stare, patiently waiting for her answer.

Sophie thought back on her parents' relationship, something she rarely did and hadn't done in years. It was happy at times, especially in the early years, and her childhood had seemed almost idyllic, with Papa always laughing, her mother greeting him each evening with a kiss and a long, lingering smile.

Until it all changed. Without warning. Then the memories became cloudy and confusing, mostly filled with her mother's tears, and later, her anger, which seemed to settle over her, defining the rest of her life.

Changing her. Not for the better. But for the worse.

"Maybe it was," she said reluctantly. "Or maybe it was infatuation. I'd like to think that real love shouldn't suddenly stop."

"You're an idealist," Gabriel observed, seeming amused.

"More like I'm a realist," she said, giving him a pointed look.

"A cynic?" He looked at her in disbelief. "But how can you not believe in love when you are here, in Paris?"

He spread his arms wide and Sophie took in the view, the people walking hand in hand, others on bicycles, weaving through the crowd, their baskets filled with flowers and books, baked goods, and notebooks. Music piped from the cafés, which seemed to anchor every street corner, and the sky was a brilliant shade of blue.

"It's as pretty as a painting," she mused.

Gabriel grinned. "That's exactly what it is."

Sophie didn't go straight back to the apartment after leaving Gabriel, only today it wasn't because she was avoiding Camille. The talk with her sister this morning had been...progress. Not great. Far from wonderful. Certainly not enough to make her envision long nights spent giggling together the way she'd once hoped to do.

But all the same...progress.

Sophie parked herself at the café *terrasse* she'd come to most prefer in their little neighborhood because of its cheerful flowers and prime people watching, feeling more comfortable each time she visited, even though she was alone. She ordered her usual, feeling a sense of pleasure that she'd been in Paris long enough to not feel completely overwhelmed, and pulled out her notebook. Since arriving, she'd jotted down various things: what she saw, what she ate, and memories that she hoped would last a lifetime.

Only today, after writing down all the details of the day, Sophie turned the page and started jotting something else.

It wasn't a continuation of her long-abandoned novel, the one that now served as a reminder of her failure, rather than a hope for success.

It wasn't much of anything at all. Just…ideas. Inspiration, perhaps.

Or maybe a feeling.

Just as quickly, that feeling was shattered when her phone beeped. And then beeped again.

Two texts from her mother were quickly followed by a third and then a fourth, and just like that, Sophie felt like she was back in New York along with all of her problems.

She stared at the screen, feeling skittish and guilty, even though she knew that she had absolutely nothing to feel bad about other than being dishonest—and the only reason she couldn't tell the truth was because she knew how her mother would react if she did.

She did the math. It was now roughly lunchtime back home. Her mother would have a short break in the day before she had to get back to her desk. She never complained about the job or the fact that she brought the same turkey sandwich and apple with her in a brown bag each day. The two weeks of vacation she accrued were the same each year: one week at Christmas, which Sophie was expected to spend at the house, one day for Sophie's birthday, which Sophie was also expected to spend with her, and one week in the spring, which was used for cleaning and gardening.

Sophie thought back to what Gabriel had said, about how Sophie's mother was just trying to protect her, and felt her heart soften a little.

She tapped out a reply, mentioning that she was having a great time and hoped that all was well on the home front.

Her mother didn't waste thirty seconds before replying, asking for a phone call, complaining that she needed to hear Sophie's voice.

The familiar tension returned to Sophie's shoulders.

She picked up the phone and again imagined a situation where she and her mother had the kind of relationship where they could talk about things adult to adult, not parent to child. A world in which she could tell her mother about everything she'd been doing here, the things she'd seen, the food she'd eaten, the conversations she'd had with her sisters.

She smiled when she thought of her mother asking her to tell her more, sharing in her excitement, and reveling in the adventure she was having.

But she knew that she couldn't tell her any of it. Not when her mother wouldn't understand.

Not when she wouldn't support it.

Sophie put the phone back into her bag and zipped it tight, then went back to her notebook.

And all the lovely sounds of the streets of Paris.

Fourteen

ISABELLE

Isabelle took her usual route home from the gallery that day, but instead of stopping by the boulangerie for a baguette, she walked past the street that housed her apartment, deciding to eat her dinner at the bistro on the corner. Sophie was probably still out with Gabriel and Camille—well, she could fend for herself. It was what she preferred, wasn't it? A life of solitude? One in which she didn't lean on anyone, didn't open up, or even love?

The only person Camille had ever truly dared to love was Flora, and that had been a surprise. A happy one, but an unplanned pregnancy all the same. Had it not been for those circumstances, Isabelle was sure that Camille never would have planned to have a child, but she'd thrown herself into motherhood, prioritizing her daughter above all others, determined to do better than their own parents. And loving every minute of it, that much was clear.

It was bitterly unfair, and Isabelle felt her eyes prickle with tears behind her sunglasses. She was grateful for the long Parisian spring days, how the sun still shone when her workday ended, extending well past eight o'clock. Once, it had felt like possibility continued. That until nightfall, there was still hope that something good or even surprising might happen that day. That it wasn't over just yet.

But her marriage was over, wasn't it? And her hope for a baby was, too.

Unless... But no. No! She couldn't possibly consider staying with Hugh just because she wanted a child. It wouldn't be fair to the baby—or Hugh, not that he was considering *her* feelings these days.

Besides, there was no telling when or if Hugh would ever grace her with his presence again. Having her sisters visiting was an easy excuse to keep him away for now, but what would happen when they left? Would he turn the key one night when his dalliance ended, claiming he was happy to be home at long last when all this time he'd been right across the Seine?

Maybe Camille was right. Maybe Isabelle had taken her life for granted. Assumed it would carry on just as it was, or even get better. She'd never stopped believing that a baby would come along eventually. She'd certainly never thought that Hugh would lie to her, or worse.

When she reached the bistro, she took a table on the *terrasse* under a heat lamp, in case she was there for a while. She ordered a glass of good red wine and then took her time skimming the menu, even though she always ordered the chicken soaked in the creamy mustard sauce.

Maybe she'd choose something different today. Embrace change. Accept that things were going to be different from now on. That the neat little life she'd made for herself was coming to an end.

Or maybe she'd hold on to the little things that still brought her joy instead.

"*Du poulet, s'il vous plaît*," she told the waiter. Her usual. She loved her routine, her life here in Paris, down to the smallest details, and she wasn't quite ready to give it up.

"*Bon choix, madame*," he replied briskly and took her menu. *Good choice.*

Was it, though? Going about her day as if nothing was different than the one before, when she didn't know the truth about her marriage? Only she didn't know the whole truth, did she? And maybe she never would, considering that her husband was so willing to lie to her.

She supposed that was part of why she hadn't confronted him yet. But the other part, the bigger part, was that knowing the truth would make it impossible to keep her life here exactly as it was. And right now, she needed to hold on to it for just a little bit longer.

Isabelle sighed and leaned back in her chair, turning to watch the passersby on the street corner but instead catching the eye of a man a few tables down. He was watching her with a small smile, and she looked away before registering that it was Antoine.

"*Salut!*" she said in surprise.

He gave a nod and then, after some hand gestures between the two of them, collected his book and glass of wine and moved over to her table.

"You don't mind me joining you?" he asked as he sat down. His soft brown eyes locked with hers.

"Not at all," she said honestly. "I could use the company."

"I wasn't sure if one of your sisters would be meeting you. Or...your husband?"

Isabelle's hand froze on her wineglass, and she slowly took a sip as she considered her response. She supposed she'd have to come up with a handy excuse, one that didn't lead to further conversation. One that didn't hurt too much to say.

"Hugh travels for business a lot," she replied. "And my youngest sister is sightseeing. And my middle sister, Camille, whom you met, is...well. She's just Camille."

She couldn't help but smile despite how upset she was with her sister at the moment. It was how their relationship worked, always had and always would. As the oldest sister, she felt protective of Camille, tolerated her stubborn behavior, and supported her without always getting the same in return. Taking care of Camille made her strong.

She just hadn't stopped to think that now Camille was following in her footsteps.

"Mini Marie." Antoine smiled. "Funny. My ex-fiancée is named Marie."

Some insight into his personal life. Isabelle felt her pulse tick with interest. She was more than happy to hear about his life rather than talk about her own.

"Was she as stubborn as my grandmother, too?" Isabelle asked with a conspiratorial grin.

"Worse." Antoine's eyes hooded.

Isabelle laughed. "What happened, if you don't mind me asking?"

She realized just how much she longed to connect with someone who may have experienced the heartache she felt. The betrayal and confusion. Really, she yearned to talk to her family, the people who were supposed to know and love her most, but her mother would be no different than Camille, saying "told you so" even if it was only with silence and a significant look, and Sophie...Sophie was young. Happy. Why bog her down with her problems?

"Not at all," Antoine replied. "We were young, in love, and broke, honestly. As the wedding day approached, I think Marie soon realized that married life was not for her. She'd rather be free."

Isabelle nodded along. "Sounds familiar." Then, seeing the question in his gaze, she replied, "My father has a wandering spirit. He loves life, and he loves love, and when he falls, he falls hard. Until something better comes along."

Talking about her father made her tense up, thinking of his pending visit on Monday, arranged to have given Camille and Sophie time to arrive over the weekend. She hadn't heard from him since she'd called to confirm the dinner, and a part of her dared to hope that this meant he would be a no-show—that she was right for not telling her sisters about the request if only to let them down in the end. But deep down she knew that he would show up, that his lack of communication was just Papa's way. He'd reach out when he was in town, assuming as always that she'd be available. That she'd have kept up her end of the promise. And he'd be right.

If she could convince Camille and Sophie not to flee back to their respective countries first.

Yes, all the more reason to wait.

Still, it didn't sit right with her. More and more, it felt dishonest, and she knew just how terrible it was to be betrayed by someone she trusted. First by Papa. And now by Hugh.

"And you?" she asked Antoine, getting back to the topic of his broken engagement. "Do you prefer being single?"

Unless...

She realized that he might have a girlfriend. Letting her gaze drift over his face, which was handsome in an approachable and friendly way, she knew that this was entirely possible—and strangely disappointing. Any woman would be lucky to have a man like Antoine in their life. She couldn't imagine him holing up in a five-star hotel on the Right Bank and pretending he was in Tokyo.

But then, once, she couldn't have pictured Hugh doing such a thing, either.

Still, there was no comparing the two men. Hugh was buttoned-up, polished, and always aware of how he came off to others. Antoine didn't seem to notice the world around him. When they talked, he never took his eyes off her.

As her heart fluttered, she almost wished he would. But only almost.

"I've grown accustomed to being alone," he said slowly.

"Oh!" she said brightly. Too brightly. "Oh, well. It's been a while, you said…"

He nodded. "I wouldn't say that I prefer it. Life is meant to be shared. So is this city."

She smiled. "Paris is wonderful. I'm trying to share it with my sisters, but Sophie has found her own tour guide in an artist from my gallery, and Camille… Well. Camille likes to do things her way."

Again they shared a smile, thinking of Marie, who wasn't shy in voicing her opinions or needs. Who liked things her way, on her terms.

Solitude could do that to a person, but with Isabelle's grandmother, it wasn't by choice. She'd been widowed, but Camille wanted to be alone.

"Where is your gallery?" Antoine asked as he sipped his wine.

Isabelle perked up as she always did at the subject. "On Île Saint-Louis. It's small, but it's all mine. I opened it when I moved to Paris last year."

"Art runs in the family then," Antoine remarked, looking impressed.

"Oh, not really," Isabelle said ruefully. "I'm afraid that I have two left hands. But I appreciate art. It was impossible not to, growing up as I did."

She smiled fondly, as she always did when she thought of her childhood, wishing that Camille was able to do the same.

"And your husband?" Antoine asked, breaking eye contact for the first time to slide his napkin around the table. "Does he like Paris?"

Isabelle took a long sip of her wine. It was becoming increasingly difficult to hold back the truth, especially when he'd shared the circumstances of his relationship. Especially when there was no one else to tell.

She looked up into Antoine's caring brown eyes, seeing no judgment or shame.

"Hugh prefers to travel. Or so I thought." She pulled in a breath. "I think Hugh does like Paris. I just...don't think he prefers enjoying it with me."

She blinked back hot tears, shaken by the sudden burst of public emotion.

Across the table, Antoine frowned before reaching over to set a hand on hers. It was warm and solid and so reassuring that she thought she really might cry then. "The man is a fool, then. Sorry. I shouldn't speak badly about your husband."

"It's fine," Isabelle said, lifting her hand to wave it dismissively. "And I'm not sure how much longer he'll be my husband. I haven't seen him in weeks. I don't even know where he is."

That was only partly true. She knew where he had been recently. And she knew he might still be right here in Paris. But it was easier to not think about that. To keep the situation vague until she was ready to confront it.

"Is he not answering his phone?" Antoine asked carefully.

"Oh, he is." Isabelle shrugged. "He just doesn't seem to want to be forthcoming with his whereabouts." She shook her head and stared into the distance for a moment, across the street, where the lights were starting to glow in the little shops. "It's funny, because Hugh always seemed like the total opposite of my father. He has a steady job, whereas Papa was always bouncing from one thing to the other. He's traditional, and Papa is anything but."

She smiled when she thought of Papa working furiously into the night on a new painting, or being stricken by a sudden burst of inspiration on one of their many weekend walks. Each time an idea hit him, he was elated, and overjoyed, his pace quickening along with his voice, like a child who couldn't wait a second longer.

When he had a new project, it became his obsession, his only focus. He gave up everything else for it: meals, sleep, birthday parties, and school events. Promises were broken but art was made.

Isabelle knew that he was like this when he fell in love, too. He gave up his family. He gave up Paris.

But Hugh…Hugh was always so measured.

She narrowed her eyes, thinking of just how strategic he was to continue to deceive her like this, to lie without flinching, for how long she still didn't know and may never, unless he was willing to finally be honest. And he might not be, even if she asked.

"But it turns out that Hugh is just as unpredictable as Papa," she said, turning back to Antoine. "And just as driven by his wandering spirit, except I didn't see it that way at first, because for so long I went with him, all over the world. And then I made the mistake of wanting to settle down, here in Paris."

And wanting a baby, she finished to herself.

"Some people aren't made for marriage," Antoine said frankly.

"No. And Paul Laurent is at the top of that list." Isabelle couldn't help but give Antoine a sly smile, but just saying his name made her stomach tighten and her thoughts of Hugh were replaced with another worry. "He's coming to visit, actually."

"Your father?" Antoine looked surprised. No doubt he'd heard his share of stories from Marie over the years. "You don't seem happy about it."

"My father and I have a complicated relationship but I've chosen to accept him for who he is rather than wish for more. I can't say the same for Camille. Or Sophie," she added, even though she didn't sense the same anger coming from her youngest sister. With Sophie, it was more of a sad resignation. "Like I said, it's complicated. He left us—all of us—when we were younger, and he's been in and out of our lives ever since. Mostly out. And…" She picked up her wineglass and took a hearty sip. "And my sisters don't know about his visit. Or that this is why I invited them to Paris."

"Why do they think you invited them?" He seemed intrigued.

Isabelle winced. "For a big gallery opening I'm having."

Antoine raised one eyebrow and then burst out laughing, a loud, rich sound that attracted the attention of a few fellow diners. And even though it wasn't funny, Isabelle couldn't help but laugh, too.

"I'm in trouble, aren't I?" Isabelle asked once they'd settled down.

"Do you want the truth?" Antoine asked plainly.

"Always," Isabelle said, meaning it. Even when it hurt.

He didn't say anything for a moment. "I'm afraid that you probably can't keep this secret much longer."

"No," she admitted. "I'm just so afraid of how they'll react when I tell them."

"When is he coming?" Antoine asked.

"In four days," she said. Then, seeing Antoine's reaction, she quickly added, "Or so he says. With him, you never know." There was a very real possibility that Papa would forget or change his mind. It wouldn't be the first time.

But something told her that she wasn't so lucky. That this time, Papa intended to follow through on a plan.

Her stomach tightened when she remembered the tone of his voice. How serious he sounded, even when he assured her that everything was fine.

"It must be quite serious for my father to insist we are all together for this visit," Isabelle said worriedly.

"He didn't give a reason?" Antoine asked. "But did he need to?"

Isabelle thought about her mother, who, while Isabelle was

still living in London, might call and suggest lunch, and Isabelle would think nothing of it.

"Papa doesn't make casual visits," she explained. "And he's never requested that all of us are together, especially when he knows that Sophie lives abroad."

"Perhaps you are right, then, and it could be serious," Antoine said thoughtfully.

Isabelle chewed her lip. A dozen catastrophic thoughts had already crossed her mind, each one more devastating than the next.

"You shouldn't have to worry about this on your own," Antoine said. "Camille and Sophie are his daughters, too."

True, all true, but again, it was complicated.

"Over the years, it seems that I've fallen into the role of being the spokesman for Papa. We haven't seen each other in a couple of years, and that was only because I happened to be visiting Istanbul and he was briefly living there. He calls at Christmas—sometimes. But I don't think he reaches out to my sisters anymore. I try to paint him—no pun intended—in a good light, because I've hoped that Camille would come around as she got older." She paused when their food arrived. Chicken for her, and a steak for Antoine. "But I've also tried to protect Camille. She was so hurt when Papa left, and then when Sophie was born just months later. Camille felt replaced, and it took a long time for her to get over that feeling. It's a fine line, knowing how hard to push."

"You sound like a mother," Antoine said with a kind smile.

Nevertheless, his words punched her straight in the gut.

"Just a sister," she replied softly. That's all she would ever be. To Camille. And to Sophie, the baby she used to push in the stroller, now all grown up.

"Well, if he's coming on Monday, then you have to tell your sisters," Antoine told her.

Isabelle nodded. Yes, she did. She knew she did. She just couldn't bear the thought of losing their company when she needed it the most.

But now she risked something worse—losing their trust.

Fifteen

CAMILLE

The first thing Camille did when she woke up on Saturday was the same thing she had done every morning since arriving in Paris. She checked her phone for any texts or missed calls from Flora—and Rupert—and then she sent Flora a good-morning text.

And then she spent a solid twenty minutes scrolling her photos, telling herself she was just looking at the ones of Flora, even though Rupert was featured in so many of them. She had even zoomed in on his face, her chest tightening every time she saw his broad smile and the way it made the corners of his eyes crinkle. The way his entire face lit up when Flora was in his presence.

Tossing the phone onto the bed, Camille pushed back the duvet and stood, stretching her back and sneaking a glance out the window into the neighboring buildings, all nearly identical, differentiated by the plants that lined the iron balconies. It was slightly overcast, meaning the weather could probably go either way, and Camille found herself hoping for sunshine, if only because it would make it easier to spend a day wandering. She'd already hit all the museums, getting lost in each one, purposefully winding her way through the halls without bothering with a map, aching for anything to distract her from the constant thoughts of her family.

Because that's what Flora and Rupert were, weren't they? However unconventional, however misunderstood. They were her family.

And that was why she had to protect them at all costs. Especially Flora.

For her daughter's sake, she would stay strong. Stay the course. Preserve their wonderful life. It was and always had been.

She wouldn't long for more. Because she'd learned a long time ago that when you wished for more, and dared to go for it, it usually only ended in disappointment.

Her sisters were already awake and dressed when Camille left her bedroom—purposefully not taking her phone with her.

"Good morning, sleepyhead," Isabelle teased.

Camille gave a guilty smile. "I needed the extra hours. I didn't sleep well last night."

That was an understatement. She'd been awake from one o'clock onward, her mind racing, her thoughts alternating from Flora to Rupert. She'd only finally found sleep once the sun began to rise, and now she'd slept the morning away.

"Get dressed and join us!" Isabelle told her. "We're going out to lunch."

"You're not going into the gallery?" Camille remarked. Isabelle had been gone from dawn to dusk the day before and Sophie had, too, on yet another date with Gabriel—leaving Camille to think far too much about how much she missed Flora. And Rupert.

Isabelle stood and moved into the kitchen to rinse her coffee cup. "Maybe I will later, but it's already Saturday, and we haven't had a meal together in days."

And this was supposed to be a bonding trip. *Sister time*, Camille believed were Isabelle's exact words. And exactly what Camille needed to keep her mind busy. She'd just been lonely, and she could only work for so many hours each day. Yes, a day of fun would cure everything and clear her head. She had no doubt that by the time she went to bed tonight, she'd sleep like a baby.

She went back to her bedroom, quickly dressed, pulled her hair back into a low ponytail, and put on a bit of mascara and lipstick, then, eyeing the phone, cursed to herself and stuffed it into her handbag, telling herself that as a mother, she had to be reachable and that she would look at it only if she was contacted by Rupert or Flora.

Rupert and Flora who probably already made breakfast this morning, like they usually did on weekends. What would it be today? Eggs and toast? But no, Rupert would probably want to do something more special, seeing as it was just the two of them.

Just the two of them. Something about that statement didn't sound right. Not when she wasn't there, a part of the laughter and the mess. The plans for the day.

Nonsense! Camille pushed out into the hallway and hurried to the front door. "Where to?" she asked before hurrying down the stairs while her sisters took the elevator.

Once they were settled at a table at a pretty café around the corner from the apartment, their drinks in front of them, their food ordered, Camille focused her attention on Sophie, because it was certainly easier than thinking of herself.

"How was your day with Gabriel yesterday? You must have

gotten in late. You were still out when I got home. Same with you," she said, giving Isabelle a pointed look.

"I was at work," Isabelle said airily, but she didn't meet her eye. She turned to Sophie. "Has Gabriel said any more about the final painting?"

"I know he hopes to finish it this weekend," Sophie said, but Isabelle looked only mildly relieved by that news.

"You'll believe it when you see it?" Camille gave her sister a little smile. "Maybe you're not quite as trusting as I thought you were."

She eyed her sister, wondering if there was more going on than Isabelle was leading her to believe.

On the surface, Isabelle's life certainly seemed perfect. She had a beautiful apartment in one of the best neighborhoods in Paris. A gallery in the heart of the city. A handsome husband who she never complained about. She never openly longed for more or expressed fault with anything.

And maybe she didn't need to. Maybe her life was just that. Perfect.

And maybe Camille's was not, because something was still missing. By choice, but still, missing.

"It's okay to trust people, Camille," Isabelle said, but again, she didn't meet her eye. Instead, she turned to Sophie. "But I was wrong for pushing Gabriel on you, Sophie."

"Oh, you didn't push him on me," Sophie protested, but Isabelle just shook her head.

"I had an ulterior motive. I did think you'd have fun. I wanted you to enjoy your time in Paris."

"I am enjoying it! Very much!" Sophie's smile was genuine, but Isabelle just stared at her miserably.

"What's going on, Isabelle?" Camille asked, growing

concerned. "I know you're worried about the show, but I'm sure your artist will deliver. He has a lot at stake, too."

Not that she would know firsthand, seeing as she'd chosen to create art on command rather than from her own heart and mind. Sure, her illustrations took imagination, and she had the books to showcase her hard work, but it wasn't the same as a gallery show, and up until now she'd been fine with that.

It was just being back in Paris, hearing Isabelle talk so excitedly about this opening, that made her second-guess herself.

But just like with Rupert, Camille couldn't go throwing away a sure thing. And she wasn't going to get lost in work, consumed with ideas and the need to put them on paper. She would not put her daughter last the way Papa had done so many times.

"It's not just that," Isabelle said, giving her a fleeting, nervous glance. "There's something I need to tell you both." Isabelle inhaled deeply and then lowered her gaze.

Camille had to restrain herself from smacking the table. She knew it! She knew that something was up, that Isabelle was keeping something from her. Trouble with Hugh? She wouldn't be surprised—well, a little, perhaps, only because it had all gone so well for this long. A problem with the gallery? She'd hate for her sister to lose something she'd poured so much into, especially when, like Rupert always said, it was all she had.

Or chose to have, Camille thought. For as much as Isabelle might think Camille had limited her journey, Isabelle was guilty of the same by never wanting children.

But the satisfaction was quickly replaced with concern. What could it be? Because from the look on her sister's face, it didn't appear to be good news. Was Isabelle sick? In financial trouble? Was it something to do with their mother? But surely Camille would have heard that sort of news first!

Isabelle let out a long breath. "I heard from Papa. He's coming to town. He wants to have dinner. With all of us."

Camille felt like she'd been doused with ice water. She stared at her sister, who struggled to meet her eye, all too aware of the pounding in her chest, the rushing of blood in her veins, and the shaking of her hands.

She couldn't speak, and the city seemed to have gone very quiet. Across the table, Sophie was just as still.

"I should have told you sooner—"

Wait.

"You already *knew*?" Camille all but shouted. Then, catching the disapproving glance from a couple at the next table, she pursed her lips and leaned forward, practically hissing. "You knew and you didn't tell us?"

Her eyes darted around the street as if Papa might materialize at any point. She checked her watch, calculating if she could pack her bags in time to get to the station and make the last train back to London.

Heck, she'd send for her bags!

"I didn't know how to tell you," Isabelle pleaded. "I worried that if I did then you might not come."

Camille glanced at Sophie, who hadn't moved and was very pale.

"Wait," she said, turning her attention back to Isabelle. "You mean to tell us that you didn't invite us to Paris for your gallery opening but because of Papa?"

"Of course I invited you to my opening," Isabelle said tersely. "It's going to be a huge event with lots of press and it means a great deal to me that you're there, especially with

Hugh..." She stopped, blinking quickly. "With Hugh not able to make it. I've worked hard on this show. It could really open doors for me."

"But you knew about the dinner with Papa before you invited us," Camille said flatly, folding her arms across her chest.

Isabelle's sigh rolled through her shoulders. "Yes. I knew. He asked me to get us all together and it planted the seed that it might be nice for us to have some time together in Paris."

"You *know* how I feel about this city," Camille said angrily as hot tears filled her eyes. "And you know how I feel about Papa."

She fumbled for the napkin in her lap. She would not cry. Not at this table. Not in public.

Not over Papa. She'd shed enough tears for him.

"Why does Papa want to meet with us?" Sophie finally spoke, her voice calm, as if she'd taken a moment to gather her thoughts. To zero in on the one question that hadn't been answered.

"I don't know why he suggested this dinner," Isabelle said.

"When?" Camille asked, adopting Sophie's need to get to the facts. It was far easier to focus on them than the emotions roiling inside her. "When is this so-called family meal taking place?"

Isabelle hesitated long enough for Camille to panic.

"Monday evening," Isabelle finally said.

Meaning she could still get out of Paris before he arrived. She'd leave first thing in the morning, Camille decided.

Feeling only slightly more relaxed, Camille reached for her wineglass and took a big slug before refilling it. If ever there was a time to self-medicate, it was now.

"This is concerning," Sophie said, glancing worriedly from Camille to Isabelle.

"It's only my second glass!" Camille replied. "And it's France!"

"I don't mean that," Sophie said with a soft laugh. "I mean... Why would Papa need to see us all in person? This could be really bad."

"I'm not sure what could be worse than having to share a meal with Paul Laurent," Camille replied, but she, too, felt worried. A gnawing sensation took over her stomach as possibilities formed. Cancer. Weeks to live. "You didn't think to ask why he suddenly wanted to get together?" Camille couldn't believe that Isabelle agreed to this dinner without pressing for more information.

But then, she couldn't believe that her sister had agreed to this dinner at all—or that she'd accepted on their behalf.

Isabelle paused. "You know Papa. He lives by his whims..."

Camille's eyes narrowed. "I do. Meaning by now he's probably already forgotten the dinner."

"Or..." Sophie's eyes were round. "Maybe he has news."

"That was my concern," Isabelle admitted. She glanced at each of them. "I was afraid to ask. Afraid of the answer. And...if that's the case, it will be easier to take the news together." She shook her head. "He sounded healthy on the phone. But I agree, it's impossible not to worry."

Camille snorted, snapping herself back to reality. "Like he ever worried about any of us!" It seemed unfair, to care more about a parent than they did about you. Unnatural, even. As a mother herself, she knew what it felt like to be on the opposing side. To care more about Flora than herself. To do anything and everything to protect her child and shield her from harm or pain, even if it was at her own expense.

Her mind drifted to Rupert, to the image of a happy family. And then to the thought of how easily it could all be snatched away. And who would be the biggest casualty in that case? Rupert would move on and find another girlfriend. She had her career and her sister—make that sisters, she thought, glancing at Sophie.

But Flora had only her. And Rupert. And Camille needed to ensure that nothing ever threatened that.

"And he hasn't given you any updates either?" Camille asked Sophie.

"I haven't talked to Papa since Isabelle's wedding," she replied. "He sent a few postcards, from Turkey, Greece, Croatia. I don't even remember. They eventually stopped."

Camille lifted an eyebrow, officially silenced.

"You seem surprised by that," Sophie observed. "You know how Papa is."

"Oh, do I." Camille chuckled bitterly. "But you two seemed to be getting along so well at the reception. You even danced together. Quite a bit."

"That was because he asked, and…it felt nice to be asked. He wasn't exactly present much in my life since I was twelve other than some phone calls and gifts. He would promise to visit but then something always came up." Sophie paused, looking down at the table as if searching for an explanation, and when she lifted her gaze, it was tired. Sad. "I didn't want to say no, I suppose. Papa was paying attention to me after so many years of being absent from my life. And…he was the only person there I knew. I…think we both felt a little out of place."

Camille felt a wash of shame, thinking of how she'd treated

Sophie at that wedding, deliberately keeping her distance and being cool, not even introducing her to Flora as her aunt, but rather just as Sophie, like she could be anyone.

She hadn't even introduced her daughter to Papa. How could she tell Flora that she had a grandfather, only to crush her little girl when he disappeared again the next day, likely never to be heard from again?

"I...just need some time to process this," Sophie said, pushing back her chair.

"Are you leaving?" Camille asked in surprise, but she felt something else. Envy. Or maybe fear.

Right now, Sophie felt like an ally. Unlike Isabelle, Camille and Sophie didn't maintain a relationship with their father. And they didn't see the good in him either, but rather, saw him for who he was. A man who had let them down. Left them. And reappeared only when it was convenient for him.

"I'm going to take a walk," Sophie replied.

"But—" But so many things. The clouds in the sky looked threatening. Sophie didn't have an umbrella with her. And her sweater was thin; maybe Camille should give her her trench coat.

"It's fine," Isabelle said, giving Camille a warning glance.

Camille kept her mouth shut, resigned to letting Sophie go, and wishing that she could join her. But she had words to say to Isabelle. And they were easier said when they were alone.

Because just like Sophie had sensed, there was a different bond that Isabelle and Camille shared. A history, a life that Sophie had never been a part of.

"I trusted you," she said once Sophie had rounded the corner, the words causing her entire body to tremble. "Out of everyone, I thought you were the one person in this world that I could trust."

Only now she realized her error. There was no one in this world she could trust. No matter how much you loved someone or thought they loved you, they always found a way to let you down.

And she'd be best to remember that before she slipped again.

Isabelle didn't argue this time or try to defend herself; she simply nodded because she knew that it was true.

Only maybe it was only partly true. Maybe there was another person that Camille had trusted—or could trust. Or wanted to, at least.

And just like that, all her strength seemed to fall into a puddle at her feet, just like it had when she was six years old and their father walked out the door of their apartment and never came back. She'd cried into Isabelle's arms then, let herself be held, rocked, and comforted.

And she needed that again now, only Isabelle wasn't the one who could deliver.

But someone else would. He always had. And even if she didn't want to depend on anyone right now, in this moment, when someone she'd cared about had betrayed her in the worst possible way, she needed to know that someone she loved still cared about her on some level.

That one person would still stand by her and pull through.

"I have to go," Camille said, pushing back her chair.

She didn't even make it to the next intersection when she pulled out her phone and called Rupert.

"Hey!" he answered in his usual bright and cheerful voice, which immediately made Camille want to weep with relief.

She sank onto a bench at a small corner park, her back to the busy street. "Hey."

"Uh-oh," he said, hearing the crack in her voice. "Is something wrong?"

Only everything, she thought. She opened her mouth to start to tell him the whole horrible story about her father, and Isabelle, how she'd been led here under false pretenses, and that the one person in the world she thought she could trust had not only let her down but lied to her, in the worst possible way.

Rupert wouldn't need an explanation for just how deep of a betrayal this was. He'd understand, just like he'd understand why the mere thought of seeing Papa would send shock waves through Camille's body.

He'd tell her to come home. That he'd be waiting, with Flora, and a hot meal. There would be a fire in the hearth, a glass of wine on the table, and a cake that Flora probably helped him bake in honor of her return. Or maybe they'd go down to the pub instead, where they'd sit at their usual table, nestled in the back, near the window, devouring fish and chips until their stomachs were full and their hearts felt a little less heavy. And she would go. Immediately. And by the end of the night, somehow they'd be laughing, and all the pain, and all the fear, and all the sadness would be gone.

And there would just be happiness. Comfort.

And...love.

She opened her mouth to tell him what had just happened, but then she heard music in the background, and people, and she realized that Rupert wasn't at home, but out, with Flora, no doubt.

"It's just been..." She swallowed hard. There was too much

to tell in a short conversation, and she'd caught Rupert at a bad time.

"I know," he said gently. "Hey, why don't I call you back later, when it's not so noisy? Then you can tell me all about it."

She nodded, even though he couldn't see her, even as the disappointment set in. "Where are you guys?" she asked.

"We're at a festival," he replied as the music changed in the background, gaining traction.

"That sounds like fun!" Camille felt a pang in her chest, wishing she was there with them instead of sitting on a park bench in Paris.

And what was stopping her? She didn't owe Isabelle anything from the way she saw it—and she certainly didn't feel any obligation toward Papa's dinner request. She could go back to the apartment now, while Isabelle was still out, pack her bags, and hail a taxi to the train station. She could be back home in a matter of hours, all her troubles forgotten, or at least behind her.

"I think I might—"

But just as she started to speak, Rupert said, "Hold on, Flora wants to say something."

A second later, Flora's excited voice came through the receiver, the smile so evident in her tone that Camille couldn't help but feel better even as a drop of rain splashed her on the forehead, catching her by surprise.

"Mum! You should see it! There are rides and a petting zoo. With baby goats! And Dad bought a bunch of tickets for the games, and he even won me a stuffed animal. One for Maisie, too."

"Maisie?" Camille went through the catalog of Flora's friends, but she came up blank. Another raindrop landed on her head, and she scooted to the side of the bench, shielding herself under a tree branch. "I don't think I remember you ever talking about a Maisie before. Is she a new friend from school?"

"She's not my friend, she's Dad's," Flora corrected her.

Another raindrop came down, landing on her cheek, but Camille felt like she'd just been punched in the chest. She blinked quickly, trying to push back the emotions that were fighting for first place. Confusion. Jealousy. Loss.

And always fear. Stone-cold, like a vise gripping her heart.

"She's super cool," Flora went on as Camille nodded along, swallowing hard, her mouth too dry to speak. "Oh! We're about to try another ride. Do you want me to pass you back to Dad?"

"No!" Camille blurted, finding her voice just when she needed it. "I mean... No, honey. You go and have fun. And reach out later. Tell me all about it."

"I will, Mum! Every single detail!" Flora said cheerfully before disconnecting.

Every single detail. Of a day spent at a festival. With Rupert. And his new "friend."

Camille sat on the bench, clutching the phone, as the rain fell harder, soaking the shoulders of her trench coat, and plastering her hair to her head, until she didn't know where the rain stopped and her tears began.

The last time she'd cried had been here, in Paris, as she'd looked back at the city that she'd sworn she'd never see again, the city she'd loved with all her heart. The city where all her happiest memories had taken place, and where all her worst ones had happened.

And she knew then and there that coming back had been a mistake. But it was one that she'd chosen. She'd asked for this—not just for the details of the day at the festival, but for this scenario. One in which she was free and so was Rupert. One in which there was space for someone to enter his world and take her place.

She'd come here and let it happen. And now she didn't know how she could bear it.

Sixteen

SOPHIE

Sophie sat under an awning at the first café she'd spotted when the rain started, a *café crème* on the table beside her, along with her notebook that she kept in her bag at all times. It was ironic, she thought, that she was finally living out such a Parisian moment, and she didn't even feel like she could enjoy it.

She wasn't the type of person who believed in things like karma, but right now, she felt like the universe was punishing her.

She'd lied to her mother about her whereabouts. And now, the man who had hurt them the most was in town...in Paris... and coming to dinner!

A part of her was excited about the idea of seeing her father again after all this time. The other part was afraid of being disappointed again. And of course, as always, she was worried about what her mother would say if she found out.

Which was why she never could. Not about the dinner. Not about Paris.

Not about any of it.

She glanced at the screen of her phone. Her mother had left

four messages today, asking for details about the conference Sophie was supposedly at, but rather than feed into the dishonesty, Sophie turned off the device. She couldn't think about her mother right now. She had plenty of time to do that when she went home.

Home. Just thinking of going back to New York filled her with dread, and she forced herself to look around, at the people, and the buildings, and to remember where she was, to tell herself that she was allowed to enjoy it, that she wasn't being punished.

That seeing her father was not a bad thing. Completely.

"Hello?" a deep voice said, pulling her from her darkening thoughts.

Sophie looked up to see Gabriel standing on the sidewalk under an umbrella, a bemused expression on his face.

"This is a coincidence!" she marveled, quickly moving her notebook into her bag to make room for him. "Come get out of the rain!"

"I don't mind it," Gabriel assured her, but all the same, he closed up the umbrella and moved under the awning.

Sophie's mood shifted as her stomach fluttered. She wasn't sure when she'd see Gabriel next and she'd been telling herself that was for the best. She had a boyfriend—sort of—back in New York. And an entire life there, too.

Even if more and more it wasn't a life she yearned to return to anytime soon.

If ever.

Gabriel's smile was guilty when he sat down. "Actually, it's not. Isabelle called and asked me to find you. Based on your last known location and the weather, I knew I wouldn't have to look far."

"She sent you to track me down?" Sophie wondered if Isabelle feared her sisters might leave Paris.

But nothing could make Sophie want to leave Paris. Not even a surprise visit from Papa.

Camille, on the other hand… Sophie frowned when she considered the possibility that her middle sister might go back to London early. She hoped that wouldn't happen, not when they were finally getting somewhere with their relationship. Sure, Camille could be a little overbearing, but it felt nice to know that she cared for once.

And, Sophie suspected, it helped to keep Camille from missing Flora, who was back in England.

"I think she just wanted me to cheer you up," Gabriel said kindly. "Isabelle mentioned that she had to deliver some difficult news today."

"*Difficult* is one word for it," Sophie replied.

"Maybe it was lost in translation?" Gabriel suggested. He gave a little smile, one that she would have found smug that first day. "Her French is not perfect, you know."

Sophie laughed, and she didn't know she was capable of that after today's announcement.

"I didn't know." Everything about Isabelle had always seemed perfect, from her marriage to her relationship with Camille, to the life she was living here on the Left Bank. Even her walk to work was idyllic compared to Sophie's smelly subway commute to Midtown. "But I think *difficult* is probably the word she meant," Sophie said with a sigh. "Our father is coming to town."

Gabriel frowned in confusion. "And that's a bad thing?"

"Not bad, but not good," Sophie said carefully. "Just…difficult."

"I take it you don't have a close relationship with him?" Gabriel ventured.

Sophie paused as a waiter stopped by the table to take Gabriel's drink order. It gave her time to consider the question—and her answer. There was a time when she was extremely close to Papa, when she would run to greet him when she returned from school. But those moments became further and further between, until one day, he was just gone.

"My father doesn't have a close relationship with any of us," Sophie replied. "He keeps in touch with Isabelle, but loosely, from my understanding. I'm not sure how much Isabelle has told you about him."

"Nothing," Gabriel said simply. "I only know him by his art, which I admire, as you know. His early work in particular was very captivating."

Hm. Yes, that was when he was working in oils, painting colorful and unique portraits. He'd been very successful for a while, maybe too much so, because he was always trying to compete with himself, hoping to outshine his former days. He started experimenting with other mediums, which had only made him restless, constantly in search of something new and inspiring.

Sophie hesitated, unsure if Gabriel was waiting for her to open up, or if she should, but then she remembered that for whatever reason, he had come when asked.

That Isabelle had thought to call him.

That maybe this made her and Gabriel friends.

"My father was married to Isabelle and Camille's mother for years," she started. "Over a decade, I don't know for sure. To hear Camille tell it, they had a perfect life here in Paris." She paused, her anger rising when she thought of the way her middle sister had always narrowed her gaze on her, for as far back as Sophie could remember. How nothing she ever did or said was right, but rather, further proof that Sophie couldn't make up for Papa's disappointments.

And that maybe she had caused them.

"Though they've never come flat out and admitted it, it's obvious that Papa had an affair with my mother. It could have been weeks, months, I really don't know." She shrugged. She'd long since given up trying to piece together the timeline of her father's transgressions, though she was sure if she asked, Camille would be able to produce a diary complete with exact dates and time stamps. "He left their mother, married mine, and I was born a short time later."

And she'd never been forgiven for it.

Neither, it would seem, had Papa.

"He left when I was just twelve. My mother...didn't take it well."

"And you didn't keep in touch?" Gabriel frowned.

"At first, yes." Sophie hesitated, unsure if she should stop there. It had been an emotional day already, opening up a part of her past that she had closed off for a long time. But there was another story that she had tried to write, or at least stop telling herself. One that she'd learned in time was best forgotten. "I was...I was supposed to study here in Paris, at the Sorbonne."

Gabriel raised his eyebrows. "What happened?"

Sophie pushed back the wave of hurt, anger, and confusion that accompanied that time in her life. She didn't like to think about it, and spoke of it even less. Her mother certainly never breathed a word about it, and Sophie saw no point in stirring up something that couldn't be changed or made right. Eventually, it was as if it had never happened.

"I had a scholarship. I was so excited." She smiled, thinking back to those weeks leading up to what she thought would be the beginning of a huge adventure, the start of her life in Paris. All her hard work and hours of studying paying off for the experience of a lifetime. For a dream she had made come true.

Just as quickly, she frowned, straight to the heart, and looked at the table. She wanted to get the next words out as quickly as possible.

"My mother could only think of her feelings at that time," she said. "She had changed after the divorce. She became closed off, bitter, and cynical. She no longer saw the world the same way, and she wanted me to see it through her lens. She still does. Me going to Paris...that was not something she could support."

Sophie hesitated, wanting to stop as much as she wanted to get the words out. It had been so long since she'd thought back to that dark time that she almost couldn't believe that it ever happened, that her dream had been within her reach, that she'd made it come true, only to have it be snatched away.

"She wrote to the school and told them I wouldn't be attending. By the time I found out, the scholarship had been awarded to someone else."

Gabriel sat back in his chair, silenced. "So you never came to Paris."

"I never came to Paris," Sophie whispered. "Until now."

Even now she could remember that feeling of certainty, of knowing that something she'd worked toward for years and had finally achieved was just gone and that she was powerless to stop it. That someone she'd trusted and loved and depended on could make that decision for her, without feeling, emotion, or remorse. That was simply that. And Sophie knew it. She didn't cry or try to argue.

It was as if by then, she'd seen how her mother had changed, who she had become, and maybe, deep down, a part of her had known all along that some dreams were never meant to come true.

Except that this one did, she thought, looking around.

She'd made it happen. Ten years later.

Sophie blinked back tears and forced a brave smile. "It turned out okay. I went to a good college, locally, of course. I got a sensible degree, something that she made sure of, which worked out, I suppose. English literature instead of creative writing, but it could have been worse. I have a good job, which she set up for me, and again, it could have been worse."

"Sophie, everything could always be worse," Gabriel pointed out.

Sophie thought about that for a moment but then jutted her chin defiantly. Her life had turned out fairly great by outward appearances. If anyone looking at her didn't know her story, they'd say she had a storybook ending.

"I have a great job in a coveted industry, honestly. A nice apartment, by New York standards, in a trendy neighborhood. Great friends..."

A boyfriend, which she didn't mention.

"It sounds like you're trying to convince yourself," Gabriel said. "Or are you really sure that you're living the life you want?"

She wasn't sure of anything, only that right now she was exactly where she wanted to be.

And this time, no one was going to ruin it for her.

Not her mother.

Not Camille.

Not even Papa.

They lingered at the table straight through dinner, something that Sophie would never tire of, this different pace, so much slower than her harried life in New York, where she was always rushing to cram down a sandwich or catch the train. Afterward, Gabriel suggested a walk. "Walking the streets of Paris at nighttime is a very different experience. One that can't be missed."

Sophie had no desire to return to the apartment and face Isabelle, not when her chest still ached from the way Isabelle had deceived her.

They walked along the riverbank so that they could take in the view from both sides of the Seine, and seeing the buildings illuminated and reflected in the water filled Sophie with a momentary sense of peace.

Until Gabriel had to go and mention Papa again.

"Do you think you'll see him?" he asked. "Your father? When he visits?"

Sophie considered the alternative, knowing that Isabelle would be seeing him and that Camille might not.

"The last time I saw my father was at Isabelle's wedding," she said. "That was five years ago. We got along fine. It was nice."

"But then..." Again Gabriel's smile was knowing.

A few days ago, she might have found it smug. But then, a few days ago, she hadn't known him. She still didn't, she supposed, but she was starting to and...she wanted to know more. About him.

About her sisters.

And this city.

"Then he disappeared." Sophie shrugged and stopped at the

famed bridge, Pont Alexandre III, beside one of the gilded statues that anchored its four points. "That's what he does best."

Gabriel leaned against the wall, standing so close that she could feel the heat from his body next to hers, the skin from his arm brushing against her own.

"Your father is a brilliant artist," Gabriel pointed out. "You already know it's one of the reasons I chose to have my first show at Isabelle's gallery. Blatant favoritism."

Sophie managed a smile. She couldn't help it in Gabriel's presence; he had a way of making her laugh even when she didn't think she could.

"It's his first love," Sophie said, nodding. Then, because she couldn't stop herself, "Maybe his only love."

"And women?"

"His weakness," Sophie said with a knowing smile. A breeze blew the hair from her neck as she continued to soak in the view. "But no one ever lasts. Not even his children. His art, though, never goes away. He's always chasing it. Always creating. It's the one thing he's willing to fight for."

"It's not his art," Gabriel said, pulling Sophie's attention. "It's him. It's who he is. It's what drives him, keeps him awake at night, and gives him a reason to get up the next morning. It's passion, sure. It's love, yes. But it's ultimately just who he is. What makes him complete."

Sophie swallowed hard. She understood. Because she'd once felt that way, too. When she was writing, it was always on her mind, even when she wasn't at her computer or holding a pen.

And without it, something was missing. Something that had been missing for many years now.

"You know, I wasn't always an artist," Gabriel confided.

Sophie looked at him in surprise. "Isabelle didn't tell me."

Gabriel gave a small shrug. "That's because she doesn't know. Few do. Only those who've known me all my life."

"And that would be?" Sophie realized that this was the first time Gabriel was opening up to her. "Parents? Siblings?"

A girlfriend? She didn't ask because a part of her couldn't bear to know. She felt a connection with Gabriel, one that made no sense and one that she couldn't explain. She knew that she could assume it was all part of her Parisian experience, that she was getting swept away by her time here, when her real life felt so far away, almost as if it didn't exist at all.

"A few friends," Gabriel said. "A brother. Parents, of course."

No mention of a girlfriend, current or otherwise.

"What did you do before?" she asked, genuinely curious. Gabriel was older than her, but still young. She'd guess his age to be somewhere around thirty-two, maybe a couple of years older, but not much.

"I was a lawyer."

She couldn't contain her shock when a gasp escaped her, loudly.

"I know." Gabriel's smile was wry. "It doesn't fit me, right?"

Sophie stared at the man before her, the one whom she'd only ever seen in jeans, at best a button-down shirt, his hair a bit tousled at all times. She tried to imagine him in a suit and tie, carrying a briefcase. Sitting behind a desk.

"It's not fair for me to say," she said. "I just met you."

He gave her a small smile as their eyes met. "It doesn't take long for two people to connect, though. To know each other on some level."

Sophie felt her cheeks flush and she glanced down. "No. It doesn't."

A woman on a bike cycled by, forcing Gabriel to move closer, enough for their hips to touch and for Sophie to sense the heat of his body. Their faces were close when he looked down at her, his lips not far from hers, and she lingered for a moment, wondering...

Clearing her throat, she took a small step back.

"Why did you go into law?" she asked. It seemed the more obvious question than why he left to paint.

"My father was a lawyer. My brother, too. It was the natural path. I was good at it, too. I'm told that I can make an excellent argument."

They shared a smile.

"But I was also miserable," Gabriel said matter-of-factly.

A chill went down Sophie's spine when she thought of her desk job, how she wasn't quite miserable, but she was far from fulfilled. How every time she read a new manuscript, she longed to write one of her own.

And not just write one, but finish it, too. To do what she'd set out to do. To be the person she not just hoped to be but needed to be.

"So you quit?" she asked breathlessly, wondering if it was just that easy. If she, too, could dare to do the same.

He shook his head, all at once deflating her hope. "I stayed with it. Joined my wife's father's firm. She was an attorney, too. We met in law school."

Sophie stared at him as his words hit her. Hard. "You were married?"

Meaning that he wasn't anymore. He was divorced. Or—

"I moved here after my divorce," he clarified. "I quit law then, too."

"But...but..." She blinked, trying to make sense of everything he'd said, all the talks they'd had, the words they'd shared. "But you seemed to believe so much in lasting love."

"Who says I don't?" he asked with a shrug. "Just because it didn't work for me."

She stared at him, wanting to ask a hundred questions but not wanting to appear rude.

Finally, he sighed and said, "She left me. I didn't see it coming. She had an affair with a coworker. Another lawyer. I guess you can say that this was what confirmed my distaste for that profession."

He slipped her a wry smile but she saw the hurt in his eyes.

"I'm sorry," she said.

"It was a long time ago. Besides, now I'm here, in Paris, doing what I love. Sometimes you have to experience hardship to find your happy ending."

Sophie considered this, knowing that as much as she wished it weren't true, that it was. And sensing that there was hope to be found in that.

"Is that what you've found?" she asked. "Your happy ending?"

His eyes met hers. "I think so."

Her heart swooped and then began to pound as his gaze dropped to her mouth, and for a moment she wondered if he was going to kiss her, right here in the heart of Paris with the Eiffel Tower lit up in the distance.

And she wondered if he'd let him.

But then he leaned against the wall and said, "You had a

notebook on the table before I arrived. Were you writing something?"

"Oh…" Sophie felt her cheeks go warm as she struggled to bring her thoughts back to the conversation. She wasn't sure what was more nerve-racking—thinking about kissing someone other than Jack or talking about her writing. Another dream lost…that she was trying to find. "I was just scribbling some thoughts."

"It helps," Gabriel said, looking straight into her eyes, "to let the feelings out. To put them on paper. Through words. Or…paint." He gave a little smile.

"For a long time I gave up writing," Sophie explained, realizing that it was easier to talk about with him than she'd thought it would be. But then, everything was easy to talk about with Gabriel. He didn't judge, and he just seemed to…understand. "It hurt too much to think about anything that bothered me, and trying to escape it wasn't working, either."

"Time is needed to have a better perspective," Gabriel agreed. "That's why I haven't given Isabelle my final painting yet."

"But you will give it?" Sophie felt a flicker of alarm, and she realized that even though she was mad at her sister, and even though she was disappointed in realizing that they were not as close as she'd hoped, she still cared about her.

And she still yearned for her approval.

"I told you," Gabriel said. "I'm a man of my word."

Sophie nodded. He was a man of many things, she'd come to realize. And of many surprises.

Seventeen

ISABELLE

Well, that went worse than expected, and Isabelle hadn't hoped for it to go well at all. Even as she stood at the boulangerie the next morning and paid for her croissants, she could still see the hurt in Camille's eyes, and she knew that she had only herself to blame this time. Not Papa.

She walked toward the apartment, and then, with her hand on the large brass door handle of the building, hesitated. Maybe Sophie or Camille were awake by now, and maybe they needed space. They'd all stayed in their bedrooms last night; it had been too soon to try to explain herself, even though she had longed to do just that. Maybe it was still too soon.

Sophie would probably hear her out, maybe even forgive her. But Camille... Isabelle's hand tensed against the metal.

Camille might never forgive her for this. She wasn't the type to turn the other cheek when someone hurt her.

Isabelle was still contemplating her next course of action when the door opened, forcing her to drop her hand and step back. It was Antoine, looking pleased to see her, and Isabelle quickly arranged her expression to look anything but how she felt, which was...miserable. And she couldn't even blame Hugh for the reason why.

"*Bonjour!*" Antoine stood outside on the sidewalk, smiling at her. "Are you coming in?"

"I..." Isabelle couldn't think straight. Her mind was buzzing and she felt at a loss for words. It was a foreign feeling and not a good one. She liked her days planned out and took comfort in her routine.

Once, she'd taken pleasure in never knowing where she and Hugh would travel, or how long they would stay. But that was before Paris.

And now, her life was as wide open as it had been all those days early into her relationship, only this time she was flying solo. She didn't know what tomorrow would bring, or who would be by her side. She didn't know if she was married or not, or if she would stay married, if she and Hugh would work it out. How could she ever forgive him? She didn't know if there would ever be a baby, or if the years would pass by her, closing the door on that opportunity. She didn't know what Papa was so eager to tell them all, and if she'd have to hear the news alone.

And she didn't know what to say to her sisters to make things right again.

"I'm going to the gallery, actually," she said, thinking of the one place she had that was hers alone. The little storefront on Île Saint-Louis was filled with art that she'd personally chosen and hung with care. The business gave her days not just purpose but fulfillment, even if neither Hugh nor Camille could ever understand that.

It's what made it hers, though, wasn't it? That only she loved it so?

"Your gallery?" Antoine looked interested. "On a Sunday?"

She gave a guilty smile. It wasn't very common in France to work on weekends. "I have that big show coming up and I still have a lot of work to do."

Yes, work would keep her away from the apartment until she knew what to do. And it would keep her from calling Hugh, too.

She wondered, idly, if he'd noticed that she hadn't been reaching out as much, but then she figured that he'd just assume it was because her sisters were visiting.

If he bothered to think about her all.

"Actually, that's not the real reason I'm heading into work today," she confided, unsure of why the moment the words slipped from her lips. But looking into Antoine's kind eyes, she did know. He was easy to talk to. Understanding.

Maybe it was because he was close to her grandmother, a link to her past. Or maybe it was because he always seemed to be around when she needed a helping hand. One that she hadn't noticed until now.

Or maybe hadn't needed until now.

"Oh?" He didn't look overly curious, but more concerned.

"I told my sisters about our father's visit." The words felt heavy.

"Ah." He winced. "It didn't go well?"

"It was a disaster," she said. "If we hadn't been in public, I imagine you might have heard us through the walls."

He laughed, and despite the ache in her chest, she did, too.

"So work it is then," he said, giving a firm nod.

"I *do* have a lot to do for the gallery," she said, more to herself than to him.

"Do you want some company?" he surprised her by asking.

She looked up at him, and without needing to pause or

think about it, she said only what she was feeling. "I'd love some."

Two hours later, with the catering menu finalized, and invitations read and sorted, Antoine stood and stretched his legs. Isabelle watched him from the desk where she still sat, entering the last of the wine orders, allowing for extra in case people decided to bring a date.

"This will be a big event," Antoine commented, taking in the guest list, which was long and impressive and made Isabelle nervous every time she looked at it. It was a show that would certainly put her little gallery on the map.

"You should come," Isabelle said. "I mean, I'd like you to come."

Please come, she thought, looking into his kind eyes. She didn't know if her sisters would even come after her big announcement, and she could use a friendly face in an otherwise intimidating crowd.

And Antoine was certainly a very friendly one.

"Really?" He looked flattered. "I don't know much about art."

"Just nod along and comment on the perspective," she whispered, giving him a wink.

He jutted his lip. "I think I can handle that."

"So you will?" she asked hopefully.

He nodded. "Wouldn't miss it."

Isabelle pulled in a breath and released it slowly, feeling instantly better about, well, everything. Still, she felt a little shaky when she stood up, bracing herself for her return to the apartment.

"I love this one." Antoine stood in front of an oil painting. It was an abstract landscape, but it was the colors and brushstrokes that had caught Isabelle's attention. "The artist has a very unique…perspective."

He turned to grin at her.

"That's one of my favorites," she replied after she'd finished laughing. "The artist isn't very prolific, unfortunately, but I think that's what makes this piece so special."

"Is it for sale?" Antoine asked, sounding genuinely interested.

Isabelle nodded. "It can be yours for fifteen."

"Euros?" Antoine looked both confused and delighted.

"Thousand," she replied with a knowing smile.

"Ah." Antoine stepped away with his hands in the air.

Isabelle laughed again. She'd laughed a lot today, thanks to Antoine. He was easy company, quiet, thoughtful, and quick with a joke or a comment that made her smile.

For a while, she'd almost been able to forget her troubles.

"Do you get many buyers?" he asked, moving on to a small modern sculpture of a couple embracing.

"It depends what you call many," Isabelle said, moving away from the piece. She'd acquired it from an artist she and Hugh had met on a trip to Madrid and now she was eager to send it back to its owner. "Mostly, I have browsers. Tourists who love to pop in and out. I have a list of clients, of course. Collectors. I know their taste and call them when I see something that I know they would like."

"How did you come to meet these people?" Antoine asked, seeming genuinely curious.

"Oh, Hugh and I traveled a lot over the years for his business. You get to meet a lot of people that way, at parties, or work events…" She trailed off, not wanting to talk about Hugh any more than she wanted to think about him, or what he was doing. Or what she was going to do about him. She had come to this gallery to escape her problems, and so far she'd managed to do just that. "I suppose I'm fortunate to have inherited my grandmother's apartment, but I can cover the rent here. I'm proud of this gallery. It's my baby, you could say."

And it might be her only one, she thought with a pang.

"You have a good eye," Antoine told her as he moved slowly around the room, careful to keep a distance from the canvases.

"It's in my blood," Isabelle said, dismissing the compliment. "My father isn't the only one, you know. My mother is a successful interior designer in London. Camille is a book illustrator, and Sophie is a writer. Or she will be. Once she believes in herself."

"That's an impressive family," Antoine said, lifting an eyebrow.

"It is," Isabelle agreed. "Though I'm not sure anyone is all that impressed with what I do." Seeing his frown, she explained, "They're creators. And I'm, well, a businesswoman, to hear Camille tell it, even though I don't agree."

"But you're happy?" Antoine asked.

Isabelle paused. There was so much that caused her unhappiness these days that she didn't know how to answer his question. But this gallery, these four walls, these paintings and sculptures that she hand-selected, they brought her joy.

"I love this gallery," she replied. "But Hugh would have preferred that I travel with him."

And if she had? Would their marriage have survived? But at what cost?

"My sister is the real artist, or she could be," Isabelle said. "I'd love to give her a show but she's holding herself back. It's as if she'd afraid…"

"Of failure?" Antoine asked.

Isabelle regarded him for a moment. "Of turning into our father."

She felt her expression drop as the heaviness in her chest returned, and this time, she knew she couldn't hide her true emotions. "As you can probably sense, there's always been some tension between me and my middle sister."

"Since you were little?" Antoine asked.

Isabelle shook her head and walked over to the cocktail cart to pour them each a glass of well-deserved wine. She usually saved the bottles for the evenings when she stayed open late and there was a buzz on the sidewalks, tourists coming in and out of storefronts, potential customers strolling her gallery, but today called for some libations, and besides, she didn't see much foot traffic through the window.

She handed him a glass of red wine. "When we were little, we were very close, but as we got older, we drifted apart. Camille had a baby right after college, and she became busy, too busy to spend much time with me."

"Ah, yes, I've lost many friends to their children," Antoine said, giving a knowing chuckle. "It always had a way of making me feel…left behind. Especially after the breakup."

"You wanted children then?" Isabelle hoped she wasn't being rude, but she longed to connect with someone who shared her plight, who had a hole in their heart that might never be filled. Had he learned to live with it, and if so, how? She needed to know. She needed...hope, she supposed.

"I still do," he replied. "Of course, that requires meeting the right woman."

Isabelle took a sip of her wine, ruefully thinking how much easier it was for men, who didn't have a clock ticking away their childbearing years.

"Hugh never wanted children," she said, finding it a relief to be able to be so open. "I'd hoped that settling down in Paris would change his mind."

"But?" Antoine raised an eyebrow.

"But I'm not sure what he ever wanted, I suppose," she replied. "He...isn't a man of his word, you could say. He's been lying to me. For quite some time. And now all I can think about is how much more he's been lying about. If anything he ever said was true."

Antoine frowned deeply and set a hand on her shoulder, leaving it there like a comfortable weight for a moment, a reminder that she wasn't completely alone.

"You know, when Marie broke off our engagement, I felt like a part of me had died," Antoine said, giving her a sheepish look. "I cried. Like a baby. For like...a month."

Isabelle wiped away a tear and laughed out loud, then clamped a hand to her mouth. "Sorry. I mean, that isn't funny."

"But it is," Antoine said with a shrug. "Sort of."

They shared a smile.

"Only in hindsight," Isabelle said.

Antoine nodded. "Only because I see now how wrong she was for me. At the time I was caught up in my feelings, in all the good I saw in her. But it wasn't reality. It wasn't even who she was. It was...who I wanted her to be."

Isabelle fell quiet as she thought about Hugh, about who he was compared to the man she always thought him to be. The Hugh she knew was not a man who would lie to her, repeatedly, about his whereabouts, and who knew what else.

"I just feel like maybe I don't know my husband at all," Isabelle whispered. "Maybe I only saw what I wanted to see. And maybe I didn't see what I didn't want…"

Like her mother. For so long her mother would make excuses for Papa's absences, airily claiming that he was staying out all night working in cafés, that he couldn't sleep when he was working on a new painting, that he found his best inspiration at night.

Was this what Papa told her or was it just what she told herself?

And how was it any different from what Isabelle had told herself about Hugh's feelings about Paris? About starting a family?

"What do your sisters say?" Antoine asked. "They must know him pretty well?"

Isabelle shook her head. "Sophie doesn't know Hugh at all. She only met him at the wedding. And Camille…Camille doesn't believe in love. Not the lasting kind, anyway. If she knew about Hugh's betrayal, she'd just say she warned me."

"So you haven't told them?" Antoine looked at her in shock, then, with a teasing wag of his finger, he said, "You have been keeping a lot from these sisters of yours."

"This is my business. It doesn't concern them," Isabelle replied, feeling a little defensive. There was no way she could share Hugh's betrayal with either of her sisters. Sophie didn't deserve to have her trip tainted and Camille— Isabelle shuddered at the mere thought of what her sister would say.

But then it hit her. Hard.

Camille would tell her the truth.

What she didn't want to hear.

Or see.

What she was afraid to admit to herself.

Antoine dropped his hand, but his eyes were still kind when they looked at her. "*You* concern them, though. They're your sisters. They're here in town to visit you."

Isabelle gave a begrudging nod. It was true. They had come to town for her—not Papa. Even Camille, who hated Paris and all it represented, had crossed the English Channel.

For her.

"What's the worst that could happen if you tell them?" Antoine asked with a casual shrug, as if it were just that easy to open up, to share. To trust.

"I suppose I'm just bracing myself for what Camille would say. That she'd confirm that I've been a fool. That Hugh never loved me. That there's no such thing as love, at least not the lasting kind. That I was naive to think I'd found it." She looked up at him shyly. "Or that I could ever find it again."

That was the part she feared the most, she realized.

His gaze was soft but intense as he studied her. Finally, his lips curved into a little smile. "Sometimes people can surprise you."

Isabelle took another sip of her wine, struggling to tear her gaze from that dark stare.

Yes, she thought. Sometimes people could surprise you.

In a good way.

Camille and Sophie were both in the living room when Isabelle returned that afternoon after a leisurely walk back to the apartment with Antoine, who took her down a different route than her usual path—perhaps even a better one.

She paused in the entranceway, relieved that they hadn't fled to their respective countries but anxious about what they planned to say to her.

"I owe you both a huge apology," she said before they could say anything. "I was wrong. So wrong. I should have told you why I was inviting you to Paris."

Camille studied her for a long moment from her seat near the window. Finally, she sighed and then patted the cushion next to her.

Releasing a breath she hadn't even known she'd been holding, Isabelle toed off her shoes and hurried across the room to join her sisters, earning a little smile of camaraderie from Sophie, who was curled up in an armchair near the crackling fireplace.

A bottle of white wine was already uncorked and poured, and cheese and bread were on the glass coffee table. Isabelle realized that her sisters must have been bonding, just the two of them, and even though the circumstance that had brought them together was one she wanted to take back, now she wondered if she really would if she could.

"You knew if you told us the truth that I wouldn't have come," Camille said. "So I understand. It doesn't mean that what you did was right, but...I understand."

Isabelle nodded, knowing it was the closest she was going to get to forgiveness.

Camille stood up and went to the kitchen, returning promptly with an empty wineglass.

Isabelle grinned. Strike her earlier thought, she thought as she accepted the olive branch. This was the true sign of forgiveness. She was being included, brought back into the fold, and oh, had she missed it.

"The past twenty-four hours have been rough," she admitted, pouring herself a glass of wine and taking a sip.

"For all of us," Camille agreed, reaching for a piece of Emmental. "At least there's cheese in France, or I might have hopped on the train by now."

"You wouldn't have, though?" Isabelle asked. "Without saying goodbye?"

Camille chewed thoughtfully. "Not without saying goodbye, no. Besides, we're sisters. We're sort of stuck with each other whether we like it or not." Here she slid a glance to Sophie, who grinned into her wineglass.

Isabelle felt a warmth wash over her skin that had nothing to do with the fire glowing in the hearth.

And as much as she hated to think of ruining this cozy moment, she knew that they had to talk about tomorrow—and what to do about it.

"We are sisters, and we do stick together, and that's why we won't have this dinner unless we all decide we should," Isabelle said, meaning it.

"Papa really didn't hint at what it was about?" Camille pressed.

"You know Papa." Isabelle felt the need to reassure her. "For all we know, he was looking through old photos, found one of us at the beach one summer, and thought, let's have a family dinner like old times!"

A whisper of a smile passed over Sophie's face. "I always

loved those days, not just because you two were visiting, but because Papa was always so happy when you came."

Camille seemed surprised by this, but then her expression folded into one of confusion, and, if Isabelle didn't know better, sadness.

"That's the thing about Papa," she said. "When he was there, he was so...present. It just made losing him so much worse."

"Present, yes," Isabelle said slowly. But she was older, and she had a slightly different memory. "But he was also so preoccupied by his art. So consumed by it. I often wonder what might have happened if he'd just stuck with his portraits. They were his signature work."

A collective nod went up in the room. Everyone in Paris knew Paul Laurent's portraits at one point in time. Everyone in Europe, and even New York.

"But you know Papa," Camille said, giving Isabelle a look.

"Yes," Isabelle said with a sigh. "He was restless. He was always in search of...more."

"Something better," Camille said.

"Maybe not something better," Sophie said gently. "Maybe just...something else."

She and Camille locked eyes for a moment, exchanging a look of understanding.

"Do you remember the ant people?" Camille asked, and all the women nodded knowingly.

The life-size metal forms had been Papa's obsession in the months leading up to his divorce from Isabelle and Camille's mother. They were meant to express Paul's belief that the human ego had become out of control and needed to be put in check, that one must be reminded that we were all living creatures, sharing this earth, that an ant people so carelessly and thoughtlessly stepped on and squished was, on some level, of equal importance to the human experience.

His ant people could be found playing musical instruments, dancing the tango, or sweeping a city street.

"The ant people were the beginning of the end," Isabelle said. They required too much explanation, their size was too cumbersome, and they didn't hold the same beauty and depth that his portraits did, those haunting paintings that looked deep inside the human soul, capturing the plight in a way that so few could.

"Well, you weren't there for the *miniature* ant people," Sophie said, her eyebrows shooting up. "When he finally gave up on the big ones, he scaled things down in an attempt underscore the humanity of the ants by domesticating their colonies."

"Oh, my," Camille said with a gulp of wine. "That sounds like Papa."

"I had to explain to all of my friends why my dollhouse was made up of an ant family instead of proper dolls." Sophie frowned.

Camille snorted and then laughed so hard that she sprayed wine from her mouth. She clasped a hand to her face, muttering an apology, but there was no reason, because Isabelle was laughing, too, and Sophie, looking a little bewildered, started to join in.

"It was actually sort of upsetting," she cried. "I tried to put little clothes on them, but nothing helped."

"Oh, my God, the clothes!" Camille screamed and pointed a finger at Isabelle.

"The clothes!" Isabelle's eyes watered from laughter. "I forgot about that."

"Forgot what?" Sophie looked from Isabelle to Camille, who was now laughing so hard that she had set down her wineglass to clutch her sides.

Isabelle calmed down enough to explain the story. "Papa went through a period of dressing the ant people. He upcycled clothing. It was all very avant-garde, actually. He was quite ahead of the times."

Camille stopped laughing to nail her with a hard look. "Isabelle, he was dumpster diving."

Isabelle licked her lip to stifle her laughter. "He was collecting materials," she explained to Sophie.

But Sophie just shrugged, completely unfazed. "Oh, he was always digging through trash. It was, like, a Saturday morning activity after bagels and lox."

The room fell silent for a split second before the women erupted into laughter again.

"Oh, my," Camille finally said, wiping her eyes and then reaching for her wine. "I haven't laughed this hard since Rupert and I—" She stopped, looking wistful for a moment.

"This was...nice," she eventually said. "Surprising. Not just because we're laughing about Papa, but because we're all here together, having, well, fun."

"At Papa's expense," Isabelle said, feeling bad.

"Oh, come on," Camille cajoled. "He had it coming."

Sophie tilted her head from side to side, grimacing. "He's an easy target. But...he tried so hard, you know?"

"With his art!" Camille retorted, her anger flashing through again.

"But it's who he is," Isabelle said, smiling when she thought back on those days when Papa was whiling away, his mind always busy, his hands always active. "And he always included us. He brought us into his world. He tried to, at least."

Camille grew quiet for a moment. "Maybe," she finally said. "Maybe he did try. In his own strange way. For as long as he could."

"As best as he could," Isabelle said quietly.

"I want to believe that," Sophie said, looking at Isabelle pleadingly, much the same way Camille used to those first few nights after Papa had left, when Isabelle still dared to believe that he would be back.

And he had come back. For this dinner. Just not when they needed him most.

Isabelle looked at her sisters, wondering if she dared to ask them the burning question. "So? Do we do it? Do we meet him for dinner?"

"It's just one dinner," Sophie said cautiously, glancing at Camille.

Camille contemplated it for a long moment before tossing up her hands, nearly sloshing what remained of her wine. "What can it hurt?"

A lot, Isabelle thought but didn't say.

And that was what she feared. For herself. But most of all, for her sisters.

Eighteen

CAMILLE

After much deliberation, the decision was made to invite Papa to the apartment rather than meet in a restaurant. While a public setting would have permitted Camille to leave the table if she wished, it also risked a public scene, which she sensed that Isabelle was hoping to avoid.

Isabelle lit candles on the dining room table, where four placings were set, along with a bottle of red wine, decanting. From the kitchen, the smell of *coq au vin* made Camille's stomach churn. It was a shame she wouldn't be able to enjoy it. She doubted she'd be able to taste it, much less consume it.

Her emotions had run from nervous to angry to sad and back again ever since Isabelle's big announcement, and now she stood at the kitchen counter slicing a baguette, hoping she didn't cut herself with how hard her hands were shaking.

She should have backed out, packed her bags and left this morning, and she would have if it hadn't been for Isabelle's big apology last night—and her conversation with Flora over the weekend.

Rupert had met someone. Someone special enough to introduce to their daughter.

And just like that, everything had changed.

Somehow home no longer felt like the place she longed to be—the place that was comfortable and full of laughter and good food and a warm fire and all her favorite things—and people. Rupert had dated in the past; they both had, very casually for her, usually only a date here and there, because she certainly wasn't looking for more. But neither of them had ever introduced anyone to Flora. They'd always kept their family life, well, to the family. To the three of them, preserving their traditions, and not letting anyone intrude.

Until now.

So no, going back to England early wasn't a choice, but sticking around for this dinner was starting to feel like an even bigger mistake than she'd already thought it would be.

Camille checked the clock once more and then eyed her sister through the doorway. Isabelle had been working all day in the kitchen between running errands or sending Camille and Sophie to various specialty shops for the dinner—a task that Sophie was all too happy to do. There was now a fresh bouquet of flowers on the table, colorful, because Papa would appreciate that, and his favorite meal cooking in the oven.

"Don't you think we're going a little overboard?" Camille asked as she walked into the living room. She stared at the table as Isabelle straightened the settings. "He's our father, not a guest of honor."

"It's been a long time since we've all had a meal together, why not make it nice?" Isabelle replied, but there was a brightness to her eyes that made Camille wonder if all this activity was her way of covering up her true emotions. If maybe Isabelle, too, was regretting agreeing to this.

"Would you hate me if I went out to a bistro and returned once he was gone?" Camille asked.

Isabelle stopped refolding a napkin and turned to glare at her. "I could never hate you, and I would probably eventually forgive you, but I'm begging you not to do that. Papa wouldn't have asked us to meet with him if it wasn't important."

This was true, and Camille was a little curious, which only added to her trepidation.

"It's so typical of Papa," Camille said, growing angry as she fluffed the flowers. Isabelle's energy was contagious, and it wasn't like Camille would be able to relax, what with her sister fluttering all over the room and that knock on the door imminent.

Her stomach heaved as she glanced over her shoulder at it now, but the only noise from the hallway came from Sophie getting ready in her room.

"He disappears for years and then when he wants to see us, he shrouds the reason in mystery," Camille said, getting worked up.

Isabelle gave a little smile. "Papa always did have a flare for drama."

"He's lured us here with a secret," Camille said, giving Isabelle a stern look to show that she wasn't able to see this fondly. "He knew that if he just told you his big news, you would tell us, and we'd have no reason to meet here."

"But aren't you glad you did?" Isabelle countered. "I mean, if it hadn't been for Papa's request, you and Sophie wouldn't have even come to Paris, because...I wouldn't have invited you."

Isabelle looked down for a moment when she said this.

"Hey," Camille said. She could give her sister a pass. Papa? Not so much. "You would never have put me in that position because you knew how I felt—I mean, how I feel—about Paris."

"But I never thought to invite Sophie," Isabelle said, giving Camille a desperate look. "In all this time!"

Again, Camille couldn't let Isabelle blame herself for this. "You knew it would upset me if you did."

Isabelle gave a nod of concession. Camille grew quiet, fighting back the guilt that crept in when she thought of all the years she refused to even say her own sister's name. She'd been young, and immature, and so wrong. But she'd also been so hurt.

"We're all here now," Camille said, trying to lift her sister's mood as much as her own. "For what it's worth, I'm glad I came. I'm not thrilled about tonight..."

"I'm happy you came, too." Isabelle's eyes filled with tears. "I'm honestly surprised that you did. Even with my excuse, I didn't think it would be enough reason to get you to agree. I know how much this city bothers you."

"Actually, the city's not so bad," Camille said. Then, seeing the light in her sister's eyes, she hurried to add, "Not that I plan to move here or anything."

"So you're glad that you came?" Isabelle asked.

"I didn't say that," Camille teased. Her stomach knotted when she considered what might have happened if she'd stayed in England. Would Rupert have still met this Maisie woman? Would he have pursued her, invited her to the festival, and introduced her to Flora?

"You okay, Camille?" Isabelle asked, setting a hand on her arm.

"What?" Camille shook her head, then forced a smile. "Fine. I mean, not fine. Just. You know."

But Isabelle didn't know. Not about Maisie. Or Rupert. Or the big mess that was her life. Isabelle couldn't understand. Camille didn't even understand it herself.

"It's tough, I know. But we'll get through this dinner," Isabelle said. Then, in an unexpected rush of emotion, she leaned forward and pulled Camille in for a tight hug.

Camille gave Isabelle a few pats on the back, even though a part of her wanted to sink into her sister's arms, the way she used to when she was little. She wanted to weep, as she had then, and share all her fears, about seeing Papa, about facing Rupert.

She pulled back instead, staying strong.

She poured them each a glass of wine from the open bottle on the table and raised hers. "To Papa. May he get stuck in that ancient elevator and never show."

"Camille!" Isabelle scolded, but she was laughing as she brought her glass to her lips and then went back to the kitchen to check on the food.

Sophie walked into the room wearing a navy dress that tied at the waist, looking fresh-faced from her shower. "Anything I can do to help?"

"You can stop me from refilling this glass before Papa arrives," Camille said wryly, taking another sip of the wine. "If he even comes."

Hope lifted her chest but just as quickly was replaced with a new worry. What if Papa didn't come after all? It was entirely possible, likely even. And as much as she dreaded the thought of seeing him, not knowing how to act, or what to expect him to say, she had also talked herself into this dinner, prepared for it, and if it didn't happen, she knew that she'd feel let down.

It was an all-too-familiar feeling. One that she'd promised herself a long time ago she would never let herself experience ever again.

For lack of anything more to do to prepare for tonight, she went back to the kitchen and returned with the bread.

"Whatever he has to say must be important for him to bother coming at all," Sophie replied. "It's not like anything in my life has been enough to get him to show up."

Camille stopped rearranging the breadbasket on the table to set a hand on Sophie's shoulder. She felt it stiffen slightly under her touch and then relax. A part of her, an instinct, really, had the urge to step forward and hug her, but she'd never hugged Sophie, not even as a child, and it somehow didn't feel right, even now.

Sophie was a grown woman, not a little girl. Even though, from the look on her face, Camille sensed that right now, they were both little girls, staring out the window, waiting for their father to come home, hoping that this was the day he would.

The doorbell rang, and Camille's entire body seized up. She locked eyes with Sophie, who looked like she might break down and cry.

"I don't know why I'm so nervous," Sophie admitted. "I don't know why I still care."

Camille swallowed hard. "I don't know why I do, either."

Up until now, she didn't think she still did. She'd thought she'd shut that part of her life away and moved on with boundaries, ones that kept her protected.

But she didn't feel protected right now, even with Isabelle now gliding into the room, wide-eyed. And she didn't know how this night was going to end. She knew only that she cared and that she didn't want to care again. That she didn't want to hurt like that ever again.

From the entranceway, they heard the turning of the locks, the opening of the door, and Isabelle greeting their father with pleasantries that came easily to her, but would be impossible for Camille.

She stared at Sophie, her breath feeling labored as her heart began to pound. "Ready?"

She linked her sister's arm, not so much for Sophie, but for herself. She needed the support, and right now, she felt like Sophie was the only one who understood. Sure, Isabelle had lived through it all, too, but somehow she'd come out of it differently. She not only believed in love, but she'd found it. A happy ending. A perfect little life.

She felt a smile grow on her face at that realization. All this time she'd thought it was her and Isabelle against the world, that only Isabelle could share the pain of her past. But it was her other sister, the very one she'd blamed for her part in it.

Slowly, they stepped into the front hall, where Paul was shedding his trench coat. It had been five years since the last time Camille had seen him at Isabelle's wedding, but he hadn't aged a day in all that time. His brown hair was still wavy, cut in his usual haphazard style that gave him a boyish charm even into his sixties. He wore his weight well on his tall frame, and when he turned to her, his gaze resting squarely on her eyes, his face broke into a grin that had the capability of ripping every wall she'd built down, stone by stone. Disappointment by disappointment.

"*Ma chérie*," he said, stepping toward her with arms outstretched.

It was the nickname he'd always used for her. His darling. Isabelle was his beauty, and Sophie, well, Camille wasn't sure what Sophie's nickname was, or if she even had one.

But hearing hers said after all this time made Camille feel like she was four years old again, riding the carousel at the base of the hill in Montmartre, or five, sharing a bench in the Tuileries Garden after a long afternoon touring museums and listening carefully as Papa pointed out which paintings he liked best and why. Or six, watching him pack his bags, and then, after a quick kiss, walk out the door of their apartment.

She steadied herself for the embrace, stiffening as he enveloped her in his arms, managing a pat on his back, nothing more.

She relaxed only when he finally stepped back, then watched as he reached, tentatively, for Sophie. Unlike Camille, Sophie hugged him back, just like she'd danced with him at the wedding.

Until Papa had disappeared on her again.

It was a reminder to stay strong, Camille told herself. To get through this night and then move on, like she always did.

Papa, in typical fashion, decided to dangle his little secret over them until he was good and ready. The man loved a captivated audience.

Camille said nothing as Papa talked about all his recent travels (Greece, Spain, pretty much the entire Mediterranean coast), the various projects he was working on (a book of poetry, illustrated by himself, and a collection of watercolors, a new medium for him), and all the delicious recipes he'd learned on his many travels.

Isabelle nodded along, asking questions when appropriate, ignoring Camille's telling glances to speed things along and get to the point of the evening.

It wasn't until the chocolate mousse was on the table that Isabelle finally took a big breath and said, "So, Papa, you've invited us all here. I have to admit that I'm a little worried about why. Is something wrong? Is it your health?"

Camille looked across the table, seeing the fear mirrored in Sophie's wide eyes.

They couldn't help it, she supposed. Caring. Because as much as Camille hated her father, a bigger part of her still loved him.

That was just the problem with love. It wasn't convenient. It didn't make sense. And it wasn't always reciprocated.

"No, nothing like that!" Papa shook his head, and there seemed to be a collective sigh of relief. "I told you, Isabelle. Everything is fine. Better than fine."

"Better than fine?" Isabelle searched his face for clarification.

Camille wondered if Papa intended to return to France full-time. If he wanted this apartment. He was the rightful heir, after all.

But would he really do that to Isabelle? Strip her of the life she'd built for herself here? Of her home?

Who was she kidding? Of course he would.

And from the stricken look on Isabelle's face, her sister knew it, too.

"The reason I wanted to meet with all of you is because I have some very good news," Papa said, smiling as he looked around the table. For a moment, Camille was brought back to all those delightful moments when Papa would announce he had a surprise or a treat. He'd hold it behind his back, his eyes always shining, the glee in his smile revealed in his voice, and Camille and Isabelle would stand before him, their hearts pounding with anticipation.

Sometimes it was a cookie. Other times, a strange little treasure, like a painted ceramic bird that he just happened to find sitting on a park bench, forgotten or discarded by its previous owner, and Camille always imagined Papa's expression when he happened upon it. How happy it made him—knowing, she thought now with a lump in her throat—how happy it would make them.

That was the part about Paris that hurt the most. It was here that he'd once loved them. And here that he'd stopped.

"I'm getting married."

The words hung in the room, while Papa smiled broadly at them all, as if he'd just announced he was going to the moon.

There was a beat of silence before Sophie cried, "*Again?*"

Camille slurped her wine. "This is hardly huge news, Papa. It's your third marriage."

Papa chewed on the bottom of his lip. Camille's eyes widened on him as she pressed into the table, feeling her eyes bulge.

"It is your third marriage, right?"

Papa's smile slipped as he took a long sip of his wine.

"There was another one, briefly," he said tersely, dismissing it with a sweep of his hand. "Barely worth mentioning."

Camille felt her teeth set on edge as she dropped back against her chair. Was that what he thought of her mother? Of Sophie's mother? Were these women just disposable to

Papa, there when it was convenient for him, gone when it wasn't?

Or was it just his children that he treated like this?

"You got married again and didn't tell us?" Isabelle looked hurt. "When was this?"

"A long time ago," Papa replied. "After I left America."

"So this is your fourth marriage," Camille clarified.

"Only if you don't count the one right after I graduated," Papa replied flatly.

"Before Mum?" Isabelle cried in a rare burst of anger.

Camille set down her wineglass, even though it didn't take a very clear head to do this math. She was shaking, with rage, confusion, and so many buried emotions that she didn't trust herself not to drop it.

"Let me get this straight," she said slowly, even as her heart began to pound. "You've been married four times."

"Technically," he said with a shrug. "If you want to get caught up in all that."

She did. Very much so.

And from the shock on her sisters' faces, she suspected that they did, too.

"Well, I guess we should just be grateful that there aren't any other siblings floating around out there," Camille remarked flippantly.

"No." Papa gave her a little smile, but then his eyes narrowed as a pinch formed between his brows. "At least..."

Camille met Sophie's gaze across the table, matching the horror that she felt.

"No." Papa shook his head again.

Camille stared him down, and her entire body seemed to vibrate. "You're sure?"

"Very sure," Papa said, almost proudly.

"As sure as you are that you're committing to this new woman? Your fifth wife?"

"I am," Papa replied with a nod to underscore it.

Camille glared at him and then reached for her wineglass again. Five marriages. Half of them hidden from her, like so much of his life. He revealed only what he cared to, and showed up only when it suited him.

"And what makes her so special?" Camille wondered aloud, not believing for a moment that this woman's fate would be any different than her mother's, Sophie's mother's, and the other two women that Papa had never even mentioned until now.

"She doesn't expect anything from me," Papa replied. "She doesn't want to change me. She loves me just as I am. As... imperfect as I am."

The words sank in, creating silence in the room.

Camille knew what her sisters were thinking. That tall, proud, unapologetic Paul Laurent had never admitted to being anything but faultless before.

Camille studied him, looking for a hint of a smile, something to show that he was joking, but all she saw was a lined, older version of the face she'd once known so well. And tried so hard to forget.

The man before her was a shadow of the man who would swing her onto his shoulders, sneak her extra sweets at the patisserie, and chase her around the fountain in the Jardin du Luxembourg, not caring if it upset the locals.

Time had caught up with him. With them all. Years had passed. Choices had been made.

Yes, Camille thought, her anger rising again. Choices had been made. Choices that had brought them to this point.

Choices that a child couldn't make but that a grown adult could.

"When is the wedding?" Isabelle finally asked, breaking the silence.

"This summer," Papa replied.

"And where will it be?" Isabelle inquired.

Did it matter? Camille wanted to ask.

But it turned out it did matter when Papa replied, "Here. In Paris. Nadine is French. This is where we live."

Now Isabelle was the one whose eyes bulged. "You've been living here in Paris and you never told me? For how long?"

Papa shifted in his chair. "Now, see, I knew you'd get worked up, which is why I didn't tell you."

Camille exchanged a glance with Sophie, who looked so bewildered that Camille had an urge to reach out a hand and comfort her. Instead, she kept it firmly clasped in her lap, digging her nails into her palm. Her heart ached for the pain and confusion that she saw in Isabelle's face.

Isabelle, who was always so strong and stoic. Isabelle, who had believed in Papa when the rest of them had stopped.

"For how long?" Isabelle ground out.

Papa let out a long breath. "Oh, I guess it's been about two or three months now."

Let that sink in, Camille thought. And in all that time, he hadn't bothered to tell the only daughter who was still willing to speak to him.

"But...those postcards!" Isabelle was breathless with disbelief.

"Vacations," Papa replied as if it should be obvious. "I was recently in Portugal."

Isabelle opened her mouth, but no sound came out.

Camille used this opportunity to comment, "I didn't receive any postcards."

"I didn't think you wanted to hear from me," Papa told her flatly.

"That doesn't mean you shouldn't have made the effort," Camille said, her voice rising with newfound anger, emotions that she'd kept trapped for so long were now boiling to the surface. "I'm a parent, too. And that's what parents do, Papa. They keep trying. They take responsibility. They take accountability. And they never give up on their children."

"I never gave up on you," he said softly, his eyes tired.

"Oh, no." She scoffed. "You just walked away! Moved across the ocean." Camille didn't even realize she was gesturing to Sophie until she felt her youngest sister's stare—and saw the hurt on her face. She dropped her arms and clutched the napkin in her lap, giving her father a long, hard look. "And then you crossed back, leaving Sophie behind, too."

Tears stung the backs of her eyes, and she willed them not to fall. She'd cried enough tears for this man, and she'd felt enough self-pity, too. But right now, it wasn't herself she was thinking of. It was Sophie. The little girl with soft brown hair, who didn't have Isabelle to fall back on the way Camille had. Who didn't have Camille, either.

Camille had made her own choices then, as a child. But she was an adult now, and she could do better. She would do better. Because they *all* deserved better.

"Isabelle, I see now that I should have reached out sooner," Papa said heavily. "It had been so long, I wasn't sure what to say. If you'd want to get together. That's why I thought it would be better *all* together."

Camille bit back a laugh. All together. That was Papa's idea? Clearly, all his best thoughts were behind him.

Isabelle shot her a look. Turning back to Papa, she said, "You should have reached out."

He nodded, closing his eyes. "I should have done a lot of things differently, but I wouldn't take it all back." He looked at Sophie. "I can't say that everything I did was a mistake."

Camille pulled in a breath and stared at her younger sister, holding a fist at her side that she slowly released.

"No," she said quietly. "Not everything was a mistake."

Papa looked at her with surprise, but Camille turned away.

"I think we should call it a night," Isabelle said quietly, already standing to clear the table with noticeably shaking hands. Sophie wasted no time in standing to help her, but Camille remained seated, glaring at her father, trying to communicate all the hurt she felt, that had been trapped for so long, with nowhere to go.

Finally, when nothing more was said, because the past couldn't be changed, Camille stood. Eventually, their father did, too.

"Maybe I'll see you girls again before you leave?" Papa asked, his voice hesitant when she was used to it being so decisive.

Papa wasn't making all the plans now. Life was no longer exclusively on his terms. Camille had grown up. They all had. And now it was him turning to them to dictate their relationship.

Now she had a choice to make. To walk away. Or to open up.

"Maybe," she said, because she didn't trust herself to make a decision one way or another right now, not when the emotions were brewing so violently inside her, not when she felt like for the first time, she didn't know who her father was.

He kissed her on the cheek and then did the same for Sophie and Isabelle.

And then, he was gone.

Only this time, it didn't feel so permanent. And Camille wasn't sure what to make of that.

Nineteen

SOPHIE

Sophie had to keep remembering to sip her *chocolat chaud* before it went cold. Her hand was flying over the page of her notebook, and she had to keep shaking her wrist to stop it from cramping. She'd started her morning at the café by transcribing the events of last night, needing to get it off her chest and out of her heart, but somewhere between the part where Papa first arrived at the apartment and then mentioned his fourth marriage, she had an idea, for a story, or maybe something more. A novel—of sorts. Three sisters. One father. And a reunion. In Paris.

Because who could not be inspired by this beautiful city?

Her phone pinged, stirring her from her world, and she looked down at the screen to see yet another message from her mother, once again asking why she wasn't responding. Heaving a sigh, she thought of last night, everything leading up to it, and all the messy emotions that it had stirred up. She was in no mood to talk to her mother or even text. She couldn't pretend that what was transpiring here in Paris wasn't happening, so for now, it was best not to reply at all.

She went back to her notebook, trying to get back into her zone, but now she was distracted by something else. The sound of her name being called out.

Frowning, she looked up, trying to pinpoint the sound, and she beamed when she saw the source.

"Gabriel!"

"I hope I'm not disturbing you," he said as he leaned down to kiss both her cheeks.

She warmed at the touch. "Not at all. A welcome distraction." There was a difference, after all. "Do you have time to sit?"

"Only for a moment, then I'm off to the gallery." Gabriel dropped onto a chair and smiled broadly. "Good news. I finished my painting."

"That is good news!" Sophie said. Isabelle would be relieved.

"Then why don't you look happier?" he asked.

Sophie let her shoulders relax. "Is it that obvious?"

"Only because I've come to know you," he said, giving her a small smile that made her stomach flutter.

He had come to know her, and it wasn't just a feeling that she alone had. He understood her. More than Jack. Certainly more than her mother.

She could talk to him. About anything.

"It's been an eventful couple of days," she began. "My father came to the apartment for dinner last night."

"Ah, so you agreed to see him." Gabriel looked pleased by the decision.

Sophie wondered what he'd have to say about what came next.

"He's getting married. Again. Not for the third time or the

fourth. But for the fifth, as it turns out." Or so he said. She still wasn't sure if she believed him. There may have been one or two he forgot to mention—or forgot in general. Surely there's been more than one woman in all the years since he'd left her and her mother and flown back to Europe on a one-way ticket.

"And you're not happy for him?" Gabriel gave her a knowing look.

"I don't know how to feel," Sophie replied. "Papa seemed happy, but then, he was happy with my mother, too, at first."

And Isabelle and Camille's mother before that.

And maybe the wife he had before her, too. Sophie would laugh out loud if she didn't feel like crying.

"You're surprised then?" Gabriel ventured.

"Yes," she replied. Though she wasn't sure why she should be. Their father bounced around, never staying put for long, never able to sit in the same place or stay with the same person before he got restless. "I guess I didn't think my father was capable of love."

"But surely he loves you," Gabriel said. "And your sisters."

Sophie had thought about this a lot over the years until she'd stopped thinking about it at all. She had one parent who was too ever-present and another who was never there. But did physical presence constitute love?

"Maybe I have it all wrong," she said with a shrug. "Maybe I don't even know what love is."

"You mean you've never been in love?" Gabriel glanced at her, causing a blush to bloom in her cheeks.

"Honestly?" Sophie thought of Jack, down on one knee. "I'm not sure that I have."

Except she wasn't so sure that was true anymore because

lately, she felt like she was falling in love. With Gabriel. With Paris. With the life she had here.

Or maybe she was just getting swept away.

"That's the thing about love," she continued. "It's not certain."

There was no guarantee. And the thing or person you loved the most could be snatched away at any time, sometimes by the very person you thought you could trust more than anyone.

"You said the same thing the last time I saw you," Gabriel commented.

Sophie glanced at him, flattered that he remembered. "I'll have to watch what I say around you," she teased, again feeling her cheeks heat.

"You can speak freely with me," he assured her with a pat of his hand, letting it linger there on top of hers, warm and reassuring. "I feel like I can be open with you, too. It's been a long time since I've been able to do that."

She stared up into his dark eyes, feeling the pull of their connection as her heart picked up speed, and she wondered for a moment if he might kiss her, right here under the awning of this café in the heart of Paris, and she realized that she wanted him to, as much as she wanted just about anything else in the world. She felt close to him, but she wanted to be even closer.

They were side by side, pressed together, and just when she thought he might lean in, the woman beside her stood up, shaking their table, forcing them to steady their belongings.

"Your father," he said after a moment, and Sophie inwardly groaned. She didn't want to think about her father right now, much less talk about him. "What part surprises you most? That he's getting married again?"

"I guess you could say that I thought my father wasn't the marrying kind," Sophie said. "But I guess he's exactly that. It's the committing part that he has a problem with."

"And to you, they are the same?" Gabriel asked.

Sophie looked at him in confusion. "Absolutely. That's what marriage is. A pact. A promise. A commitment for life. Otherwise, it's just…a relationship. Otherwise, there's no point in getting married."

Isabelle and Hugh were a perfect example of two people who were not just in love but committed to each other for life. She had seen it in their eyes at their wedding, and she saw it when Isabelle spoke of Hugh, which was admittedly not very frequently, but then again, this was sister time.

"Do you think your father sets out to end these marriages?" Gabriel asked pensively.

Sophie had gotten used to Camille's support when it came to their father, and she grew quiet while she contemplated Gabriel's question.

"No, I think that Papa just gets swept up in the moment," she finally said, just like she was, she supposed. It was easy to do, especially here in Paris, on a beautiful blue-sky day with the tulips in bloom and the river across the street, sparkling in the morning sun, and a handsome, understanding man at her side.

"Maybe he just loves the idea of love," Gabriel said. "Just because he can't make a marriage last doesn't mean he is incapable of love."

Sophie nodded slowly, thinking back to when she was young and her father used to take her mother by the hand and twirl her around their small backyard when a song he liked came on the radio. Her mother was a different person back then. She was more carefree. Happy even. She used to laugh and light up around him. She'd been, Sophie supposed, a woman in love.

And now, she was a woman who had been burned by it.

"He lives life big, to the fullest, but only for the day," Sophie said. Papa never stopped to think about how his actions might impact tomorrow—or who they might hurt. "He's in love, so he wants to get married. Again. But once the honeymoon is over, so is the marriage to him. His feelings change over time. And Papa always lets his emotions be his guide."

Gabriel looked at her thoughtfully for a moment. "You have high expectations of marriage."

Sophie considered this. "Maybe I do. But shouldn't everyone before they take that step?"

"I don't know," Gabriel said. "I don't ever plan to get married again."

Sophie wasn't sure why this proclamation bothered her, but it did. It wasn't like Gabriel was a boyfriend or anything more than a friend. He hadn't kissed her, had never even held her hand. He owed her absolutely nothing, yet somehow she couldn't help but feel...heartbroken.

"You don't?" she asked, willing him to change his mind.

"No," he said simply.

"But if you met the right girl..." She stopped talking, not wanting him to think that she was referring to yourself. "You'd be open to it then, surely?"

"I don't think so," Gabriel said.

Sophie took a sip of her hot chocolate, finding that it had now grown quite cold. She wasn't in love with Gabriel—surely not. She was just caught up with being in Paris, with a man who was attractive and charming and easy to talk to. She hadn't even considered a future before this trip with him, but hearing him announce that he never wanted to get married made her realize that there never could be a future with him.

And that maybe...she eventually did want to get married.

But maybe just not to Jack.

Twenty
ISABELLE

Isabelle was grateful for her meeting with an up-and-coming artist the next day because right now she needed something to take her mind off the dinner last night—and everything else. She'd discovered this woman while walking the streets of Montmartre a few months ago; she'd been immediately captivated by her fresh angle on landscapes, focusing on the windows of Paris, and had been delighted when the woman agreed to a show at the gallery.

"Amazingly, I can look at this city all day long and always see it with fresh eyes," Isabelle said as she admired the pieces the artist had brought with her today. The collection was nearly complete, and they set a date for the opening two months from now.

Two months, Isabelle thought when she was alone at her desk with her calendar. What would her life look like in two months? It would be the start of summer. Gabriel's show would be over, and maybe her marriage would be, too.

She looked at her phone, thinking of how easy it would be

to call Hugh—if he would even answer. To pretend like everything was fine, the way that he seemed to be doing.

Two months. Not so long ago she might have hoped she'd be entering her second pregnancy trimester by June. That she'd be shopping for nursery furniture and sweet little stuffed animals.

Now, her entire future seemed uncertain. Maybe it always had been. Maybe she was wrong to think that anything in her life was as she thought.

The door opened again, and she looked up, expecting to see the artist returning because she'd forgotten something, or a tourist looking to browse, but instead, Gabriel stood grinning at her.

And holding something in his hands.

Isabelle's heart began to drum as she came around her desk. "That's not what I think it is, is it?"

He grinned wickedly, holding the brown-paper-wrapped canvas out of reach. "Depends on what you're expecting."

"I'm expecting the final painting in the collection," she said warmly. She looked him in the eye, sensing his doubt and feeling a need to put him at ease. They both knew that this show was going to change things for both of them, but especially for Gabriel. There would be press at the event, but there would also be critics. She was sure that all the reviews would be favorable, but try telling that to the artist himself. "And I know that it's going to be wonderful, just like the rest."

"Are you sure?"

She hesitated. How could anyone be sure of anything? She'd thought she was sure of Hugh when she married him, and look how that had turned out. Her mother had probably been sure of Papa, and Sophie's mother had felt the same. She'd signed

Gabriel for the gallery after seeing just one of his paintings, and nothing else.

She'd taken a leap of faith. And against all her better judgment, for some reason, she felt very sure that in this case, at least, it would all work out.

And that maybe, somehow, all hope wasn't lost for everything in life.

"I'm sure," she said firmly. She held out a hand, and after a moment, he handed over the painting.

Isabelle wanted to unwrap it right then and there, but she sensed that Gabriel would rather not be judged face-to-face, so instead she set it on her desk.

"So, are you playing tour guide with my sister today?" she asked conversationally.

Gabriel looked evasive for a moment as he wandered the gallery, stopping to look closely at a few paintings she knew he'd already seen a dozen times before. "Oh, I just saw her, actually, at a café."

That didn't answer her question, and she wondered if something was going on that he wasn't telling her. But then she thought of Sophie's boyfriend, and she knew that things were complicated. That life was this way for everyone, not just for her.

"You seemed a little surprised to see me," Gabriel said, tilting his head. "Did you think I wouldn't pull through?"

"Oh..." Isabelle started to shake her head and then realized that there was no use denying it. She was a terrible liar, unlike her husband, and she had been nervous. More than she could admit. "A little."

Gabriel grinned. "I wouldn't do that to you."

She nodded, knowing that now. Wishing she could have

believed it then, like she had blind faith in the quality of his work. "I guess I'm still working on trusting people."

"I understand," Gabriel said, the amusement leaving his face. "But I've learned that sometimes, when you least expect it, people can surprise you."

They could.

Even Papa had surprised her. And not in a good way.

But Camille had, she thought. She could have fled back to England, but instead, she'd stayed in Paris, for the dinner, for Isabelle.

For both her sisters.

Isabelle waved Gabriel off and waited a few minutes until she was sure he was truly gone. Then she carefully unwrapped the canvas and stared at the painting, feeling her shoulders relax as the breath she'd been holding left her body.

Yes, people really could surprise you, even when you didn't think they could. And Gabriel had done just that, not just by delivering this painting when she'd all but given up on him, but by surpassing even her expectations of him.

What he didn't know was that by creating this, he had surprised himself. He might have spent the past few years painting for the joy of it, but he didn't truly know how good he was, and in just a few short days, he was about to find out.

And then, his life would change. She could only hope for the better.

That's all she could hope for any of them.

Isabelle walked over to the window and looked out onto the street, thinking of what Antoine had said, and now Gabriel, about people surprising you. With that in mind, she packed her bag for the day and headed home.

Maybe Camille would surprise her again.

Both of her sisters were home and in the kitchen, making dinner, when Isabelle pushed through the door.

"We thought we'd do something nice for you," Sophie said brightly, but there was pain in her eyes.

Pain that Isabelle had brought upon her.

"If anyone should be making up for last night, it's me," Isabelle said.

"No, it's our father who should," Camille said firmly. "And you were the one who made the effort for him."

She still was, Isabelle thought bitterly.

With a heavy sigh, she leaned against the counter. The kitchen was so small that the three of them could barely fit inside together, yet somehow they had, day after day, for more than a week.

Isabelle had grown used to having her sisters here, and she realized just how much she would miss them when they were gone.

"It's hard to believe that you'll both be leaving this weekend," she said sadly.

"I know," Sophie said, blinking quickly as she chopped a carrot.

"I do miss Flora," Camille replied with a wistful look. She grew quiet for a moment and then smiled broadly at Isabelle. "Are you all ready for the opening?"

Isabelle bit her lip, watching her sisters work in silence to prepare a salad. One of them had been to the boulangerie, because a fresh baguette sat on the counter, waiting to be cut.

"About that...I wanted to check with you both first," Isabelle said. "But I'd like to invite Papa to the show."

She was almost afraid to look at either of her sisters for fear that they would tell her what she didn't want to hear, that they didn't want their father there. And if they did, she knew that she'd be compelled to honor their wishes. Papa had hurt them. He hadn't been there when they'd needed him. But he was here now. And he was trying. And Isabelle could only hope that it wasn't too late for a second chance.

"It's your gallery," Sophie said, glancing nervously at Camille. "You should invite whomever you want."

Isabelle gave her a small smile and then skirted her gaze to Camille, whose expression was unreadable.

"Camille?"

Camille didn't speak for a moment but then said, "I can't stop you if you want to invite him. It's no different than your wedding."

The mere mention of her wedding day made Isabelle stiffen, and she was grateful when Camille gathered the plates from the cupboard.

"I'll set the table," Camille said, beating Isabelle to an excuse to leave the room.

Isabelle didn't argue. Camille needed space; it was her way. She didn't show her emotions but instead chose to hide from them.

Isabelle took her time gathering up the food with Sophie before joining Camille at the dining room table. Camille said nothing as they all sat down, but it was clear from the frown she wore that she had much to say.

"I still can't believe that Papa has been living in Paris all this time and that he never told you," Camille said, uncorking a bottle of wine. "I thought you two talked."

"Only occasionally," Isabelle replied, watching as Camille poured her a glass of wine.

"More than the rest of us," Sophie said, doing the same.

Isabelle detected the hurt in Sophie's voice, the longing for something she didn't have but maybe now could. She looked at her youngest sister, hoping that Papa's presence wasn't upsetting her trip to Paris. But she didn't dare to hope that seeing their father had made this visit better, either.

It was complicated at best. For all of them.

And sitting here, at this table, felt far too familiar to last night.

Isabelle glanced at the chair that Papa had occupied, now empty, as if reminding her of his steady absence.

"Do you want to eat over near the windows instead?" Isabelle suggested. "We could set this up on the coffee table."

Camille and Sophie wasted no time in grabbing their plates and moving, and everyone seemed more relaxed once they were curled up on the sofa and armchairs, food plates untouched on the coffee table, wineglasses in hand.

"I had no idea Papa was in Paris," Isabelle finally spoke. "It was a shock. And I won't deny that it hurts."

Sophie's look was one of sympathy. Camille simply glared.

"And you've never run into him, in all these months," she said, sounding almost surprised. "I know that Paris is big, but it's not that big, not when you have favorite spots and can rule out the touristy areas."

"I have a routine," Isabelle commented. One that she hadn't considered until now was maybe her way of keeping her world contained and safe, much like Camille.

So much for that, she thought.

"But you're living in Papa's childhood home," Sophie pointed out.

"It's true," Camille said. "This was Papa's stomping grounds when he was young. I can't believe he wouldn't be drawn back to this neighborhood in all these months."

"Maybe he didn't want to be seen until he was ready," Isabelle replied. She stared at the glass in her hands, not taking a sip. "He wouldn't be the only one."

"What does that mean?" Camille asked.

Isabelle took a deep breath. Her chest was so heavy, so filled with confusion and worry and fear of the unknown. And the two people who might love her most in this world were sitting in this room. Maybe they wouldn't understand.

But maybe, just maybe, they would.

"Hugh hasn't been traveling like I told you," she blurted. "Or like I thought. It turns out that all this time, he's been right here in Paris, across the river, living at one of his company's properties."

"What?" Camille gasped. "Why didn't you tell us you were separated?"

"Because I didn't know we were. I don't know what we are. Or ever were," Isabelle said, her voice cracking. "He told me that he was in Tokyo for business. I had calls and texts from him, and all that time, he was right here in Paris."

"But how do you know?" Sophie asked worriedly.

Isabelle hesitated, if only because recanting the details made it real. "I called his office to get the name of his hotel in Tokyo. They told me he was in the office that day. They even offered to transfer my call!"

"When was this?" Camille asked.

"Two weeks ago," Isabelle replied. "And before you ask, yes,

I've spoken to him since, and he's still pretending to be in Japan."

"Is it possible that he just popped into town for a few days before heading back?" Sophie asked with such hope in her voice that Isabelle almost felt bad for letting her down.

Sophie was young, but she wasn't naive. Like her and Camille, she'd understood heartbreak from an early age. That you couldn't always depend on people who were supposed to love you.

Isabelle had learned that lesson. But somehow she'd chosen to forget it. Or believe that somehow Hugh would be different.

"I mean...it's possible." Isabelle wasn't convinced.

"Wait." Camille set her wineglass on a coaster. "You're telling me that you've known he's here in Paris for weeks and you haven't said anything to him about it?"

"I haven't known what to say," Isabelle replied, but saying it made her realize how lame she sounded. "I didn't want to ruin your visit. I wanted to enjoy it. And then there was this business with Papa and this dinner. And my gallery show. I'll be in a clearer space in a week."

"A clearer space!" Camille stared at her. "Isabelle, you don't know what's going on with your husband! If he's here in Paris, then why is he in Paris, and why hasn't he told you?"

Isabelle looked at Camille frankly. "Do I need to spell it out to you of all people?"

"There is a possible explanation," Sophie said tentatively.

"What's that?" Camille asked.

Isabelle sat up straighter, too, holding on to the last thread of hope. She wanted to see the world through Sophie's eyes, not just Paris. And, she realized, glancing across the room, maybe Camille did, too.

"If there is an explanation, I can only think of one," Isabelle replied with a sigh. As much as she'd love to deny it, she knew that it was time to face reality. "He must be cheating on me."

"You don't know for sure," Sophie insisted. "You won't know until you talk to him."

"She's right," Camille said. "You can't avoid him forever. What have you even said each time you talk on the phone?"

"As little as possible." Isabelle sighed. "I've stopped asking him how the food is in Japan, that's for sure."

She managed a brittle laugh but neither of her sisters joined her.

"Besides, who knows what he'd even tell me if I asked him," Isabelle said. "If he's been lying about where he is, what's to stop him from lying again?"

"True." Sophie let out a heavy breath.

"You know what I think," Camille said, picking up her wineglass again.

Inwardly, Isabelle groaned. She knew exactly what Camille would think of all this, which was another reason she hadn't said anything, not that she would admit to it. This was Camille, her kid sister, a woman she loved, even if she had hardened her heart and saw the world as an unsafe place. Assumed the worst in people.

But wasn't that what Isabelle was doing? Assuming the worst about her own husband? A man she had promised to love and cherish until death did they part?

She didn't know what to believe. She just knew that somewhere, deep inside her, a tiny bloom of hope still existed, and she wasn't ready for it to be lost just yet.

"That you always knew Hugh would do this to me and I

was a fool to ever marry him much less fall in love with him?" Isabelle ventured.

Camille didn't bother to look hurt by the assessment. They both knew where she stood when it came to matters of the heart.

"I think you need to scout him out," Camille said firmly.

"You mean...follow him?" Isabelle almost laughed until she realized how serious Camille was. Beside her, Sophie nodded with enthusiasm. "No! Absolutely, not!"

"Yes! Sit outside his office, see where he goes for lunch, or after work," Camille said. "Take a few photos if you need to."

"This isn't a detective movie," Isabelle replied with a firm shake of her head. "This is my life."

"And that's all the more reason you need to find out what's going on with your husband. If he isn't going to tell you the truth, you need to discover it on your own." Camille turned to Sophie. "We'll go with you, won't we?"

Well, great. Isabelle had finally managed to get her sisters together and now they were teaming up against her.

Sophie looked startled but then nodded forcefully. "Of course. Absolutely. I only met Hugh one time and that was at your wedding. He might not even remember me or what I look like. I could easily follow him, sit beside him at a café even..."

Isabelle thought about this for about half a second before dismissing it. "He might not recognize you, Sophie, but he'd notice you. And he'd notice that you resemble me quite a bit."

"We'll keep our distance then," Camille said. "Let's just see where he goes."

And with whom were the unspoken words.

"I don't have a say in this, do I?" Isabelle asked.

"It's your life, Isabelle," Camille said, looking at her frankly.

"And you're not a helpless child anymore. You absolutely have a say in it."

Isabelle let those words sink in as she quietly sipped her wine. Camille's idea may be crazy, and they might even get caught, but if they did, then so did Hugh.

"You know what I'm going to say, don't you?" she said, giving her middle sister a rueful look.

Camille sighed audibly. "That it's a crazy idea and that you'll deal with Hugh on your own when you're ready."

"It is a crazy idea, and I will deal with Hugh when I'm ready," Isabelle said, "but that's not what I was going to say."

"It wasn't?" Camille blinked.

Isabelle shook her head. "I was going to say thank you. Just…thank you."

And she knew from the looks on both of her sisters' faces that no other words were needed. That despite their differences and physical distance, they had a bond, a shared understanding, and a loyalty that couldn't be broken.

And that they all knew they were going on that stakeout.

The thing about Camille was that when she said she was going to do something, she followed through, and on Wednesday morning when Isabelle awoke, she knew that even the rumble of thunder wouldn't keep them from stalking her husband.

"Maybe we should have waited for another day," Isabelle said, fighting against the knots that were forming in her stomach as she emerged from the metro station and popped open her umbrella.

She looked around the 1st arrondissement nervously. It was

her first time on the Right Bank since learning that Hugh was here in Paris, and she felt jittery like she might see him at any moment, even though they were several blocks from his office.

"Nice try," said Camille with a look of disapproval. She held her umbrella high over her head and her gaze firmly in front of her. She looked like a woman on a mission.

If Isabelle didn't know better, she'd have thought Camille was stalking her own husband, not Isabelle's.

"You can take off the sunglasses," Isabelle said as they joined a group of tourists hoping to blend in (and failing miserably) as they crossed the busy street. What had Isabelle been thinking by wearing her usual trench and favorite scarf? Hugh would spot her from two blocks away!

"And show my face?" Camille tutted.

"It is raining and gloomy," Sophie pointed out.

It *was* gloomy, and the mood fit the task. But right now, all Isabelle wanted to do was get back inside her warm and dry apartment and pretend that none of this was happening.

At the very least, she wanted to get on the other side of the river where she suspected Hugh wouldn't dare cross until he was ready to—what? End their marriage? Or end his affair? Because Isabelle was sure that was what was going on here, and today would only confirm it.

She put a hand to her stomach, feeling suddenly sick. She would turn around, dash into the metro station, go back to the apartment, and deal with this another day.

But her sisters were now ten paces in front of her, and if she turned back, there was no telling what Camille would do. Confront Hugh? March into his office and demand to see him and know what was going on? Camille wasn't afraid of a fight.

But Isabelle was. Ironic that all this time Camille thought

that Isabelle was the strong one when she just masked her fear with denial.

Even now.

"I'm just saying that the sunglasses make you stand out even more on a day like this," Isabelle hissed when she caught up to her sisters. "I thought we were supposed to blend in."

"Fine," Camille said tersely when they reached the café they'd agreed upon in advance as their stakeout point. She folded her umbrella before dropping onto a seat that faced the road. Isabelle reluctantly did the same, flanked by Sophie at the end.

At least it was Paris, where sitting in a row was even more acceptable than facing each other.

Only today, there would be no pleasant people watching. No kir royales, much as they were needed. No cheese, either. Today, they were on a mission. An unpleasant one.

Rain dropped down from the edge of the café awning, but underneath it was dry and warm from the heaters that hung below the sturdy fabric. The women all ordered a round of *café crèmes* to ward off the chill, but when the drinks arrived, none of them reached for a sip.

"I don't know why I feel nervous, but I do," Sophie admitted, her eyes wide as she glanced at Isabelle.

Even now, when Isabelle felt like she was being twisted into a knot and her heart was going to pound right out of her chest, she felt comforted by Sophie's presence.

"It will be okay," she assured Sophie, setting a hand on her arm.

Wishing that she could be so sure herself.

"We should have brought binoculars," Camille suddenly

said. "Grand-mère kept a small pair for the opera. I'm sure you still have them, Isabelle."

"I do," Isabelle said. They were tucked away in a box in a bedroom closet, along with some of the other treasures she couldn't bear to part with just yet—if ever. She'd told herself that she'd have to clear out more of the past to make room for a future baby, but now that future didn't feel full. As she sat staring at the passersby, waiting for her husband to appear, it felt bleak. "But something tells me that would be more suspicious than dark sunglasses on a rainy day."

She managed a hint of a smile, which Sophie shared.

"How will we see Hugh if he's under an umbrella?" Sophie asked after a few minutes of silence and scrutinizing passersby.

"Good point," Isabelle said, seizing the chance. She reached for her handbag, eager to pay and get away. Just being in this neighborhood made her tense. At any moment, Hugh could spot her. Maybe he already had.

But then she thought of how ridiculous this was, to be hiding from her own husband.

About as ridiculous as the fact that he was also hiding from her.

"The rain is letting up," Camille said, tipping her head toward the sky. "Look, there's a bit of sun poking through the clouds."

Isabelle studied the clouds, wishing she could read some meaning into the turn of the weather. That there was hope for her as well as the afternoon ahead.

"Maybe Hugh won't come out," she said after another ten minutes had passed. People had put away their umbrellas, and the early lunch crowd was growing thick. They'd planned their timing for when her husband was most likely to come outside and have a social break in his day, but they hadn't discussed what they would do when they saw him.

"Maybe he has a working lunch," Sophie commented.

At this, Camille and Isabelle both exchanged a look and then burst out laughing.

"What?" Sophie asked, staring from one sister to the next.

"Honey, this is France, not New York. Food is a pleasure, meant to be enjoyed," Isabelle said, once again grateful for her youngest sister's presence, and the brief moment of distraction it had given her.

"No one is cramming down a turkey sandwich while tapping on the computer here," Camille agreed. "Hugh will come out. We just have to be patient."

"And then what?" Isabelle said, her panic rising now that they were here and a confrontation was imminent. "What happens when he does come out? What then?"

"I think you'll know what you want to do when you see him," Camille said with confidence.

"If he sees you first, you'll have to think fast," Sophie warned her. "Are you a good actress?"

Isabelle blinked at Sophie and then jabbed Camille with her elbow. "Give me your sunglasses."

"But I thought—" Camille started to protest.

"Hey, the sun's out," Isabelle reminded her. And she needed to hide. Fast.

What *would* she do if Hugh saw her first? And what would *he* do? Pretend he hadn't seen her, most likely, even though they'd both know he had. And what if he decided to cross the street, dust off his own acting skills, pretend that he'd just flown into town that morning and had decided to make a quick stop at the office before going home?

How would she react then?

A phone rang, causing her to jump and nearly spill her coffee.

She pulled her phone from her pocket, half expecting it to be Hugh saying he was looking down at her from his office window, but it was Sophie who was staring at her phone with a frown.

"It's just my mother," she said tersely. "I'll call back."

They resumed their watch, until another phone rang, this time Camille's. Isabelle was acutely aware that hers was the only device that wasn't chiming, and that both of her sisters had a life waiting for them when this week was over—people waiting for them. And what did she have left for her when they were gone?

"Is that Flora?" Isabelle asked, seeing an opportunity to shut down this stakeout—at least until she'd worked out how she wanted to handle things with Hugh. "You should probably take it."

"It's not Flora, and I don't need to take it," Camille replied tersely. She swiped the phone screen, ignoring the call, but not before Isabelle had a chance to see the name of the caller.

"Aren't you worried that Rupert might have something to say about Flora?" Isabelle pressed.

Camille eyed her sternly. "Aren't you always telling me I worry too much? Besides, if it's an emergency, he would text or try calling again. And that's not happening."

"I just thought since he called, it must be important," Isabelle hedged.

"He's just returning my call from the other day," Camille said, staring straight across the street. Her focus was on spotting

Hugh, and it was clear that nothing—and no one—could pull her from it.

"Should we order food?" Sophie asked when the waiter looked over at their table.

Isabelle hadn't eaten yet today, but she was too anxious to be hungry. Camille narrowed her eyes at the street and then shook her head.

"Eating will only distract us," she said. "We can eat after."

After. Meaning after they had seen Hugh. Because it was clear from the lift of Camille's chin and the set of her jaw that they weren't going to be leaving this table until they did.

"I don't know if I can do this," Isabelle said as a heave of nausea hit her full force. "I don't know what to say, or—what I want."

Except that wasn't true. She did know what she wanted. She wanted the life she thought she had just a couple of weeks ago.

A beautiful apartment here in Paris. A daily walk to a little gallery that she was proud to own. A husband who she loved. And a baby.

It wasn't asking for much, was it? But right now, it felt like the impossible.

"That's why we're here," Camille reminded her, pulling her gaze from the sidewalk to stare at her. "You need to see him, Isabelle. Only then will you know how you feel."

"You mean...if I still love him?" Isabelle was angry with her husband, but she hadn't stopped to consider the root of the reason why. Was it because he lied? Or because he'd hurt her? Or both?

Or was the person she was really angry at herself? For trusting him? For wanting more than he'd told her he could offer? For believing that in time they could want the same things?

For daring to think that anything was possible?

"Look! A bunch of people are coming out of his building," Sophie said in an excited whisper.

Camille and Isabelle both whipped their heads toward the building on the corner, curiosity winning out over Isabelle's fear of being seen.

Sure enough, a small crowd of men and women in business attire pushed through the doors onto the sidewalk. A few balding businessmen, women who walked quickly, laughing at what their friends were saying, and a man with his shirtsleeves rolled up, his nut-brown hair flopping over his forehead, looking intensely at a tall, thin blonde while she talked.

It was Hugh. With another woman. And before Isabelle could try to convince herself that it was just a professional acquaintance, Camille tutted and turned to her.

"He's holding her hand," she said, pinching her lips in anger. "What are they...twelve?"

Isabelle stared, no longer caring if she was seen. Wishing, for once, that she might be. That he'd notice her. Remember her. Consider what he'd done to her.

She stood, feeling her sisters' shocked stares as she did, but her eyes were locked on Hugh. Hugh, who had stopped at the crosswalk to kiss another woman, right there on the open street of Paris. Her Paris. The city she loved. The city she'd asked him to live in, with her.

"They're not twelve," she finally said. "They're...in love."

Something she'd experienced once. Until it was lost.

Like so many other things.

Twenty-One

SOPHIE

"Let's go back to the apartment," Sophie suggested after Isabelle finally sat down, and Hugh disappeared, and enough silence had passed that it was clear even Camille wasn't going to chase him down and cause a public scene. She was wet and sad for what had transpired this morning, and she didn't think that any of them needed to see anything more, especially Isabelle.

Isabelle barely nodded, but Camille's jaw set defiantly.

"I'm hoping to run into my dear brother-in-law and have a few choice words with him," she said angrily.

Sophie rather wished she would. He certainly deserved it—and then some. She saw the fire in her middle sister's eyes—and the hurt in her eldest's—and she understood more than she ever had before. Camille might be a fighter, but she also fought for what she believed in, and for whom she loved.

"Please don't," Isabelle said wearily. "I'll...deal with Hugh."

"Will you, though?" Camille asked as they approached the metro stop.

Isabelle paused at the top of the stairs. She looked so pale and small in her navy raincoat and stylish floral scarf tied at the side of her neck that Sophie felt like the roles were reversed, and that for the first time, she was the big sister, the one whose life was established and in order, which was almost comical considering that Sophie's life was a complete mess.

But compared to Isabelle's, she supposed that it was...safe. Secure. Everything that her mother wanted for her.

As they descended the stairs in silence and then rode the metro back to their stop, Sophie watched her sisters and contemplated this, wondering what was worse: having and losing a life you loved or never having one at all?

She'd thought that Isabelle and Hugh were the ideal couple.

But then, she'd once thought the same about her parents, and look how that turned out.

Maybe, she thought, matching Isabelle's frown, there really was no such thing as lasting love. But did that mean it was any less real?

Isabelle's mood, however, shifted when they arrived back at the apartment. "Antoine!" she said to a handsome man standing near the mailboxes. "Have you met my sister Sophie?"

But before Antoine could reply, a woman who had been standing with her back to the door turned. A woman with shoulder-length brown hair, a no-nonsense beige jacket, and sensible sneakers stood stiffly clutching the handle of a large suitcase.

"Mom?" Sophie felt her heart lock up in her chest as she ground to a halt, causing Camille to crash into her back.

She stared at the woman who had raised her, mostly on her own. The person whom she spoke to daily and saw weekly, but who now seemed like a stranger, completely out of place in this marble lobby.

Her mother's voice lacked its usual warmth when she said, "Hello, Sophie."

Camille edged closer to Isabelle. Sophie edged closer to Isabelle. Antoine gave a little smile to Isabelle and then a bow to the ladies before making his excuses and quickly exiting through the front door, leaving Sophie to wish that she could join him.

Sophie stared at her mother, whose steely gaze never left her, and then glanced at her sisters, who no longer seemed to be so worried about Hugh or his whereabouts or that woman he was with earlier.

"Mom, you remember Isabelle. And Camille," Sophie said.

Her mother adjusted her features and managed a polite smile. "Of course. You're all grown up. Such lovely young women." She gave each of them a brief hug, but stood back before she reached Sophie.

"Are you staying long, Patricia?" Isabelle asked diplomatically. "I can take your luggage upstairs and get you settled?"

"I'm staying in a hotel just down the road," Sophie's mother replied. "But this was my first stop after arriving. I wanted to check on my daughter and make sure she was okay."

"Of course she's okay," Isabelle said with a small laugh, sounding surprised.

Sophie closed her eyes briefly. She didn't know how her mother had found her. Or why she had come. She didn't even know why she should be in trouble, other than the fact that she hadn't been honest. But she clearly was.

"Mom, why don't we get some air now that the rain has stopped," she suggested. "There's a great café around the corner. I think you'll love it."

"You know I don't drink coffee." Her mother sounded put out by the suggestion.

"They have tea," Sophie said, feeling suddenly as exhausted as Isabelle looked. "Or hot chocolate. The most delicious hot chocolate you can ever imagine!"

Her mother pursed her lips and glanced at Isabelle and Camille, as if weighing the lesser of two evils. Eventually she gave the slightest nod. "Fine."

"Your luggage will be safe here," Isabelle assured her. She gave Sophie a sympathetic look as she moved toward the elevator, and Camille toward the staircase.

Outside, Sophie knew she could speak freely, but when could she ever really speak freely to her mother?

She stopped just outside the door. The rain had subsided for now, and she had no real interest in going to that charming café that had come to feel like a second home and tainting it with a negative experience. Her time in Paris—even this morning's strange experience with her sisters—had brought out a side of her that she didn't want to deny anymore. She didn't want to go back to being the person who hid from her passions, or her true self.

She didn't want to go back to her old life at all.

"How did you know where I was?" she asked. That seemed like a fair question, all things considered.

"I have a tracker on your phone," her mother answered, as if that were an obvious answer. "When you stopped replying to my texts, I checked it."

Sophie gaped at her mother. Seconds seemed to pass as a woman on a bicycle rode past, spraying water onto Sophie's legs, not that she minded. No, what she minded was that she was nearly thirty years old, she had come to Paris with her own money, on her own vacation time, and that somehow, once again, she was being denied the experience.

"You track my whereabouts?"

"You're my child!" her mother said indignantly.

"But that's just the thing, Mom," Sophie cried as her heart started to pound. It was the first time she had dared to speak up for herself, and she was outside of her comfort zone, but maybe this was long overdue. "I'm not a child. And I haven't been one for some time."

Her mother didn't seem to hear her as she shook her head.

"You lied to me," she accused, her eyes narrowing. "Telling me you were in London."

"Because I knew how you would react if I told you the truth," Sophie said with a sigh. "I knew how you would react if I told you I was going to Paris."

"Yet you went, anyway! You didn't care one bit about *my* feelings!"

Sophie stared at her mother, officially silenced, because she knew that there was nothing she could say at that moment that could ever make her mother understand.

"And what about *my* feelings?" she tried, hoping to get through to her mother once and for all, but suspecting from the look on her face that she wouldn't succeed. "What about when I got into the Sorbonne? What about how hard I worked all through high school to get that scholarship? Did you ever think of how I felt then? I was so excited, Mom! It was my *passion*. It was my dream! And it came true. Until you took it away. And you didn't even care."

"I did what was best for you," her mother said with a lift of her chin. "Look what passion and dreams got me. Trouble, that's what."

"No." Sophie was shaking now, from head to toe. In all these years, they had never once discussed what had happened.

Sophie had just been forced to accept it, knowing that nothing could change the outcome, that it was easier to just forget her dreams and to accept reality. But she couldn't do that anymore. "You did what was best for *you*, Mom."

She took a step back toward the apartment building and her sisters. Her mother took a step toward her.

"Where do you think you're going?" she asked in a tone better served for a misbehaving four-year-old.

Sophie stopped and sighed. "I'm going to get your suitcase, Mom. And then I'm going to get you a cab. And then I'm going inside to be with my sisters. Isabelle needs me, and…I think Camille does, too."

She smiled a little, but her mother only scowled deeper.

"But I flew all the way to this godforsaken place!"

"Then I suggest that you make the most of it," Sophie said lightly, even though her entire body was so tense she felt like her veins were on fire. She'd never liked the way her mother spoke to her, and she'd always known that it was different than how her friends' mothers treated them, that it had grown worse in time, starting when Papa left, and escalating with each passing year, until now. The breaking point.

She'd finally set herself free. Found the life she wanted to live. And nothing and no one could make her give it up.

"Paris is a beautiful city," she said. "It's everything I dreamed it would be and more. Take a walk. Eat the food. See the sights. Just wander."

"Wander?" Her mother looked appalled. "You plan to *abandon* me when I crossed an ocean for you?"

"I'm not abandoning you, Mom," Sophie said, forcing herself to stay strong. "But I have plans for the day, and I didn't know you were coming."

She didn't have any concrete plans, and she knew that her sisters wouldn't mind if she spent the afternoon with her mother—but she minded. She couldn't imagine compromising this vacation by sharing it with someone who didn't support it.

Or her.

"Well!" her mother huffed. "At least you'll be back in New York where you belong next week and all this nonsense will be over."

New York. Where she belonged.

But was it? It was home. It was where she grew up. But it wasn't where her heart was. And it wasn't where she was happy.

Her mother seemed to collect herself for a moment, her expression softening as much as possible. It wasn't an apology; her mother didn't do those. It was, perhaps, a concession. "We'll just...forget it ever happened."

A wave of fresh anger surged, and this time, Sophie knew that she couldn't forget. Not the present. Not the past. Not the future she'd always wanted.

"Like my scholarship?" Sophie saw the flash in her mother's eyes and had the courage to say, "We never talked about you did."

"I did what was best for you," her mother said firmly.

"Best for me or best for you?" Sophie dared to ask.

Her mother looked startled before quickly recovering. She waved a hand through the air, giving a dismissive smile. "What are we even talking about this? That was years ago, Sophie! And everything turned out for the better. You went to a great school. Got a great job. Met a great guy. I can't believe you even remember that." She shook her head, still smiling, giving a hint of an eye roll.

The feelings that Sophie had buried rose to the surface,

along with her dreams and her deepest desires, the ones that she'd been forced to neglect, to tell herself didn't matter. She pictured herself a week from now, back in New York, sitting at her desk, clocking a day that was too long to leave time for little else other than a nightly call with her mother, maybe a meal with a man she didn't know if she loved, and a book that would never get written.

And then she thought of her sisters, upstairs right now, and of Papa, who was somewhere in this city, no doubt wondering if they would welcome him into their lives or turn their backs, the way he had done so many times to them.

And she thought of Paris. And all its possibilities. And how she felt every morning when she woke up here. And how she wanted to feel like that every day. Or at least for as long as she could.

She played out the scenario as she grabbed her mother's luggage and pulled it back onto the street, then hailed the nearest taxi.

She'd rewritten her own story once. She wouldn't do it again.

"Actually, Mom," she said, "I'm not going back to New York."

Her heart began to pound just as it did when she made the decision to come to Paris. When she'd made the leap, taken the chance, and believed in herself enough to think that somehow a dream could still come true.

"What?" Her mother went pale. "What are you talking about? Of course you're coming back to New York. You have to come back!"

"But that's just the thing. I don't," Sophie replied, standing a little taller, forcing herself not to lose her nerve, because it would be so easy just to give in, be the good daughter, do the right thing, and pretend that this conversation never happened, which is what could happen if she let it. "I'm an adult. And I have my entire life ahead of me. The life that I want to live. And I'm half-French, so I should have no problem getting dual citizenship."

Her mother's mouth fell open, and for the first time in a very long time, she was at a loss for words.

"I can't believe you would do this to me, Sophie," she finally scolded, narrowing her eyes.

"Oh, Mom," Sophie said sadly, because a part of her genuinely did feel sorry for what her mother had become—not just for what her father had done to them, but for what her mother had let him do. He'd stolen her spirit and broken her down. Instead of reclaiming the life she wanted, she'd chosen to spend her time in bitterness and negativity, keeping her world small and expecting Sophie to do the same. "I'm not doing anything to you. I'm doing it for me. I just wish that you could see that this is what makes me happy. And I hope that someday, somehow, you can be happy, too."

She walked over to her mother, kissed her on the cheek, and then walked back inside the building.

And toward her future.

Twenty-Two
CAMILLE

There wasn't enough brie in all of Paris to make up for Hugh's indiscretions, but still Camille and Sophie both went above and beyond, raiding the local fromagerie while Isabelle took a hot bath, and then setting up a board with fresh baguette, grapes, and, of course, plenty of chocolate.

By the time Isabelle emerged from her bedroom wrapped in a soft ivory robe, the wine had been poured.

Camille couldn't help but notice that even after realizing her husband had been cheating on her (not that Camille was surprised in the least, given his recent behavior), Isabelle looked completely composed and downright pretty in her pale pink satin pajama set. Had this happened to Camille, she'd have been stumbling around the apartment in threadbare gray sweats, with a blotchy face, clutching a wine bottle by the neck and eating ice cream straight from the tub.

But then, this would never happen to Camille, because one could only have a husband cheat on you if one actually had a husband.

With a pang, her mind went to Rupert, and again, she

pushed it quickly from her mind. Her sister was in distress, even if she didn't look it. Her attention was needed here.

"Well, Isabelle, you may be in touch with your French roots lately, but there is no denying you are your mother's daughter," Camille remarked when she handed Isabelle her wine.

Isabelle managed an almost imperceptible smile.

"In what way?" Sophie asked as she settled on the sofa.

Camille realized that she and Isabelle never talked about their mother around Sophie. Somehow it had always felt disloyal to the woman who raised them, however loosely, to do that. Now, she saw that it left Sophie on the outside, not quite a sister, but instead a relative who didn't share in the bond that Camille had with Isabelle.

"Our mother never shed a single tear when Papa left," Camille told her, glancing at Isabelle to see if she'd protest.

But Isabelle didn't seem to mind that Camille was opening up about their mother. She had bigger problems at the moment.

"It's not that she didn't care," Isabelle explained to Sophie. "It's that she's always composed."

"Cold," Camille said, hearing a bitter edge in her tone.

She reached for a piece of bread and slathered it with brie, then popped it into her mouth. Rupert would love this, she thought, longing for him once again. They spent many quiet winter nights over the years in front of the fire, after Flora had gone to bed, drinking wine, enjoying cheese, reading books, or watching a movie. Sometimes talking, sometimes not talking at all.

And as nice as it was to be here with her sisters—yes, even Sophie—she couldn't help but wish that right now she was with Rupert.

He was the person she loved most, she supposed. Other than Flora, of course.

But was she in love with him?

And if she was, she shouldn't be, because he had moved on.

And even then, she couldn't be in love with Rupert. Or so she had always told herself.

"Not cold," Isabelle corrected her, sipping her wine. "Just..." She paused, searching for a more delicate word. "Guarded."

Sophie nodded as if she understood, and Camille didn't see how she possibly could. Sophie's mother was the complete opposite of theirs; honestly, Paul Laurent was as eclectic in his taste in women as he was in his style of art. Whereas their mother was classically elegant, Sophie's mother was bohemian —even if she didn't appear so today.

"My mother is very closed off, too," she said. "After Papa left, she changed. She stopped laughing and smiling. Stopped working in the theater. She shut everyone out. Except for me. The more consumed she became about constraining her own life, the stricter she became with me."

"How was your visit with her?" Isabelle asked. Sophie had been quiet about it all afternoon. "You didn't stay out long."

"Oh, she was tired from the flight and the jet lag," Sophie said but then shook her head. "Actually, that's not true. Not at all. My mother...she tracked me down. Against my wishes. She didn't know I was coming here."

"But why not?" Camille asked, immediately thinking of her daughter and how she would feel if Flora traveled abroad and failed to mention it.

"My mother would never have allowed me to come to Paris," Sophie said simply.

Camille frowned. "But you're a grown adult. She can't stop you."

"Technically, no, but, with my mother, it's complicated." Sophie looked down at her wineglass. "It's often easier to just give her her way. If I don't, she makes me feel guilty. I'm her only daughter, she's done so much for me. She'll go silent on me, or sulk, and it's always up to me to smooth things over. It's...well, it became my job to make her happy after Papa left."

Camille and Isabelle exchanged a wide-eyed glance. This wasn't the woman they remembered from their summer visits, though in fairness, they hadn't interacted with her very much, especially Camille. Back then Patricia was full of energy, consumed with Sophie, of course, but happily so.

"When I was in high school, I was obsessed with moving to Paris," Sophie started to say as a wistful smile came over her face. "I was the best student in my class. Not to brag," she rushed to say.

"Not in the least!" Isabelle said, grinning. "You should be proud of yourself!"

Sophie's face fell. "My mother didn't see it that way. Papa had left by then, and I suppose she saw it as some sort of betrayal that I had any interest in anything French."

"But you're half-French," Isabelle pointed out. "It's part of your heritage."

"It's more than that," Sophie said, leaning in. "It's who I am. It's what excited me. It always did. I used to have posters of Paris up in my room, all over the walls, until I saw how upset they made my mother, so I took them down. I knew she'd never support me coming here, so I worked hard to make it happen for myself. I aced all my classes, even won an award, and...a full scholarship to the Sorbonne."

"What?" Camille gasped, once again looking at Isabelle. They both knew that this was Sophie's first time in Paris. She certainly hadn't been shy in showing her enthusiasm. "But you didn't go."

"No," Sophie said, shaking her head. "I didn't."

"What happened?" Isabelle asked.

"My mother happened," Sophie replied. "Without me knowing, she told the school I was passing up the scholarship. By the time I found out, they'd already given it to someone else."

"But how could she?" Camille's voice rose with anger. "She's your mother! I can't imagine!" She pictured her little girl, who worked so hard at her various passions and interests, and then she tried to imagine Flora ever earning such a significant achievement only to strip her of that accomplishment. Of that dream.

Her imagination was big, but even she couldn't fathom it.

"It's just how it is with her," Sophie said with a sigh. "It's how it always has been. But...not anymore." Her mouth twisted into a little smile as she looked at Isabelle. "I've made a decision. A big one. I'm...not going back to New York. I want to stay here, in Paris. That is if you don't mind letting me have the room until I can figure out a job—"

"Of course you can stay!" Isabelle exclaimed.

"But..." Camille couldn't help but think of everything that Sophie had told them about her life back in New York. "What about your boyfriend?"

"I feel horrible admitting this, but I don't miss Jack. At first I thought it was because I was here, in Paris, at long last, and I didn't have time to think about him, but now I think there's more to it." Sophie sighed. "Jack proposed to me before I came here. It's why I came here. To get away from him. And to avoid having to make a decision about the future of our relationship."

Another thing Camille had in common with Sophie, then.

"Do you think this has anything to do with spending time with Gabriel?" Isabelle asked.

Sophie shook her head. "I don't think so, not directly at least. But Gabriel said something that made me wonder. I used to think that I didn't believe in love, but now I think it's that I haven't found love yet."

"When you find it, you'll know," Isabelle said with a sad smile. "You'll forget all your fears because the only thing to be afraid of is the thought of living one day without that person."

Camille took a slug of her wine. "But isn't that the fear that holds people back?"

Because it was for her, and maybe it was for Sophie, too.

"Only if you let it," Isabelle said, holding her eyes.

"Don't tell me you're talking about Rupert again." Camille sniffed, pushing back the building emotions, no longer sure how much longer she could fight them. "Besides, it doesn't matter because he has a new girlfriend. Flora says she's lovely. It sounds quite serious, actually."

She was talking quickly, and the glass in her hand was starting to shake.

And one glance at Isabelle told Camille that she was fooling no one. Not even Sophie, who didn't know her at all, but somehow seemed to understand her more than anyone.

Sophie's eyes widened with sympathy as she reached out and took Camille's free hand.

"Rupert is what people would call a good egg," she said.

"How do you know?" Camille asked. What she meant was

how could anyone be sure of anyone, but given their history, Sophie took the question differently.

She didn't know Rupert, after all. Camille had made sure of that.

"I didn't know anyone at Isabelle's wedding other than Papa," Sophie replied. "Rupert came over to me a few times, cracked a few jokes, and made sure I had a refill of wine."

That sounded like Rupert, Camille thought, looking down at her hands.

"I was honestly surprised that Papa came to your wedding," she admitted to Isabelle.

"And now we have to ask ourselves if we should return the favor," Isabelle replied.

They all exchanged a glance. There was still the topic of Papa and his upcoming wedding, and what to do about it. Another problem for another day, their silence said.

For now, they each had enough to deal with. But for once, they didn't have to handle it all on their own.

Camille had always thought she had a lot to lose if she dared to let Rupert fully into her life and made a proper family of their little trio, but now, thinking of him out with this other woman, one who was probably funny and pretty and would no doubt appreciate everything about him that Camille did, made her realize that she still had a lot to lose. And that maybe, this time, her worst fears were coming true, and that she really was losing Rupert for good.

"So you're really going give up your life in New York, just like that?" Camille imagined what it would feel like, to take a risk so big, or to be so sure of something after such a short time. She stared at her younger sister, aching for guidance, or maybe direction.

Sophie nodded triumphantly. "I'm not giving up my life. I'm starting my life. The life I want to be living."

The life she wanted to be living. Camille let that sink in as she sipped her wine. Was she doing that? Shuffling Flora back and forth from Rupert's house to her own? Crawling into an empty bed after closing the door on the person that made her smile on even the darkest days, and made the best ones even brighter?

"Well, I for one couldn't be happier for you and for me! The room is all yours for as long as you'd like!" Isabelle exclaimed, giving her first real smile of the day, if not the week. But just as quickly, her face crumbled. "It's not like I have any other purpose for it."

Sophie looked at Camille, alarmed.

"Oh, Isabelle, Hugh isn't worth it. Punch something if you want. Here." Camille handed her a throw pillow.

Isabelle waved it away. "I'm all out of tears for Hugh," Isabelle finally said with a sigh. "He's a cheat and a liar. Sound familiar? I should have seen it sooner."

Camille sighed. "We see what we want to see, I suppose."

"And sometimes we choose not to see what's obvious." Isabelle gave her a long look, and Camille knew that she was thinking of all those nights when they sat at the window, staring out onto the streets of Paris, waiting for Papa. Did Isabelle really think he would come home, or did she just want to believe it?

"Deep down I knew that this was the case," Isabelle said. "There was no other reason for him to lie the way he did, and for so long."

Camille held back from commenting on the fact that Isabelle didn't even know for sure just how long Hugh had been cheating on her, or if it was even the first time, but she also knew that it didn't matter. Hugh had lied and been unfaithful. Details would just add to the pain at this point.

"Isabelle?" Camille asked gently. "What is it?"

Isabelle, to her great surprise, started to weep. "It's the room. Sophie's room. The empty rooms. I'd...I'd been hoping to have a baby!"

Camille stared at her sister, who now wiped tears from her cheeks as they started to fall.

"I didn't even know you and Hugh were trying to start a family," she said slowly. Isabelle had never hinted at such a thing, never confided in her, of all people, and not just because Camille was a mother, but because she was her sister.

But then, Camille supposed that she hadn't trusted Isabelle with the things closest to her heart, either.

She hadn't trusted anyone with her heart. And that was just the problem.

But Isabelle had wanted a baby, all this time, while Hugh was kissing another woman on a street corner for all of Paris to see.

"And to think that he went and pulled this while knowing that!" she seethed.

"But that's just the thing," Isabelle said, wiping her eyes. "We weren't planning to start a family."

Sophie took a long sip of her wine. Camille tipped her head in confusion. "I don't understand."

"Hugh never wanted children. Just like he never wanted to settle down in Paris. Those were things that *I* wanted. I thought that once it all happened, he'd see how happy he was, and he'd come around..."

"Oh, Isabelle." Camille pulled in a long breath. "You know that I can attest to the fact that an unplanned pregnancy can be very complicated."

"It wasn't like I was trying to trick him. I just thought...if it happened, it happened. And that it would be wonderful." Isabelle's voice broke on the last word as fresh tears started to flow.

Camille set down her wineglass and pushed out of her chair, moving to sit next to her sister, who was crying harder than Camille could ever remember seeing her do, even when they were young and Papa had left. Even when they'd packed up the Paris apartment and moved to London. Even after that awful first day of school in England, when they didn't know a soul but each other.

"I didn't even know you wanted a baby," she said, feeling miserable as she admitted it.

Once, there had been a time when she and Isabelle shared everything. But that was a long time ago. And she was just as guilty, wasn't she? She'd held Isabelle at arm's length for years, sensing that Isabelle couldn't understand her life, when it now seemed that Isabelle actually craved it.

And even now, she'd kept the most personal thing from her sister. Even denied the truth when Isabelle tried to speak it, when she talked about Rupert and her art.

About the life that Camille wanted and wouldn't let herself have.

"I wanted a baby," Isabelle said sadly. "Just like I wanted to settle down here in Paris. Once I inherited the apartment, it all seemed to make sense. To me at least."

"Well, you can still have a baby without Hugh," Camille told her sister.

Isabelle shook her head. "I'm older than you, Camille. And we've—I mean, I—tried recently. I think that I just have to accept the fact that my window of opportunity to have a child has come and gone."

Sophie looked like she might be the one to cry now, even though Camille was the one who wanted to. She thought of Flora, back at home, in the little cottage that they'd made their own—her, Flora, and Rupert.

Even though he didn't live there full-time, his markings were all over it, from the framed photos of the three of them on holidays that Camille set on end tables and the mantel, to the little things, like the fresh flowers he made a point of picking up every week and she set in a vase on the kitchen table.

Flora had been a surprise, and Camille had often been afraid to even think of what her life might have been like if it had gone according to plan.

Because the plan was never to let anyone in. Never let anyone get too close. Never to fall in love.

And fall in love she had. With Flora. And, she knew, with Rupert.

Twenty-Three
SOPHIE

The day of the gallery opening had finally arrived. The purpose —or so they'd been led to believe—of this trip to Paris. Sophie and Camille had both spent the last two days helping Isabelle with the last-minute details, which entailed everything from ordering the wine and setting up tables, checking the lighting and going over the guest list, to making calls to anyone who hadn't responded to the invitation so they had a final head count.

When the trays of assorted cheeses and bread were delivered, the wine chilled and uncorked, and the glasses polished and waiting, the women finally had a chance to stand back, breathe, and admire their work.

And Gabriel's.

"He really is a gifted artist," Sophie admitted, stepping closer to look at the painting she admired the most, a colorful abstract landscape of what she now recognized to be the Montmartre neighborhood. His entire collection was a love letter to Paris, something that had surprised her at first.

Like her, Gabriel had come to Paris in search of something.

And like her, he had found it. The city had made him whole again. It reminded him of what he loved most, what made him feel alive. What made him who he was.

And this, this art, this city, these brushstrokes and colors, were all Gabriel.

"I'm sorry he let you down," Isabelle said, coming to stand beside her. There was disappointment in her tone that only a sister could understand and share.

"Want me to have a few words with him when he comes in?" Camille asked, giving Sophie a suggestive look.

Sophie couldn't help but grin when Isabelle swatted her sister playfully. "Don't you dare. I need to sell every one of these paintings now that I'm going to be on my own."

"You won't be completely on your own," Sophie reminded her. "You'll have me."

Isabelle gave her a grateful smile, but her eyes were tired from more than working around the clock to make tonight's show the success that Sophie hoped it would be.

"And maybe someone else," Camile said with a waggle of her eyebrows.

Before Sophie or Isabelle could ask what she meant, Camille stepped aside, revealing a man lingering outside the gallery on the sidewalk.

"It's Antoine!" Isabelle gasped. Her cheeks flushed and she quickly set her hands to them. "I'm blushing, aren't I?"

"Yes," Camille and Sophie said in unison and then laughed.

"Well, go on," Camille said, giving her sister a light shove. "He's your first guest. Don't leave him standing out on the street."

Camille winked at Sophie and popped a bottle of champagne while Isabelle went to open the door. "I'm glad he came. Isabelle needs all the support she can get right now."

"I'm glad *we* both came," Sophie said, giving Camille a meaningful look. She knew that Camille was scheduled to leave tomorrow and that it was inevitable. She was a mother; her daughter needed her. Not long ago, she would have dreaded the thought of having to see her middle sister, and now she felt close to tears at the thought of her going.

"I am, too," Camille said, locking her eyes and grinning. "You're not so bad, kid. Actually, you're kind of cool."

"And you're pretty wonderful," Sophie said, meaning it. "And so is Isabelle. I just wish Hugh could have seen that."

"That's not how life works, sadly." Camille slugged her drink and turned to face the room, which was quickly gathering a crowd of unfamiliar strangers, all chattering in rapid French, making it impossible for Sophie to understand a word of their conversations.

"No, I suppose not," Sophie said, thinking of her mother, of Camille and Isabelle's mother, and, of course, of Gabriel. She glanced at the door again, looking for a glimpse of him, knowing that at any moment, he would arrive.

And then what? She'd congratulate him. Be civil. There was no reason to be anything but polite.

But there was no reason to be anything more than that either, was there?

"I'm looking forward to meeting this Gabriel at long last," Camille said, unable to hide her coy smile.

Sophie could only shake her head. "I'm afraid nothing is going on between the two of us."

"But you wish there was?" Camille asked.

Sophie hesitated. "Where does wishing for anything get you?"

"Paris," Camille said simply. Her eyes sparkled. "Sometimes you just have to fight for what you want."

Sophie raised an eyebrow. "Maybe it's time to take your own advice."

"What's that supposed to mean?" Camille stared at her.

Sophie hesitated, not wanting to upset their relationship, but decided that Camille needed to hear it. "You fight for everyone else, Camille. Me, when you were worried about Gabriel. Isabelle, with Hugh's terrible behavior. But why not fight for yourself? For what will really make you happy?"

Camille grew quiet as she sipped her wine, her gaze flitting to the door.

"Between you and me, I'm a little anxious about tonight and I didn't want to say so in front of Isabelle," Camille said.

"Oh?" Sophie was both flattered that Camille was confiding in her and terrified by what Camille was about to say.

"Isabelle invited Papa," Camille said.

Sophie nodded. "Yes. That's what she said."

Camile dipped her chin and gave her a hard look. "And what would be worse? Him coming or being a no-show?"

Sophie pulled in a long breath and then took a much-needed sip of wine, but only a small one because by the way this night was gearing up, she'd need to keep a clear head. She'd wanted to believe that Papa would show up to support Isabelle, if only because this was his scene. But now, hearing how Camille put it, she had to wonder if Papa would go back to his old ways, and if her sister would end up disappointed by more than her husband tonight.

"Maybe he'll surprise us," she said brightly.

"Oh, Sophie," Camille said, laughing.

"Well, why not?" Sophie said, leaning into the idea. Maybe it was the wine, or maybe it was being here, chatting with a sister who had once been a stranger and who was now a true friend. Or maybe it was the spring air filtering in through the open door, the soft music playing in the background, and the buzz of French conversation all around. Or maybe it was just Paris. And the feelings it brought out in her. She had every reason to be nervous and anxious and to assume that tonight could be a complete disaster, but right now, she was choosing to be optimistic. She was choosing hope.

"Why can't tonight be full of surprises?" she insisted.

Camille shrugged begrudgingly. "Let's just hope that they're good ones."

Half an hour into the event, there was still no sign of Papa. Or Gabriel.

At least one of the two artists had to make an appearance tonight, and Sophie was bracing herself for his imminent arrival. She had just topped off her wine when she saw him appear in the doorway, wearing his signature leather jacket.

She couldn't help herself; her heart started to pound, and she struggled to keep up with the polite conversation she was having with Antoine. She had half a mind to slip into Isabelle's storage room and park herself there, but just then Gabriel's eyes slid to hers and stayed there, locked from across the room.

She waited to see if he'd look away, but before she could first, he gave her a slow smile and then started walking toward her.

Sensing a shift in her attention, Antoine touched her elbow and made his excuses. He was a keeper, that one.

"You came," Gabriel said in that smooth voice of his that still managed to make Sophie's insides turn all warm and soft.

"Of course! My sister owns the gallery!" She saw the shadow cross over his face and added, "And I happened to hear the artist she's featuring is extremely talented."

He gave a modest shrug but he couldn't fight his smile. "So you've seen my work, then. Cat's out of the bag, as you say."

"It's beautiful, Gabriel, honestly," she said. "Congratulations. You've earned it."

He pulled in a breath and nodded. "It was a long journey, getting to this point. Not one that I took for granted. I'm just honored that your sister believed in me."

"And she's honored that you chose her gallery for your first show," Sophie said. "Your first of many, from what I can tell."

They looked around the room. Sophie already saw several red dots next to Gabriel's paintings, meaning that they were sold. She watched as he noted this, too, his eyebrows shooting up in surprise.

"Between you and me, I was a little worried it would be a disaster," he said, lowering his voice. "I wasn't even sure I wanted to come tonight, especially with so many big names here."

She frowned at him, surprised at his admission. "You were worried? But...you've always been so sure of yourself. So confident in your work."

"So confident in what I do, sure, but in the results?" He shook his head. "Not so much. You see, you can love something, or someone, but it doesn't mean that it will be a success. Or that it has merit."

She fell quiet, understanding now. The reason for the delay of his painting. His hesitation for opening his heart again. He might come across as a man who had it all figured out, but he was still finding himself, just like the rest of them.

"I wanted to say that I'm sorry, Sophie," Gabriel said. "For how we left things the last time we saw each other."

She brushed a hand through the air. "It's fine," she said, even as her heart leaped into her throat. She felt the emotions brewing close to the surface and she worried that her voice would give it away. She looked around the room, not wanting him to see the hurt in her eyes.

Hurt eventually faded, she knew. With time and effort, it was forgotten. Or at least buried. But it was always there, wasn't it? All the setbacks and painful parts of life, just like the joyful and good moments, were always a part of you.

Part of your story.

One that she was still waiting to tell. And write.

She let out a sigh, knowing that this, too, would pass. That she'd be all right. It might take time, but eventually, she'd end up right where she needed to be. Just like she'd finally ended up here in Paris.

"The truth is that I haven't wanted to get close to anyone since my divorce," Gabriel went on. "Until you."

"Oh." Sophie turned to look at him sharply and felt her cheeks grow warm. She hadn't been expecting that. But then, she hadn't been expecting a lot of things about this trip.

"You had so much excitement for this city, and for life." He smiled. "It reminded me of how I used to feel, so alive and open to the future. So eager to see what it held. I haven't felt that way in a long time, and thanks to you, I wanted to feel it again. To believe that anything was possible."

"And anything is," she pressed, stepping closer to him.

"There's no point." Gabriel shook his head. "You live in New York. And I live in Paris. And I'm realistic enough to know that an arrangement like that couldn't work."

It wouldn't have, but she'd started to learn that just because two people were not together didn't necessarily mean that there was never any love between them.

"Probably not," Sophie admitted, seeing the light leave Gabriel's eyes and wondering if he'd been hoping that she'd disagree with him. Only she didn't have to. "But I'm not going back to New York."

He looked at her with surprise. "You're not?"

She shook her head, smiling broadly. "I'm staying in Paris. It's where I was always supposed to be, it just took me a little while to get here."

He was smiling, too, now, standing closer to her, until it felt like they were the only two people in the room, even though the gallery was filling up by the minute, the door opening and closing, the small space growing warm and crowded.

"I wish we could get out of here," Gabriel whispered.

Sophie laughed. "But it's your show!"

"It's just a part of who I am," he said. "A big part, yes. But you...I hope you'll be a big part of my life, too, Sophie."

She pulled in a breath, feeling more complete than she had in her entire life, and gave one firm nod.

"I'd like that," she said.

Only that wasn't true. Because really, she'd love that.

Twenty-Four

CAMILLE

"Aw, look at that," Isabelle said wistfully as she came to stand beside Camille, who had been watching Sophie from across the room, ready to pounce on Gabriel at a moment's notice should the need arise.

Camille pursed her lips. "I don't know. I can't help but worry."

Isabelle didn't bother to hide her smile. "Of course you can't."

"What's that supposed to mean?" Camille asked, turning to give her sister her full attention.

"I mean that you care about our sister," Isabelle said simply.

This time it was Camille who smiled. "I do. I just wish it hadn't taken me so long to figure that out."

She wished it hadn't taken her so long to figure a lot of things out, she thought sadly, stuffing a piece of cheese into her mouth. She'd probably need to go on a diet once she was home, but then, why bother? The man she loved was dating Maisie now. Maybe he'd marry her.

Maybe, given how her life was going, she'd be asked to stand up at their wedding, give a toast and everything. Maybe she'd even like Maisie. They'd be an even bigger unconventional family. Maybe she'd even manage to convince herself she was happy. That it was enough.

Oh, who was she kidding?

"But you don't need to worry about Sophie," Isabelle promised her. "She's going to be just fine. We all will."

Camille wished she could be certain, but now, just like when they were still children, she hung on to her sister's words, needing the reassurance, holding on to the confidence in Isabelle's tone.

"How can you be so sure?" she asked in a small voice. "After everything you've been through? How can you still believe in a happy ending?"

Isabelle pulled in a deep breath and let it out slowly. "Because of tonight. Because of this. Because of you worrying about Sophie when for years you couldn't even stand to hear her name. Because of you being here in Paris when you swore you would never come back. Don't you see, Camille? Anything is possible."

Camille laughed in spite of herself and leaned her head on Isabelle's shoulder for a second before lifting it again, stiffening when she saw the door open.

"It's Papa!" she hissed.

Isabelle, however, didn't look surprised. "Of course it is. I invited him."

"Yes, but—" But she didn't think he cared enough to actually come.

Camille blinked rapidly but Isabelle was already weaving her way through the crowd to greet their father, who was standing near the doorway in a rumpled linen suit, looking a little dazed.

His face lit up when he spotted his oldest daughter, and he leaned down to kiss her cheek.

Camille hung back, clutching her wineglass, then glanced at Sophie across the room, wishing that she could catch her attention, her unexpected ally in this strained family dynamic. But alas, it was too late. Isabelle was dragging a rather reluctant Papa by the arm, pausing here and there so he could greet a familiar face, because this was their scene, of course, their world. The very one that Camille had shunned for her cozy little attic studio and her happy little animal watercolors.

Her safe place.

Her happy place.

She felt her eyes well up with tears when she realized just how much she missed it. As much as she'd enjoyed this time with her sisters, she ached to be back at home with Flora.

And Rupert.

"Camille." Papa stood before her, looking hesitant and almost repentant, if she didn't know better. She eyed him suspiciously, thinking of how they'd left things off after that awful dinner, and how they'd left things off after every fleeting interaction in the years prior.

With silence. And distance. Until the next brief chance meeting.

And she thought of Sophie. And the time lost. And the family gained. And how her heart had never felt so full, yet had never ached for more.

And for the first time since she was a little girl, living in this very city without a care, believing that this world was a safe space and that the people she loved would never let her down or hurt or disappoint her, she dared to take a risk.

"*Bon soir*, Papa," she said, giving him a small smile at first, which turned bigger, warmer, and more genuine when she saw first the surprise in his eyes, and then, the love.

It had been there all along, she supposed. But like her, Papa just hadn't quite known what to do with it.

She'd learned more than how to hold a paintbrush from this man, it would seem.

When she looked back on this moment, she wouldn't remember who opened their arms first, but she also knew that it didn't matter. The past was finally in the past, and the future, for perhaps the first time in her entire life, was wide open.

"*Je t'aime*, Camille," her father said. *I love you*.

Camille nodded but then stopped herself. Those were words she had been capable of saying only to her daughter all this time. Not to her mother, who never said it either, and not to Isabelle, who knew she loved her without words.

Not to any man. Not even to Rupert.

"*Je t'aime*, Papa," she whispered, feeling the tears fill her eyes. She looked up to see Sophie standing beside Isabelle now, and Papa pulled back only to greet his youngest daughter, who accepted his arms, his words, and his unspoken apology a little more easily than Camille.

"This was a surprise," Camille muttered to Isabelle, wiping her eyes quickly. Really, she wasn't that much of a sap. She was still her mother's daughter, stiff upper lip and all. This trip hadn't changed her that much.

"That's not the only one," Isabelle said. She jutted her chin over Camille's shoulder. "Look."

Frowning, Camille turned, her mouth falling open when she saw Rupert and Flora standing in the doorway, looking shyly at the family drama unfolding.

"Flora!" Camille exclaimed, thrusting her wineglass at

Isabelle before rushing over to her daughter, who didn't seem embarrassed about greeting her mum in public for once. She held her daughter to her chest and stared at the man before her who looked even more handsome than she remembered him with his lopsided grin and kind eyes that were so familiar her heart hurt.

She missed him, even though he was right here, she'd never felt further away from him.

Her childhood family was just behind her, but the family she'd made, the family she loved, was right here. Just the three of them.

"Rupert! I…I…" She didn't even know where to begin. Or if it was too late.

"I hope you don't mind," he said.

"*Mind*?" she said. "How could I ever mind?"

Only that wasn't true, was it? Because she'd come here to get away from him, to get space and clarity, and oh, had she gotten it.

"Rupert, I—" *Need to fight for what I want*, she thought. If she wasn't too late.

"Flora!" Isabelle said, coming over to greet her niece, who was all too excited to see her aunt. "And Rupert." Isabelle gave him a friendly hug after Flora finally let her go.

Camille snapped out of her fog. Of course. There were introductions to be made. Conversations to be had. But not all of them here, perhaps. Not all of them tonight.

"Flora," Camille said. "I want to properly introduce you. This is my other sister, Sophie."

Sophie stepped forward and looked fondly at Flora, and it was only then that Camille saw the physical resemblance between the two. They both had the same dark hair and big, bright eyes. The same excitement for the world. A certain...*joi de vivre*, she supposed.

She looked from her daughter to her sister and gave Sophie a nod of encouragement.

"That makes her your aunt Sophie," Camille said. "She's American."

"American?" Flora looked impressed. "Cool!"

At that moment, Papa shyly stepped forward. Camille saw Isabelle flash her a nervous look.

"And...this is your...grandfather," Camille said stiffly.

Flora's eyes went round. "I have a *grandfather*?" Rupert's father had passed away from a sudden heart attack when Rupert was in high school, and Flora had only ever known grandmothers until now.

Had Camille failed to even mention her father in front of Flora? It had been easier that way, she supposed. But what was easy wasn't always right, was it? And sometimes it was downright empty.

"Of course you do," Camille said lightly. "He just...travels a lot. He's an artist. A very talented one. I learned from him, you see."

She felt her father smile at her and looked up to see tears in his eyes.

"Why don't you and your grandfather go get some snacks?" Camille suggested hastily before her emotions got the better of her, too. What was she thinking, getting all misty-eyed in public like this?

She watched as Flora took Papa's hand and they wandered across the room together, a sight that she'd never thought she'd see, one that she'd tried to protect her child from, and now, one that filled her heart with more joy than she could have ever imagined.

"This was quite a surprise," she finally said.

"Which part?" Rupert asked, widening his eyes.

Camille gave a small laugh. "All of it. You didn't tell me that you'd be coming!"

"Flora missed you," Rupert said with a shrug.

"Oh." Camille felt her expression drop but she recovered quickly. Of course. Her child. Her daughter. She'd missed her. "Of course. Well, thank you for bringing her."

"And...I missed you," Rupert said, locking her gaze.

Camille felt her heart begin to thud against her chest. Not long ago, she would have made up some excuse, claimed the room was too hot (which it was), and run outside for some much-needed air. But she wasn't running anymore. Not from her feelings. Not from her heart. Not from the places and people she loved most.

And not from what she wanted more than anything.

"I missed you, too," she said breathlessly. "So much."

But just as quickly she remembered Maisie and she felt her stomach drop like a stone.

"What is it?" Rupert frowned.

"But..." Camille blinked, wondering if she'd misunderstood this entire conversation. "What about Maisie?"

Rupert tilted his head. "Maisie?"

"Flora told me about her," Camille explained. When Rupert didn't take the bait, she added, "From the festival? Your girlfriend?"

Your super cool girlfriend, she thought miserably.

But Rupert's frown just deepened before a huge smile split his face.

"Girlfriend?" He laughed. "Is that what Flora said?"

"She did," Camille said, not finding any of this funny. She peered at Rupert, wondering what he was getting at. "Our daughter doesn't keep secrets, you know."

"And neither do I," he said, growing serious. He took a deep breath and looked her in the eyes. "Camille, Maisie is my new neighbor. She was on her own for the weekend and feeling lonely because she doesn't know a soul in town. She's a really friendly girl. You'd like her. She's young. Only twenty-one."

Oh, great. It just got better and better.

"She's loads of fun."

Mm-hmm. Camille sipped her wine.

"And she's married."

Wait.

"To a woman." Rupert raised an eyebrow. "And do I need to elaborate further?"

"Oh, so...not a girlfriend," Camille said, too pleased to feel foolish. But then, she could never feel embarrassed around Rupert. She could only ever feel like herself.

Happy. Content. Safe.

"Definitely not a girlfriend," Rupert said with a nod.

"But...you have had girlfriends," Camille said slowly. "So you can understand why Flora jumped to the conclusion."

Rupert nodded begrudgingly. "I have friends, and some of them are women, but that's all any of them are, Camille. That's all any of them can ever be. No one stands a chance of being anything more because none of them are you."

Camille stared at him as the room around them grew quiet, and even though she knew that her entire family was within reach and that her daughter was only a few feet away, for one magical moment, it felt like she and Rupert were the only two people in the room.

His eyes didn't waver, and for once, she didn't want to look away. Or run away.

She just wanted to stay right where she was. With the man she loved. For now. For always.

Forever.

"Mum! You won't believe how we got here," Flora said as she came running back over to them. Forcing Camille's attention away from Rupert. "We took the Chunnel. It's a train that goes through a tunnel under the English Channel! Isn't that super cool?"

Camille thought back to how terrifying she'd found that experience just a mere matter of days ago and could only look at her daughter's shining eyes and smile. "It really is cool when you think about it."

Terrifying, but rather cool. Like the ancient elevator in the apartment building.

Like falling in love.

"Paris is so close to London, Mum," Flora went on. "And Aunt Isabelle lives here. And they have the best croissants and food. And people here speak French. And they're so chic."

Camille lifted an eyebrow at Rupert.

"Why haven't we visited before?" Flora inquired.

Good question, Camille thought. And one without a very good answer.

"That's going to change, honey," Camille said as she slipped her hand into Rupert's. She looked across the room and saw her sisters giving her a smile of encouragement. "A lot is going to change."

And only for the better.

Twenty-Five
ISABELLE

"The event is a success," Antoine said once Isabelle finally had another moment to slip away from her guests.

She looked around the room, at the familiar and not-so-familiar faces. The art critics and reviewers, the journalists and magazine editors, the fellow gallery owners and other artists, some of whom she'd featured, some of whom she hoped to. And her family. Camille—and Rupert! And little Flora, who was not so little anymore. Sophie. And Papa.

And...

"Hugh." Her heart felt like it was stuck in her throat for a moment as she watched her husband glide through the open door, look around the crowded room, and then, spotting her, hold his hand up in a wave, oh so casually, as if nothing was amiss.

For a moment she wondered if she was going crazy. If she had it all wrong. If his assistant had misspoke. If she'd seen someone else kissing a woman on that street corner the other day. It would be so easy to believe, and Hugh, being here, walking toward her, weaving his way through the groups of people, huddled together, clutching wineglasses, talking animatedly, would have her believe so.

She could go along with it. Live out the life she'd created in Paris. Maybe even have that baby she wanted so badly.

"Hugh?" Antoine's voice was deep with confusion, close in her ear.

"My husband is here," Isabelle said, her eyes still locked on the man coming her way, approaching one step at a time until suddenly, a couple parted and there he was, standing right in front of her. She looked up at him, at the familiar light brown eyes she'd stared into for the past six years, the ones that had always seemed so transparent, so readable, and then lower, at the lopsided smile that had never seemed to carry a hint of malice but now seemed to possess a bit of smugness, a sense that he'd gotten away with something, perhaps, that he knew something that she didn't.

Only he was wrong about that. And she had been wrong about a lot of things.

"Hugh," she managed to say, her tone one of reasonable surprise. "You're here."

Why, she didn't know. He'd been hiding out for weeks, possibly longer, and he decided to show up now, of all nights, at the most important event of her career. Had his girlfriend suddenly dumped him? Rather timely, if she did say so.

He bent down to kiss her on the cheek, and for once she was pleased that Hugh had never been one for public displays of affection. At least not with her.

A memory of that passionate kiss on the street hit her full force and she felt a wave of sickness pass through her as his cologne washed over her. She pulled back, needing to get away from it, from him. She wished he'd never come.

She should have listened to her sister. She should have confronted him sooner.

But she hadn't been ready then. Seeing him now, she remembered something Camille had said about how she would know how she felt when she saw Hugh again. And oh, her feelings had never been more clear. Crystal.

"I just got in. Dropped my bags at the apartment and came straight here. Didn't even stop to unpack." Hugh grinned.

Isabelle stared at him, in awe of how easy it was for him to let the lie roll off his lips, wondering just how many times he'd done it before, and how many times she'd believed him.

"You didn't need to," she told him, her tone frosty but polite. They were in a public setting, after all. There was press. Journalists. Reporters. She didn't want to take the spotlight off the art, and she certainly didn't want to shine it on her divorce.

Because that's what was happening here.

She was going to leave Hugh even though it didn't seem that he intended to leave her. No, it seemed that Hugh planned to continue as he had all along, living a double life, stopping at the apartment to visit her when it suited him, and dashing off to Tokyo or Berlin or...the Right Bank...when he saw fit.

That was the life that he wanted.

And it wasn't the life for her.

"I knew how important it was to you," he said, standing a little straighter.

"Yes," Isabelle said, nodding thoughtfully. "And you also knew how important this marriage was to me."

The smile slipped, along, Isabelle thought, with the mask. He stared at her, his eyes narrowing, assessing what she might know, or what she simply suspected, calculating his next move.

"The game's up, Hugh," she said, deciding to make this easy for them both. "I know you weren't in Tokyo."

He opened his mouth, but she held up a hand to stop him.

"Please don't insult me again by continuing to lie. I know the truth. Not all of it but enough." She stared at him, waiting for the emotion to set in. For her heart to start pounding, for the tears to fill her eyes, for...something. But instead, she felt nothing. Not for this man, at least. It was as if all the emotions that she'd ever felt for Hugh had been spent, used up over time, exorcised in the weeks since she'd discovered his betrayal. The man standing before her might be named Hugh, and he might look like Hugh, but he certainly wasn't the man she married, and he wasn't the man that she loved.

Maybe that man had never existed. Or maybe he had, for a little while.

Either way, he was gone.

"Isabelle, you know I love you," Hugh said urgently, reaching for her hand.

She snatched it back, taking a deep breath. She looked up at him, straight into his eyes, and knew that the next words she spoke were important. "Maybe you do, Hugh. But actions have consequences."

"What are you saying?" he asked, his brow furrowing.

"I'm saying that it's over, Hugh."

"Come on," he said, giving a little smile. "Let's go somewhere and talk. After the event."

"I don't see a reason to talk when your word means nothing," she told him, trying to back away.

He stepped toward her, but this time, Papa stepped between them. "I believe my daughter has asked you to leave, Hugh."

Isabelle looked up at her father in alarm, but a warm glow

washed over her when she saw the twitch of his jaw and the set of Hugh's. Camille was watching it all in shock, and Rupert was standing by, ready to intervene, but Isabelle knew both of these men.

Papa wouldn't back down. He was passionate about the things he loved. And the people, too.

And Hugh. He was a coward.

Eventually, Hugh held up his hands, surrendering, giving her one fleeting look before moving to the door. Isabelle just shook her head and turned back to her family, letting them all surround her with the love and support that she needed. Everyone who she needed was right here.

But she realized with a skip of her pulse that one person was missing.

Someone who she had come to count on, and looked forward to seeing. Someone who she wanted in her life, not just for tonight, but for tomorrow, and the day after that.

Isabelle weaved her way through the crowd, which seemed to have grown even thicker in the time she was arguing with Hugh. Had she invited this many people? The gallery was small. Too small to hold this many. She shouldn't complain. The show was a hit. Her career would be a success. But what did it matter if she had no one to share it with?

She managed to get to the back of the room and poked her head into the storage closet, but it was empty aside from the paintings and pieces that she stored there. She stood on her tiptoes, trying to see over the crowd, but it was no use. She wasn't exactly tall, and most of the men in the room had at least six inches on her, if not more.

She moved through the groups, trying not to interrupt conversations, her eyes flitting and searching as her heart pounded.

He'd come, for her. To show his support. To be her friend. Maybe even to be something more.

And so had her husband. Her soon-to-be ex-husband. A man who hadn't been much of a husband at all for a very long time. Just one who had floated in and out of her life, never planning to stay for long, only ever playing the part.

She plucked her phone from her small handbag and checked for messages, but there were none. Everyone she knew was either here tonight or knew she was busy with the event.

Fighting back tears of frustration and loss and overwhelming emotion at the highs and lows that had occurred in just a matter of hours, she stepped outside into the cool night air and stopped.

There, sitting on a bench just a block down, under the glow of a streetlamp, was Antoine.

"Antoine?" she said breathlessly. She wasn't sure if she should approach him, but then, he hadn't gone home yet, so she walked across the cobblestone, her steps quickening when she saw the encouraging lift of his smile. "I thought you had left."

"Just needed some air," he said. "I...needed some space. And...I thought you did, too."

She nodded and then sat down beside him. "Space, yes. But...not from you." She glanced at him shyly, seeing him frown at her uncertainly. "You missed quite a show back there. My father and my husband—I mean my soon-to-be ex-husband—almost got in a fistfight."

Antoine's eyebrows rose. "*Non!*"

"*Mais oui.*" Isabelle nodded, then, remembering the scene, started to laugh. It wasn't funny, not in the least, but it was so unexpected in every possible way that the only thing she could do was laugh, because if she didn't, she might cry.

And she didn't want to cry tonight, because tonight was too good of a night to waste with tears. It was a night that she wanted to remember for being the start of her next chapter. With her family. With her gallery.

And maybe with her heart.

"I suppose you should probably get back inside in case there's any more drama," Antoine said.

Isabelle felt her smile fade. He was giving her a hint. A polite one, but a hint all the same.

She nodded and then stood. He did the same.

"With my family, you never know what can happen," she said, trying to keep things light, even though her chest felt heavy. "Thank you. For coming. And...for everything."

Antoine gave a slow smile. "If it's all right with you, Isabelle, I think I'll stay."

"Oh?" Her heart fluttered with that old familiar feeling. Hope. She'd never let it go, even when others had, and even if it might have made sense to, she still kept coming back to it. She still believed.

In good. In people.

In love.

That was the thing about her, she supposed, as she looped her arm through the crook of his elbow and walked back into the gallery, admiring the colorful paintings that filled the space.

She saw beauty and goodness and potential in every moment of her life here in Paris, even on the difficult days, even when it made more sense to focus on the gloom and the rain. And she believed in love, even when it was complicated, and even when it was fleeting, and even when she had every reason not to.

Life, like art, was full of beauty and infinite possibilities, if you were willing to open your mind and sometimes look below the surface.

Epilogue

CAMILLE

Paul Laurent's fifth (but who can really be sure?) marriage took place on a rainy June morning in Paris in the living room of Isabelle's apartment. The entire family was present for the occasion, with Flora serving as the flower girl, and Antoine as the officiant.

The vows were long and handwritten, and Camille managed not to roll her eyes, cough into her hand, or even object, because Papa and his bride had already legally married at town hall earlier that day, and because she liked Nadine, who seemed sensible and wise and acutely aware of the exact type of man she marrying.

"I can't believe that I'm saying this," Camille said after meeting the happy couple one weekend in May on a long overdue trip to Paris for Flora, "but I think that Papa has finally met his match."

"And I think," Isabelle said with a knowing look, "that you have, too."

It was true, and perhaps the real reason why, when Papa slipped the ring onto Nadine's finger, Camille felt her eyes tear up not with fury, but with another emotion, one that could only be described as hope, because there, across the makeshift aisle, serving as one of the best men to balance out the bridesmaids, was her other half, her better half, the yin to her yang, the lid to her pot, as all those sayings she never used to believe in went.

"You have to admit that it was a beautiful wedding," Isabelle said afterward while she and Camille retrieved the champagne from the fridge.

"Only because you planned every detail," Camille remarked, but she exchanged a rueful look with her sister. They both knew that it was a touching ceremony and that it had nothing to do with the stunning floral arrangements and everything to do with the people who were there.

All of Paul's daughters were in one room. And all of their newfound loves, too.

"Almost enough to make you want to get married," Sophie said, breezing into the kitchen in a lovely soft pink dress that brought out the color of her cheeks. Since moving to Paris full-time she had a permanent glow about her, one that Camille noticed each time she visited, and the two times that Sophie had come to England.

"Are you and Gabriel already talking about marriage?" Camille whispered.

"Not yet," Sophie remarked, but it was clear by the light in her eyes that it was possible. Someday. "I was talking about you."

"Please. You know that Rupert and I don't need a piece of paper to confirm how we feel about each other. We're fine just as we are."

And they were. They were the same happy family that

they'd always been, just a little more official now that they were all living under the same roof seven days a week. Rupert had given up the apartment in town, and the cottage was now home to the three of them, as it always really had been.

"But..." She leaned against the counter, wondering if she should tell her sisters and then deciding that she had no reason to hold back anymore. She never did. "Just because we don't need to make it official doesn't mean we won't."

"You mean you're getting married?" Sophie squealed, then slapped a hand to her mouth, realizing it might be a surprise.

Camille nodded. "At the end of summer. You're all invited, of course."

"Oh, Camille." Isabelle's eyes filled with tears as she and Sophie leaned in to hug her. When she pulled back, she wiped her eyes. "I'm afraid that if you expect me to be a bridesmaid, you may have to alter my dress by September."

Camille stared at her sister for a moment, trying to understand what she meant, until understanding unfolded. "Do you mean?"

Isabelle nodded excitedly, biting her lip. "It's early days. Very early. I just took the test, yesterday. I know it's a little scandalous, what with my divorce so fresh, but I'm not getting any younger, and Antoine and I didn't see a reason to waste any time."

"You don't need to explain yourself to me," Camille said. "You're in love. With someone who loves you back. And with someone who wants to share the life you want to live. Oh, Isabelle. I'm so happy for you."

"Of course, that won't stop me from running the gallery," Isabelle said. "As you all know, I have a very important opening in a few weeks..."

Camille groaned. "Is it too late to back out?"

"Don't you dare," Isabelle said. She pulled up her phone and flipped to the photos of the paintings that Camille had sent her, the preliminary work of her first collection. A series of family portraits, starting with early days, light and happy, leaning into darker, cloudier pieces, and then, her later canvases again showing bold, bright colors. "It's brilliant, Camille. *You're* brilliant." She looked her in the eye until Camille had to look away.

"I wouldn't have had the courage to do it without you," she said.

"I wouldn't be where I am without all of you," Isabelle said, placing a hand on her stomach.

"And I wouldn't have just sent off a first draft of my very first book to my old boss without either of you," Sophie said with a shy smile.

"You didn't!" Isabelle cried.

Sophie nodded, laughing. "I did. I really did it. I made it happen."

"Just like Paris," Camille said proudly. She reached for the champagne. "This calls for a toast."

"What are we drinking to?" Sophie asked as Isabelle filled her own glass with water.

Camille handed Sophie a flute and then poured herself a glass. They raised their arms in a toast and paused for a moment.

"To Papa," she said. "Who taught us to follow our hearts, and who never stopped looking for love. Because thanks to him, we all finally found it."

About the Author

Olivia Miles is a two-time *USA Today* bestselling author of heartwarming women's fiction and small town romance. After growing up in New England, she now lives on the North Shore of Chicago with her family and an adorable pair of dogs.

Visit www.OliviaMilesBooks.com for more.

www.ingramcontent.com/pod-product-compliance
Lightning Source LLC
LaVergne TN
LVHW030317070526
838199LV00069B/6488